Secret of the Apostle Islands

David Fabio

David Fabio

2011

Avid Readers Publishing Group
Lakewood, California

Secret of the Apostle Islands

Avid Readers Publishing Group

http://www.avidreaderspg.com

ISBN-13: 978-1-61286-004-6

Printed in the United States

/ı chateau boutin bayfield Wi

Contents

Chapter		page

Author's Note:

Writers of mysteries and fiction books usually spend considerable time researching their books before writing them. This is especially true for writers that include specific locations in their books.

I would like to thank the many people in the Bayfield area that assisted me in selecting the tales that made this book come real. Without their help, it would have been just one of those fictitious books.

I hope you enjoy the many paths this book attempts to lead you.

The story written in this book is fiction, and any similarities to any real characters are totally by coincidence.

List of Characters

Henry Longknife and Hank – trappers

Stan Moline – writer

Jane Moline – Stan's sister
        Nate Duncan – Jane's boyfriend

Miss Jean Larson – innkeeper

Barbara Fontaine – blond in ponytail
        Anthony Fontaine – husband

Vivian Jacobs – Barbara's mother
        Friends – Marcella and Edna

Gilbert Miller – Bayfield County Deputy Sheriff

Agent Mark Lawson – FBI agent

Sheriff Wayne Bradley – Bayfield County Sheriff

John Morley – Cornucopia Marina manager

Captain George Morrissey – Royal Canadian Mounted Police

Deputy Francis Knudson – Royal Canadian Mounties

William O'Brian – boat owner in Thunder Bay, Provincial engineer

Morley Cox – Buzz, of Marathon, Ontario, worker at dredging company

Jacques Laroche – Marathon, Ontario, worker in road construction

Carl Harris – NSF

Charles Ziemanski – boat owner in Cornucopia

Francis Ramona – Shorty – man in Red Cliff

James Dufault – man in Mexico

Raymond Sandberg – designer

Doug Johnson – ferry deck hand

Paul and Linda – visitors to the inn

Arthur Jones – hood in Chicago

Raul and Rosemary Baron – friends in Chicago area

Chapter 1

Visions

The great waters of Lake Superior had not been kind. Henry Longknife was exhausted as he paddled into the opening of the Baptism River. It had been three long days of paddling. He and his friend Hank had averaged over 20-miles a day, coming down from Grand Portage. The icy winds of spring had been blowing up the shoreline and into their faces.

He reached his fishing shack near the mouth of the Baptism River late in the day, where a couple of his long time hunting friends met him. They told him the sad story of how his girlfriend had disappeared over a month ago. Rumors about her had circled like the crows overhead, in the trees.

* * * * *

Similar rumors had been foretold last summer that Henry Longknife had perished hauling a load of pelts to the Hudson Bay Company at Fort Williams, in Canada.

The severe storm that hit the area had taken the lives of many of the trappers that were taking their furs north, and the rumors had reached Henry's girlfriend. When he failed to return as expected three weeks later, she feared the worst. Thinking back on the trip up lake last summer,

1

the terrifying experience replayed in Henry's mind and weakened his already broken body.

With the results of six months of trapping laced into his canoe, Henry and his friend Hank had paddled up the lake only to run into a severe storm that seemed to come up from no-where. With lightning and high winds, they were trapped along the rocky cliffs of northern Minnesota near the Canadian border.

If they pulled into shore, they would surely lose all their possessions, as the big waves would pound the large freighter canoe into the rocks. If they stayed out, they would meet sure death. Their only hope was to reach the cove of a small river that entered the lake. There they could find shelter.

As the storm intensified, the weary travelers realized they would not make the cove. Now, the waves were six to eight feet high and getting stronger. The canoe was taking on water. Within an hour, the lake had gone from almost calm to a raging sea.

Finally, the canoe was too heavy for the waves and capsized, spilling its cargo and occupants into the water. Now they watched as the pelts that they had worked so hard to find, spread all over the water like sticks bobbing in the waves. Saving them was becoming less and less of a concern. Survival was now at the top of their list.

By the time they got their bearings, the waves had viciously picked up and tossed them into the rocks along the shoreline. They tried for almost an hour to find a way to climb the high cliffs along the lake.

The cliffs were too steep to find a safe way to climb. While being constantly battered by the waves, both trappers took a severe beating against the rocks. Bones were breaking and blood was coming from gashes on their heads, arms and legs. Most people would have given up the fight, exhausted from the effort, and drowned.

The waves carried them past a small rocky island, not 30-feet from the shore. To the men, it felt like it was across the lake as they tried to swim with the parts of their bodies that were still willing to put up the fight.

When they reached the rock, which extended 20-feet out of the water, the waves somehow lifted them high enough to find a flat area, allowing them to get out of the water. There, they waited to see who would win, the storm or fate. With no shelter on the rocks, they were exposed to the winds, rain, and later the sunshine.

Three days later, two Indians from the reservation found them on the rocks and brought their broken bodies to their village. It took the entire winter for them to recover. The pelts, which they spent a whole winter trapping, were lost. It was going to be a harsh year with little money.

* * * * *

Now as Hank continued up the shoreline to his home, Henry returned to his fishing hut, limping as he walked. It was the result of his poorly set broken leg. All the rumors he had heard along the way, as he ran into his friends that his girlfriend was gone, appeared to be fact. He sat on a rock overlooking the great lake and watched as the stars came out at night. All of his struggles to heal and return seemed to have lost their meanings.

The north star and big dipper shown so clearly that night that he felt that he could have almost used the dipper to collect water from the big lake.

The cold night air from the lake was settling into his weary bones and muscles, like rainwater absorbing into a marsh. Finally, after almost

3

falling into the water, he came back into his shack and built a small fire to stay warm during the night.

The smoke rose from his small heating-stove, filling the night air and seeping back into the shack through the small cracks in the walls. He lay there half-asleep for several hours. As the full moon rose high in the sky, he could hear the loons calling to each other out in the great lake.

With the smoke gathering in the shack from the fire, it reminded him of his youth, when his father – an Ojibwe Indian, had taken him into the sweat lodge for the first time. There, several men sat around talking about the old ways of the past and the visions of the future.

While he was thinking about the smoke in the sweat lodge, he heard a great horned owl outside. It was calling for its mate. It was like a vision. Perhaps he was imagining himself calling for his girlfriend to return.

The night was long and he did not sleep. He would drift off only to be awoken again and again by the owl.

Just before morning, he had a vision. It was of a beautiful girl that was so saddened by the loss of her friend that she leaped from a rock into the icy waters. The vision was so real that it startled Henry as he sat up, looking around for her.

In his dream-like state, he could almost feel her soft hand as it reached out for him. He longed for her touch. He sat there looking into her dark brown eyes, until they started to fade. Then, he realized what he had seen. It was his girlfriend, and she had revealed to him that she had jumped off the high rocks of the cliff into the water.

He slowly climbed out of the warm bed. In the faint light of pre-dawn, he walked wearily in the dark to the high cliff, just down the lake. There, he found the image he had dreamt about.

She had taken off her hand-sewn moose-hide boots, placed them under three stones to leave a message to those that followed, and jumped off the rock into the water. In her utter despair, feeling that all was lost, she had taken her own life.

The End.

Jane Moline had tears in her eyes as she laid down the book she had just finished reading. It had been a book about a strained love affair between two people in the early 1800's. She started it early Saturday morning, and it was now 3:00 am. Sunday morning. It had been a good book. Her brother Stan had asked her to proof read it before he sent it to a publisher.

As she looked at the clock, she figured that Stan could wait a few more hours before she gave him her review. So far, this was Stan's best book. She was so entranced that she read the entire book in one sitting.

* * * * *

Later that day, Stan came over for pizza and the answer he was hoping to hear. He had labored almost six months to finish the book, and he knew that his sister would give him an honest review.

Jane made a special pizza for that evening. She carefully made sure that two pieces had considerably more garlic and red peppers than the rest of the pizza. These, she covered with several pepperoni slices. It would make it easier for her to spot, so she could make sure Stan got the chosen pieces. It was Jane's way of getting back at her brother, for killing off her favorite character in his book.

"You had me in tears again," she told Stan. "When are you going to write your next book?"

"Does that mean you liked this one? I need to get this book finished and published first. Getting them into bookstores is a lot of work. I have some ideas for another book. I might get a chance to get it going in a few months," he answered. "Besides, I just break even on these books with all the costs and travel. They keep telling me that most authors do not break even until they have six to eight books published. I'm still waiting."

Jane gave him his answer, "I did! I think it is one of your best so far. Just don't forget all the fun time you have traveling and writing off the costs," his sister reminded him.

The rest of the evening, Jane told Stan about the areas of the book she enjoyed the most, and gave him ideas about how he could make the emotions run even higher.

As they ate the pizza, Jane could see the red glow in Stan's eyes as they started to water. She knew that he had hit the peppers.

She laughed. "That's what you get for killing off the girl in the end," she told him.

Stan got a good laugh out of it. He knew his sister liked happy conclusions in all the books she read. In this case, he wanted this one to end in sadness.

For Stan, it had been a long winter of writing and revising. Now, he was looking forward to getting time to rest from all the re-reads of his book.

Chapter 2

Writer's Itch

Summer was almost in full swing before Stan Moline had allowed himself to think about writing again. He knew he had to get away to nurture his thoughts.

He had been promising to write his next book for months and was still looking for the framework that would be the central theme for his next novel. Now, he finally had that opportunity. The freelance writing job he had been working on the past month, for a local magazine, was over.

His summer enjoyment had always been riding his bike around the lakes in Minneapolis. The paved paths around Lake Calhoun, Lake Harriet and Lake of the Isles were the summer favorites for many bicyclists. Unfortunately, when he stopped for a snack near the concession stand last week, he discovered someone had stolen his bike. The bike shop told him it would take three weeks to get in the replacement model he wanted.

Stan was disgusted and upset. That bike was his pride and joy and he did not like the thought of someone else riding it. Now, three weeks would keep him from enjoying the trails in the middle of the summer. By the time he got a replacement, and got it tuned the way he wanted, he would be looking at biking in the fall season only.

To Stan, everything was pointing to the fact that it was time to get away, change his attitude, and research his next book. He had run out of excuses.

Stan searched and found a room at a bed and breakfast in Bayfield, Wisconsin. It was available for the next two weeks. This would give Stan the quiet time he needed to research his ideas and start his next fiction novel, a series of adventures along the Great Lakes.

Stan loved reading about the Great Lakes. Its history was well-known to many people. To write a great fiction book, you needed an area with a rich history and folklore to make the characters become real. Lake Superior was especially well suited for Stan's novels. In addition, for his new book, he planned to spend a lot of time talking to the local people, picking up on the fine details that he could weave into a fantastic story by winter time. He wanted it to be a fiction book set around historical facts, intertwined with a little mystery and romance woven into the framework.

Once he got started on the book, he knew that he could use the cold months of January and February to edit and finalize anything he composed this fall, while waiting for the next "paid" writing job to come along.

Stan enjoyed making quick decisions, just like dropping everything and heading up to Bayfield. Maybe that was why he never settled down into a long-term serious job, other than writing. At least when writing, he could start and stop his projects as he wished.

His older sister, Jane, kept bugging him about getting a permanent job.

His answer had been, at least up to this point; "I'm keeping ahead of the bills. Maybe someday I'll be famous enough to do this full time."

Jane kept a close eye on her younger brother, ever since he had moved to Minneapolis. Stan followed her to the University of Minnesota two years after Jane left Texas. They stayed in contact with their parents in Texas; however, Jane talked to them much more than Stan did.

Stan packed up his laptop, iPod, camera, cell phone and notebook. Along with a well-worn set of hiking boots, some jeans, shorts, and a few shirts, he was almost ready to go. He preferred to travel light and just fit in with the locals when he was doing his research. The trip from Minneapolis to Bayfield would take five to six hours, since it included stopping and talking to people at cafés, and snack/gas stations on the way. Small tales and stories had a way of interweaving into intriguing yarns.

Because of this, Stan was always looking for something interesting or different. On the last trip, he heard people at the next table joking about changing the markings on a snowmobile trail so that a friend would go off a six-foot jump into a ravine. With a few twists to the story, Stan figured that he could work the tale into something in one of his next books. He filed away all these new ideas into his computer.

On a Saturday morning, the weekend right after the 4th of July, Stan traded his noisy apartment and busy phone for a couple of weeks of quiet, and headed up to northern Wisconsin.

As he pulled out on the freeway, he left a message on his sister's cell phone, "Hi, I'm heading up north to research a book. Talk to you later." Somehow, Stan felt that was his way of letting her know where he was.

He found the trip enjoyable once he got off the freeway and traveled the smaller, back roads. The freeway was always quicker. Yet, there was something special about those back roads. Lots of trees, hills, lakes, and occasionally a deer could be spotted along the edge of the tree line. It was not the kind of road you wanted to drive late at night with all the wildlife that could wander out into the road. However, in the daytime it was exactly what Stan enjoyed driving.

He enjoyed seeing the sun reflecting on the ripples of the small lakes, and the reflections of the tall white pines in the sky-blue water. The lakes forced the small road to weave back and forth; going around the lakes and ponds instead of right down the middle like the freeways.

Even the smell was different. He noticed it immediately. The smell of the diesel trucks was gone. Now, it was the smell of the pine trees and grasses that passed through the open windows of his car. He tried to ignore the smell of a skunk that had been flattened on the road.

The drive to Bayfield was a very pleasant ride. Stan listened to his iPod all the way up. It had a connector that played through his car speakers. Stan's favorite singing groups helped him start to relax and forget the rush of the big city as he headed out of town. After a quick stop at a café in Webster, Wisconsin, he was back on the road. Stan decided to listen to a short story on his iPod – it had only been six cd's when he copied it to his iPod. He knew he did not have time to finish it before he arrived in Bayfield. However, he figured he could finish listening to it later in his room, as he tried to get to sleep.

Before he knew it, he was in Bayfield. He arrived mid-afternoon. Stan quickly located the small bed and breakfast he had contacted from home. It was not fancy. However, for doing research, he hoped it would be just what he required; a room with a view of Lake Superior, a good comfortable bed, a table he could work at, and best of all – quiet.

The Lamp Post Inn was not the most popular tourist lodging. That was why he picked this location. He would let the tourists stay at the fancy expensive spots; he just required some comfort and quiet.

Miss Jean Larson, the owner and manager, met him as he opened the door. "Welcome to the Lamp Post Inn," she shouted in a warm spirited greeting.

Stan glanced around the lobby and saw her in the hallway. The grayish-haired, 70-ish owner was all dressed up in Scandinavian clothes, including an apron that had Swedish flags sewn into it.

She had just finished cleaning the floor and was putting away the mop. "Got a little rain last night and I guess some of the mud got tracked in. With all the red clay in the area, if you don't clean it up quickly, it might stay a long time once it dries. I'm Jean Larson. Now, how can I help you?"

"I'm Stan Moline. I have a reservation for a couple weeks. Hopefully, you have my room with a view of the lake ready."

Stan glanced around and noted that all the decorations were Scandinavian in the lobby area. There were Dahl horses and straw goats on the window ledge. Above the windows, were flags of all the Scandinavian countries. Stan only recognized Sweden and Norway. He had seen them watching the Olympics.

"Sure do," she replied. "I've been expecting you. Most people just stay for a day or two. It is nice to have someone stay for a while. Let me show you the way. You have the Sweden room. All the rooms are named after the Scandinavian countries and the interiors bear the countries colors."

She led him up the stairs to a corner room on the second floor of the older looking house, located at the corner of the street. "Best room we have," she told him.

As she opened the door, Stan could see what must have been the master bedroom of an old majestic house built back in the days of the lumber industry. There was lots of oak trim including the stairs and banister. There was a queen size bed with a high pillow top mattress covered by a quilt with yellow and blue colors.

In one corner was an armoire to put his clothes in, along with a closet. In the other corner was a sitting area formed by a bowed out, curved set of windows with a table that allowed the visitor to get a full panoramic view of the town and the ferry dock on Lake Superior.

The manager informed him, "This room has a private bath. No TV, and no air-conditioner, just as I told you. However, we do have internet. Just use your WIFI to connect to the unit downstairs – no password. Breakfast is at 7:30 am. Please be prompt. I'll change the bedding every three days and fresh towels every other day. Right now there is only one other guest. However, that can change in a blink of an eye. Any questions?"

Miss Larson was rather to the point Stan thought. "I think this will do just fine. If I have any questions as to where to go or people to visit in town, mind if I ask?"

"Ask as you wish. I have put some literature on the table, just like you asked when I talked to you on the phone. I guess I know about everyone in town. Born and raised here, you know, so I've seen most folks come and go." With that, Jean turned and headed back downstairs to finish her cleaning.

Stan made a couple trips to the car and set his computer on the table. What a view. If this was the cheap lodging, he wondered what the expensive place on the hill must be like. For now, this was all he needed. He decided to drive around town and check it out, before finding a quaint restaurant for supper. It did not take long. Bayfield extended only a mile or so each way from his room.

He drove down to the ferry dock and parked in an area that gave him a view of the 5:00 pm. ferry. It was just arriving from Madeline Island, which was to the east of Bayfield. He sat and counted the cars as they came off the ferry.

The island is one of twenty-two that makes up the Apostle Islands. These islands provided valuable shelter to the early mariners that traversed Lake Superior and gave them protection from the legendary big waves that frequently accompanied the storms on the big lake. Bayfield soon became known as a safe port from storms because of the protection provided by these islands.

There was a marina at the dock area, one north of town and another to the south. The Bayfield area had become a very popular region for renting sailboats and touring the Apostle Islands.

Now, it was time to make the big decision of the day, where to have supper. He had the choice of a restaurant overlooking the ferry dock or one he had discovered a couple blocks away, which looked a little more colorful. Stan decided on color. He wanted to hear stories, not just listen to tourists talking about how their feet hurt from looking at all the knick-knack shops.

When Stan opened the door to Maggie's, he got a little more color than he expected. Well, he should have realized it when he looked at the outside of the restaurant. The bright pink paint, with yellow trim, should have been his first clue. The second clue would have been the pink plastic flamingos in the yard or the metal flamingo in the parking lot.

As he looked around the inside, he decided he could probably write a short story on the history of this restaurant, all by itself. It was definitely a collection of everything in the area, yet it had a diverse menu. He spent the next 10-minutes looking at the items inside the restaurant/bar.

It had a great old oak bar – if you could find it. It was hidden behind the pink and blue bar stools. Behind the bar were all sizes of flamingos. All were pink and white. Some were wood, some were stuffed, and some were on ropes. Christmas lights lit up the bar and restaurant areas where more flamingos could be found. Just to make it a little more strange, a large-scale railroad ran around the bar room, high along the ceiling. There were pictures here and there showing Bayfield years ago.

Stan was almost certain this was a place where the locals would come, when the tourists were gone. In fact, it seemed that there were more than a few at the bar already.

After a delicious order of Lake Superior whitefish, he was all set to start his challenge. He needed to find at least three things about the area unique enough to write into his fiction novel. Then he would have to find the connections to the past that would make things believable.

His waitress was his starting point. When she came to discuss desserts, he asked her about any interesting points around town. In minutes, he had a map of Bayfield and a short description of most of the historic buildings in town.

She showed Stan some of the main points of interest and said, "The Old Rittenhouse Inn is one of the main landmarks. It is an old mansion on the hill overlooking the town and dock. Historically, the town was linked to the lumber industry. It was built as a summer house for some senator. However, today it is a bed and breakfast – the fancy one in town.

"There is also a nice walking path through town that goes under the steel bridge. There is a great view from the old steel trestle. Just outside of town is the Big Top Chatachaqua. It is a combination music and cultural event where major singing groups come and perform for events all summer."

At the bar, Stan could hear two people talking. They were fishermen that had come in from the days fishing. Apparently, it was a poor day for fishing because of some winds the night before. He heard them say they only had half as many fish as normal.

His waitress saw that Stan was interested in their conversation. She told Stan, "The fishing dock is only two blocks away. They usually fish for either lake trout, whitefish, or herring."

Stan was starting to acquire some of the local culture he was looking for. It wasn't quite what he needed, but it was a starting point. From this basis, he could start asking questions – why is this important? Where did the people come from?

Stan headed back to his room, and was met by Jean Larson as he opened the door to the inn. "Made it back without getting lost I see. Did you find a good spot for supper?"

"Yes! I ate at Maggie's. Interesting place, to say the least. Good food though."

"Good choice! I know the owner," Jean responded. "She really changed the place when she bought it and put a lot of her charisma into it. Not your normal restaurant. Most of the locals gather there in the winter, when all the tourists leave. By the middle of October, this town all but rolls up the sidewalks.

"I put the weather forecast on the board for everyone to see each day since we do not have televisions in the rooms."

She pointed to a slate board in the corner. It showed hot and windy for Sunday – 90-degrees. Monday was 88 and windy with thundershowers late. Then Tuesday cooled off – 65 and a gusty north wind. It looked like Wednesday would be nicer at 75 and only light breezes.

Back in his room, Stan decided it was time to look at the local maps Jean gave him, check the internet for any interesting information on the historical sites, and then get a good night's sleep.

He took time to call his sister, Jane.

"Hi, just thought I would let you know I'm up in Bayfield working on a new book," he told her.

"About time you called," she told him. "From you last message, I couldn't tell if you were heading to Alaska or Maine. Couldn't you be a little more specific than, I'll be out of town?"

Jane was planning on working late the next few days, and was glad that Stan had finally called. After giving him a hard time, she told him he could use his cell phone to call her on Wednesday or Thursday. By then, he could fill her in on everything he had found out about Bayfield and Lake Superior.

Stan hoped that he would have found something really interesting by that time, to tell her. For now, the bed looked extremely comfortable.

At 9:30 pm, the sun set behind the hills. Stan's head hit the pillow and in minutes, Stan was out.

Chapter 3

The Local Feel

Sunday morning caught Stan by surprise. He had slept all night, without waking up. There were no sirens, no phone calls, and no road noises to disturb his sleep. He awoke to a bright sunny day.

Stan rushed down to breakfast, not wanting to be late. Jean had breakfast all ready for him when he arrived. Breakfast that morning was a quiche with rolls and home-made jam.

There was only two other people there with Stan; a husband and wife about 40-years old. They had the other room that Jean had rented last night.

Stan introduced himself, "Good morning. I'm Stan."

"Morning, I'm Paul and my wife is Linda. Did you just come up yesterday?" Paul asked.

"Yes. I'm here to check the area out," Stan replied.

As they started to eat the warm quiche that Jean had prepared, Paul told him about their adventure.

"We arrived late Friday night, and unfortunately, have to leave after breakfast. Yesterday, we took an eight-hour sailing excursion around the islands."

"It was the most enjoyable thing we have done in a long time," Linda told Stan. "The captain was very experienced and made sure we were not out in the large waves. He even gave me a chance to try skippering the boat, which was a lot harder than I thought. We had made reservations a full month ago.

"I told Jean that we would like to come back next summer and stay longer," she said. "Are you here on vacation?"

Stan told them, "Actually, I am up here researching a book, which I am trying to write about Lake Superior. I like writing historical fictions, and this area has a lot of interesting history to tap into."

"Wow! I'll have to look for your books and see what you came up with," she told him.

Stan gave her one of his cards. "Here, you can watch for it on my website."

After the leisurely breakfast and friendly conversations, Stan decided to walk to the local Lutheran church, which was only a couple of blocks away. When he stepped outside, he discovered something the locals knew. The forecast can change quickly, with the direction of the wind. It was only 63-degrees. He poked his head back in the inn and asked Jean about that forecast.

"Hey Jean, where did you hide that warm weather?"

"Just wait til afternoon," she said. "Wind was off the lake last night. Later in the morning, it is supposed to come off the mainland. By the time you get out of church, you'll be looking for your shorts."

Stan knew that the more time he spent with the locals, the better the odds were of hearing something he could not find in print. He was worried about the casual clothes he had packed.

When he arrived at the church, he noticed that slacks and a short sleeve shirt fit right in. He did not need to have fancy clothes for the tourist season.

The church service was small in size and length. Apparently, the pastor knew that no one wanted to listen to a long sermon in the summer. The service only lasted 45-minutes. After the service, there was coffee and cookies. Stan enjoyed talking to some of the members. When he told them he was in town to research a book, several of the ladies came up with great historical stories about their families. It seemed that everyone up here had relatives that were the original ones that settled in the area, and had tales of survival.

Stan did not realize that everyone up here had family members that came over on the Mayflower, or was it the Viking boat, and were the founding fathers of the Bayfield peninsula. To listen to them, you would think that was the case. Unfortunately, the stories were not what Stan was looking for. They were interesting though. Maybe if he combined a few of them, they could be used for fill-in stories in the book.

Walking back from church, his eye caught the sight of a young, blond-haired jogger, with a ponytail, running on the road. Whether it was the ponytail or the white jogging suit that first caught his eye, he was not sure.

Somehow, she seemed out of place. She would have probably fit right in, running on the trails that went around the lakes in Minneapolis, in the fall. However, up here, in her white suit, the outfit didn't quite fit in. Cargo shorts and tee-shirt or sports-bra maybe. He politely said "hi," and gave her a smile as she ran by.

Back at the inn, Stan changed into comfortable jeans for exploring, grabbed his camera and a small note pad. He decided to check out the views from the iron bridge and then see the Old Rittenhouse Inn.

The walk to the iron bridge was about five short blocks. By the time Stan got there, the temperature was already up to 73-degrees. It did not take long to find it.

It was an old road bridge, which had been closed to traffic in the 1960's due to its wood-plank deck, and was restored for use as a walking bridge in the 1980's. On the bridge decking were several benches that had a great view of the town and the harbor.

The bridge was built high over a ravine that had a small creek running through it, and a walking path that seemed to lead up the ravine. This was the one his waitress had told him about. The bridge had become a favorite for both local photographers and tourists. Stan had seen it in one of the pamphlets Jean had left for him in the room.

While sitting on one of the benches enjoying the warmth of the sunlight, Stan noticed the same runner, with the ponytail and white jogging suit, heading down the road towards the bridge. He quickly grabbed his camera and took a picture just as she got to the bridge, with the sun glimmering through her blond hair. It would have made a great picture for an advertisement for Bayfield – a runner, a bridge, and a view of the lake. What more could the Chamber of Commerce ask for?

She appeared to be about his age, around 27 years old. She was short and slim – about 5-foot 2-inches. As she approached, he once again politely said "hi" and gave her another smile as she jogged past. This time she replied with an equally polite "hi."

Stan took a few more pictures from the bridge. He got one of the ferry heading back from Madeline Island, another one with a wide landscape showing the island and the town, and a third picture of the ravine under the bridge. He could use them as reference points at a later date, when he started writing. The view of the ferry dock, Madeline Island, and the town put their locations into perspective. The more things he observed, the easier it would be to weave a story line around them. There was also an interesting storage cave under the bridge. It said something about an old apple storage shed. He made a mental note to check into its history.

From the bridge, the walk to the Old Rittenhouse Inn was a short one. That was one thing nice about a small town. Everything was close. The Rittenhouse was a unique old house with great woodwork on the inside. It was an old Victorian home with a large wrap-around porch that looked like a guest should just crawl up in one of their wicker chairs and get lost in a book. If you were not into reading, you could just let your mind get lost deep into the Apostle Islands, while gazing out over Lake Superior. There was an excellent view of the water and town. Obviously, things were maintained year around on this building, including the landscaping at the inn.

Stan stopped for a short tour of the building.

Inside, Stan found that it was built in 1890, as a summer cabin for former Civil War general Allen Fuller. He was a senator at the time.

When Fuller built the house, he did not put in central heat. He figured it would be a waste of money since he did not think his wife would ever stay at the summer house in the winter time. All the rooms had fireplaces to take the chill off the Lake Superior air.

In 1975, it was purchased, and converted into what was then a new business, a Bed and Breakfast Inn.

Stan checked out the beautiful wood in the main lobby and dining rooms. The old art of craftsmanship shown through. Later, he walked around the outside of the mansion. For a house that was over 110-years old, it was in great condition. They had tried to keep the original look of the old mansion. It had twelve guest rooms. Glancing over the literature, a couple of them were bigger than his whole apartment.

The host at the front desk gave Stan a little more information about some of the events that they had during the year. He said, "We have a dinner concert, called the Wassail Concert at Christmas time, which is put on by the Rittenhouse Singers. The inn is specially decorated for the Christmas Season – from the end of November until the end of December. Thirteen people wander from room to room singing to the guests as they eat dinner. In the lobby, we decorate a concolor-fir tree. It would stand 15-16 feet tall."

Looking around, Stan noticed that the three dining rooms were individually decorated in red, green, and blue décor. Even the deck was decorated with hanging plants and flower beds.

After a short tour of the old mansion, he decided to hike back to get his car and explore Madeline Island. The next ferry was due to leave in about one hour. It would be a short ride, only about 30-minutes over to the island. However, the ferry was the only way to get to and from it. This was probably the reason it was a tourist attraction. He drove down to get in line at the ferry terminal.

While he was waiting, he decided there was just enough time to stop at a small shop to get an ice cream cone he could snack on, and a sandwich, which he could eat over on the island.

He left his car in line at the ferry, so he would not lose his spot, and walked over to get his snacks.

As he got to the shop, the jogger with the blond ponytail entered the deli, just before him.

The small shop specialized in carryout. To increase their profits, they also carried a few items like sunglasses, hats, and suntan lotion that people heading on the ferry might purchase. The menu was fairly simple, they had five choices of sandwiches – two with meat and three without. You could see they really catered to the tourists. The clerk at the counter took both Stan's and the woman's order at the same time.

It took about five minutes before his was completed and packed to go. Once again, Stan gave a smile to her, as they had crossed paths a couple times earlier in the day.

As he was waiting for the ferry, Stan took a picture of the unique sculpture on the end of the ferry dock. It was a ship's mast with a number of seagulls in flight, all welded in place.

The ferry ride was short. It took almost as long to get on and off the ferry as it did for the 30-minute ride from Bayfield to Madeline Island's dock. He could stay in his car; however, he could not run his air-conditioner. For safety reasons, everyone had to turn off their engine until they reached the other shore.

For the fun of it, he turned on his GPS in the car. To Stan's surprise, it showed the route to the island as well as telling him how fast the ferry was going. It was travelling at 12-miles-per-hour.

Stan realized that the routes were based on UPS trucks delivering packages. Obviously, one had delivered a package to someone on the island, and the truck had mapped the route on the GPS's database.

So far, the temperature was mild once he opened the windows. On the way back, it might be a different story as the temperature was still warming up quickly.

Once he got off the ferry, Stan drove around the island checking out the views and establishments. Except for a few shops near the ferry landing, Stan was disappointed not to see many other places he could stop and talk with some of the locals. There were a number of houses on the island, including an Indian reservation on the one tip of the island.

He found a nice park with lots of hiking trails on one corner of the island. The trails wandered along the shoreline and went by some sea caves. This was what tourists loved; however, this was not what Stan was looking for.

Stan wished that he had his old bike with him. He also realized that if he did, he would have been off exploring the trails and not trying to find unique points of information he could use for the book.

The views from the hiking paths along the park were great, but now he needed to get back to his task. He did not want to have to walk up to someone's house to start talking to them, and the only other place he found people congregating was at the ferry terminal.

After a couple hours of looking around the island, he got in line to take the 5:00 pm ferry back to Bayfield.

This time, as soon as Stan got onto the ferry, he decided to get out of the car instead of sitting inside. The hot evening sun was shining in through the windshield and it was getting warm. His car had been the first in line for boarding.

As he got out of his car, he had a chance to talk to the deck hand – whose job it had been to make sure all the cars on the return crossing were parked exactly where he wanted them, to maximize the load.

The deck hand looked like a retired person from the area that wanted an easy job – at least in good weather. He wore safety boots, long grey pants and a vest – the kind highway crews wear to make sure people can see them.

The name on the deck hand's vest was Doug Johnson. Stan took the opportunity to talk to him on the way back to Bayfield. In a short time, he provided more information on the area than Stan had found so far. In the brief 20-minutes they had to talk, Stan learned all about the ferry and its history. On top of that, it was better than sitting in the car on a hot afternoon. Stan wished the crossing would have taken a few hours instead of just 30-minutes.

Doug told him he had been working on the ferry for over 10-years. He used to work for the county doing roadwork in the summer, and snow plowing in the winter. Now, he worked for the ferry company until the ice ended the season. When it froze over sufficiently, he plowed a path out to the island for an ice road. Most of the winters had allowed people to drive back and forth for several months. They could even haul larger items over by truck when they did not want to pay the boat fees for hauling.

This was some of the interesting first-hand information Stan was looking for.

After explaining he was a writer and was looking for interesting stories, Doug Johnson made a suggestion to him. Stan could buy a non-vehicle, one-day ticket, and they could talk on the way over and on the

24

way back. He could tell him as many stories about the area as Stan wanted to hear. He had a lot of stories about the past, when people lived on the islands and made their livings on them.

Stan thought that might be a good way to get some first hand information that might not be available any other way. He told him he would try to see him later in the week.

Doug suggested a mid-morning time when he returned. That is when it is the quietest on the ferry. The weekends are just too busy to be able to spend a lot of time talking.

Chapter 4

Fact Finding

When Stan reached the Bayfield shore, he decided there was just enough time to drive up to Sand Point, which was about 18-miles away on the northern tip of the peninsula. From there, he could see a couple more of the Apostle Islands, as well as a view of the open water of Lake Superior, before it got dark. The more he saw, the easier it was to try to put everything together for a story.

The literature he picked up earlier on Lake Superior provided him a good starting point for information on the lake. It included; a length of 350-miles, width of 160-miles, and a depth of 1,332-feet. Stan was amazed at the fact that as a drop of water enters the lake from the many streams, it takes 191-years for the lake to completely change all the water. In addition, Lake Superior contains 10% of the earth's fresh surface water. Looking at all his literature while looking over the water, provided Stan with one more tidbit for his knowledge.

Among the other facts in the literature on Lake Superior, Stan saw a number of discussion points. Being one of the largest fresh water lakes in the world, it had long been known as a loved and feared lake. The water was as clear as well water. Looking at a topographic map of the bottom of the lake, reminded him of the Rocky Mountains. Only, you have to cut the tops off the peaks and tip them upside down into the bottom of Lake Superior. Lake Superior's peaks extend down – over 1,332-feet from the surface. Hundreds of ships have sunk in storms over the past 150-years in the great lakes.

In Lake Superior, the story has always been that it rarely gives up its dead. The reason is because of the lake's depth. The bacteria that cause gasses to form in the body are retarded by the temperature. The lake water stays so cold the dead bodies rarely bloat up. Because of this, most of the sailors that drown rarely came back to the surface. Instead of a lake with temperatures in the 60's and 70's, Lake Superior stays close to 38-degrees when you get below the surface water.

The "big lake" they call "Gitche Gumee" – had been feared by mariners dating back to the Native Americans that used to travel its shorelines in large freighter canoes – up to 38-feet. Actually, the Ojibwe Indians called the lake *"Gichigami,"* meaning "big water." It wasn't until some writer – Henry Wadsworth Longfellow, wrote the name as "Gitche Gumee" in The Song of Hiawatha that the name stuck.

(*Stan got a chuckle over that fact. Amazing what the power of a pen has done to history.*)

French fur traders used the lake to transport furs from Minnesota and Wisconsin to the Hudson Bay Company in Canada. Now, the big ore boats glide down its long passage. The famous winds of November scare even the best of the 1,000-foot ore boat captains.

On the way back, Stan admired all the pine and popular trees that covered the hills. It really was beautiful. With all the green trees and blue color of the sky and water, no wonder the settlers wanted to stay.

At the inn, Stan put the record of his bills into his computer. He kept track of all his expenses so that he could write them off on his taxes. As he was inputting the sandwich shop bill, he noticed it was about $15 higher than it should have been. Somehow, they charged him for things he did not order. He would have to stop back there tomorrow and get them taken off.

Before heading off to bed, he stopped down stairs and talked to Jean about the Big Top Chautauqua event. Just in case it was something he should attend, he wanted to know the history of it, and what it was all about. It sounded interesting.

She told him, "It's an old time music festival under a huge tent. Sometimes the music goes on long after the event – sometimes all night. Since you came all the way up here to find the heritage, you really should go to it. The one playing right now talks about the history of the area. You might learn something."

Since it only played a few months a year, he thought he would attend one before he headed back home.

Chapter 5

Suggestions

Monday morning was omelet day. Jean made a huge omelet for her guest along with hash-brown potatoes and a biscuit. Stan was her only guest, so Jean asked if it was OK to join him. She sat down with him and asked Stan about his stay in Bayfield.

Stan explained to Jean, "I am trying to write a fictional adventure novel about life here in the Bayfield area. To do this, I need to find a lot of background information to fill in the color of the book."

"Fiction, you say. Well, if you give me a month, I can tell you the history of this area from the time it was founded, until the last one turns out the lights in November. It's what the locals call it when everyone leaves, except those that love the country when it gets cold enough to freeze over the lake, all the way to the islands. That's when you should come up here and hear the stories from the old folks.

"Many of them just sit around having coffee between the times they have to split wood for their heating stoves. Course, now we have some that come up for snowmobile season, which is from Christmas to the end of February. That gives us some work in the winter. Before that, it was mighty quiet up here."

"If you were to go see things around Bayfield, what would you put on your list?" Stan asked.

"Well, in the winter, I would say the ice caves along the high cliffs on Lake Superior – just to the west of Sand Point. The ice is safe for hiking only a few weeks of the winter. The National Park Service makes sure it is safe before they allow people out on the ice. When the wind changes, the ice sheet can go from thick safe ice to open water in a day.

"The caves are interesting in the summer also – just different. There are also sea-caves on a few of the islands.

"I guess the major thing for this area in the summer is sailing on the lake. Some people like diving in the clear water. You know you can see down almost 30-feet at noon on sunny days. Some areas you can see even deeper.

"The old light houses are interesting. Unfortunately, they don't use most of the lights anymore. Electronics kill everything. Now GPS guides the ships away from the islands and reefs, so they do not wreck. There are a lot of shipwrecks along the islands. They built the lights to help the boats navigate into the bay, back in the era of lumbering. After a few years and a few more shipwrecks, they built lights on the outer islands to guide the boats that were traveling farther down the lake, away from the islands to other ports.

"If you are looking for something to write about, the lighthouse on Michigan Island might get you going. It was built in 1857. The government commissioned it for Madeline Island. Once it was built, the government could not find it. After asking around, someone told them there was a lighthouse that looked like the one they were supposed to build on Madeline Island, on Michigan Island. Sure enough, they built it on the wrong island.

"In 1888, the foghorn on Raspberry Island saved a steamer from hitting the rocks. The weather was so bad that they could not see the light. They heard the foghorn just in time.

"You should take time while you are here and take the excursion boat out to one of the lighthouses. The one on Raspberry Island is interesting. It stands about 80-feet over the water and flashes every 90 seconds. They say it can be seen for 21-miles out on the water.

"The foghorn is a 10-inch steam whistle. You didn't want to stand too close to that one when it went off. The trip to the islands usually take you by some of the sea-caves as well."

"Well, maybe I will," Stan answered. "This might be a good day since it is sunny with little wind. Thanks for the information and great breakfast. One more question, weren't there only 12 apostles? The literature says there are 22 islands."

"Far as I can remember. I guess the person that named the area could not count.

"Let me know if you have a good time," Jean said as she got up from the table and gathered the dishes.

Stan gathered a few things in his room before heading down to the dock, to see about catching the excursion boat. He hoped it would not be sold out for the day. A lot of tourists took the excursions, especially on nice days. He was starting to realize that the only way he was going to find the information he needed was to talk to someone like Jean, and get the history before actually checking it out.

As he left, he grabbed his receipt from the sandwich shop by the ferry terminal. *"Might as well try and get some of my money back for something I did not purchase,"* he thought. Then he slid into his car and drove the four blocks to the dock. Seemed like a waste of gas. He really could have walked. However, his big city instincts told him to jump into the car and drive.

As he parked in the city lot, he walked over to the sandwich shop to get a refund. To his surprise, when he opened the door, the same woman with the blond ponytail was in the shop ahead of him. This time she was dressed a little more casual.

She took one look at Stan, abruptly turned towards him, and asked very indignantly, **"Why are you following me?"**

It took Stan by surprise. "Who, me? Sorry, but Bayfield is a very small town. Actually, you seem to be the one that is running all around town. I'm not following anyone."

Then, she turned back to the clerk, ignoring Stan. It appeared as though she was having a hard time returning something she had purchased earlier. Stan heard her complain that this was just not her day.

The clerk tried to explain to her that she could not return a hat without a receipt. To this, she complained that she had only purchased it yesterday. Somehow, the clerk had messed up the receipt and the items were wrong.

Stan looked at his receipt and edged closer.

"I hate to interrupt, especially since I am following you all over town, but yesterday you were ahead of me in line – just like today. My receipt had some things, which I did not purchase, and I was coming back for a refund. Perhaps our bills were mixed up."

She turned and stared with a look of amazement at Stan. Her ponytail may have been lying down, but the hairs on the back of her neck were probably standing straight on end at this point. She had been upset with both the clerk and Stan.

The clerk looked at Stan's receipt, and then, at the women's receipt. Sure enough, they had paid for each other's purchases the day before. The clerk apologized for the mix-up, as he accepted the returns and corrected the credit card bills for both Stan and the young lady.

She stood there with a look of complete surprise.

With that, and brushing aside her ponytail, she turned to Stan and said, "I can't believe what just happened. I think I owe you a real apology. I'm not sure where to start. My name is Barbara. I'm sorry I jumped on you."

"Thank you Barbara, I accept your apology. My name is Stan. It is nice to finally meet you other than saying 'hi' as we pass in the wind."

"I really am sorry, I thought you were following me. It is just that …"

"Yeah, I guess it was getting to the point that it was a lot of coincidences," Stan interrupted. "Even worse; to have each other's receipts. What are the odds we would both go back to the store at the same time?"

"Well, in a regular town probably astronomical" she told him. "I guess in this small town, it just happened. Can I buy you a drink to make up for it? I really do feel badly about what I said."

Stan wasn't sure what to say. "Well, tell you what, how about if you buy the drink and I'll buy dinner? That way we can both feel better about the situation."

Barbara was still cautious of the stranger. She still did not know anything about the guy she had just met, except for one thing, she had noticed that he had a camera and took pictures.

What was he doing with the pictures? Was he married? Where was his wife?

Cautiously, she said, "Well I guess that's the least I can do. Would it be OK if my mother came with? She is up here with me and I would hate to leave her alone."

"Fine, what time, and where are you staying?"

"How about 5:30 pm. We are staying at the Chateau," she replied.

"Five-thirty it is. We can decide then, where to go," Stan said. "Oh, it might be nice to get your last name. It might be hard for me to go to the desk and ask for Barbara."

"You are probably right. It's Fontaine."

"Thank you. By the way, my last name is Moline."

With that, they left the sandwich shop.

Stan felt a little strange. It almost felt like he had made a date with someone and her Mother was included. How was he going to explain this one to his sister?

Well, she was a good-looking blond, and the dinner was actually an apology for the situation he did not create. Maybe it was a good thing that her mother was going to be there. Maybe Barbara would not be as defensive.

Chapter 6

Dinner Guests

The excursion boat was filled for the early trip and only had a few openings for the later trip to Raspberry Island. Stan decided that he would have to delay the trip since he had just made arrangements for dinner, and the boat got back less than an hour before he would have to be ready. It gave him a little more time to wander and try to find some of the interesting stories of the past.

He visited a few shops in town and talked to the clerks at some of the antique shops. From his experiences, he had found that the antique shops were a good place to pick up information about historical happenings. The owners tended to know everyone, and that was how they got their leads to buy valuable items before the public found them. Many of the shop owners suggested Stan purchase some of the books they had on the shelves about the history of Bayfield.

When he got back to the inn, Stan asked Jean for suggestions for dinner. Jean gave him three choices between Bayfield and Washburn, which was only 20 minutes away.

* * * * *

Barbara had hiked back to the Chateau and met her mother, who was walking out in the gardens that surrounded the pergola. It was an area that was used for weddings at the inn.

Barbara's mother, Vivian Jacobs, was not too keen on the newly decided dinner arrangements when Barbara informed her.

"Barbara, did you know that they used to have two fountains here that were fed by underground streams? I have been trying to find out some of the history of the inn. I ran into one of the inn's gardeners, Bob, and he told me all about the garden area.

"The grassy area behind the inn was used as a tennis court, and the pink and yellow roses that grow along the wall, date back as far as anyone can remember. They have worked to keep the original plants alive.

"The carriage house in back is said to be haunted. I hope they fix it up. It would be fun to stay there. Who knows who you might run into.

"He also told me that the breakfast over at the Rittenhouse is 'to die for.' We will have to go over there some morning. You can find all kinds of information by asking people that you run into.

"Tell me more about this man that invited us for dinner. You see him here and there in the town, then, twice you both visit the same deli at the same time. Now, because he says he is not following you, you believe him? What does he do? What makes you think he is a man you can trust? In my day…"

"Yes Mother, I know. However, he really could not arrange getting the wrong receipt and both of us paying for each other's purchases. Sometimes things just happen. Besides, you are coming along. You can stare at him and make him as uncomfortable as you like."

"OK," Vivian said. "But, nothing late."

* * * * *

At 5:30, Stan pulled up to the Le Chateau Boutin, or the Chateau as everyone called it.

He had missed this bed and breakfast on his quick walking-tour the other day. The sign said it was owned by the Old Rittenhouse B&B.

It had a spectacular spot overlooking the harbor with nothing in the way of the view. When he walked inside, he was surprised. It was actually fancier than the Rittenhouse was, except they did not serve meals in the dining room. It was used only occasionally for the guests at special occasions. Perched on the hill, from its porch's wicker chairs and swing, it had one of the best views of the lake. There was an oval window in the front door with leaded glass windows above it and to the right of the entry door. Once inside, Stan saw a main foyer with a round oak table filled with literature of the area placed there for the guests, and oak wood trim everywhere, including the beams on the ceiling. Spectacular!

He met Barbara and her mother – Vivian Jacobs, in the lobby. She was a rather elegant woman that Stan guessed was probably about 60-years old. Her well maintained white hair and stylish clothes gave the impression that she was definitely a classy person.

"Thank you for allowing me to come along," Vivian said.

"Glad to have you with," Stan responded. "Mind if I glance at the inn a second before we go? I haven't been inside the Chateau before."

Barbara replied, "Yes, please. Let me show you around. In fact, we can show you our rooms. They both have spectacular views."

Vivian just rolled her eyes. *"She'll never learn,"* she thought.

Starting on the main floor, Barbara showed Stan the library that was just to the right of the foyer. It was a small reading nook with curved glass windows that overlooked the lake and a matching curved, padded, oak seat, which matched the curvature of the window for reading. The wood in all the rooms looked like it was in perfect condition.

"If your rooms look like this, I can understand why you wanted to stay here," he told them.

"Well, wait until you see my room. This must have been a magnificent house when it was built." Barbara told him

"Across the hallway from the library, is the music room."

She showed Stan the room. The stained-glass windows looked alive as the light came through them casting their light on a grand piano. There was a fireplace with the words Harmony in the stone, just above the fire. It looked so inviting with leather chairs, wood floors and dark green wallpaper, that Stan felt like sitting down and putting his feet up.

"I was told that the owner used to play the viola, and had music concerts in this room. Now, they keep up the tradition with summer concerts at the Chateau called 'Mainly Thursdays' in July and August.

"The living room is over here," Barbara pointed out.

Vivian was standing in the room surrounded by elegance. Stained-glass windows, a fireplace, and leaded-glass bookcases revealed the expertise of the builder. So far, everything in the house looked like it was still 1900, with the exception of the lights having been converted to electricity.

"There is a dining room and kitchen at the inn. However, they are used for special occasions only. The dining room still has the original table and chairs. In the stained-glass cabinets are crystal-ware for use at weddings."

"Where do I sign up to be part of the family that owned this house?" Stan jested.

They took him upstairs to see their rooms.

The grand stairway, with its oak railing up to the second and third levels, looked like something out of the movies. When they reached the third floor, Barbara showed him her room first.

As she opened the door, Stan saw the difference between where he was staying, and the Chateau. It was three times the size of Stan's room at the inn, where he was staying.

"Wow! Looks like you have the Grand Suite."

"No, that's on second floor," she told him. "It was reserved already. Actually, most of the rooms are this big," Barbara replied. "The ones that they have like this at the Rittenhouse were taken and they only had some smaller rooms left. I like the view of the harbor from here. That's why we preferred it to the Rittenhouse. The Rittenhouse is nice, but we did not need their restaurant. We can walk over there and use it if we would like. It is only a few blocks."

"What exactly do you do for a living," Vivian asked Stan. In her mind, she was still questioning her daughter's decision to go out to dinner with him, and was now she had taken him up to see their room.

"I'm a writer. I write fiction novels," Stan replied. "I'm up here doing research for my next book, which I hope to have based in the Bayfield area. So far, I am just in the initial stage of the book, trying to establish the background for the setting of the novel. You have to have a good setting to make the characters believable."

"You have written books before?" Vivian asked.

"Yes, this is my sixth novel. My last two have been good sellers in this area. Maybe you have heard of <u>Tales of a River's Bend</u> and <u>Search and Seizure</u>."

Vivian was feeling a little less apprehensive. Maybe she was wrong about this stranger. Still, you have to be careful.

Barbara was looking cautiously for a change in her Mother's expression.

They continued the tour of Barbara's room. It was the South Suite. It had a Jacuzzi, a fireplace, a king size bed and a wonderful view of the lake and town from its two alcoves that were set up with reading chairs. In the middle of the room was a davenport that faced the fireplace. From her room, it was easy to see Madeline Island. You could almost see parts of Ashland, Wisconsin, down at the end of the bay. At night, the lights of Ashland would be visible. It was definitely a room designed to be spacious, comfortable looking, and with a unique view.

Next, she showed Stan Vivian's room, which was in the southeast corner of the third floor. It was the Turret Suite. Inside he saw a very large room, with a rounded reading room in the corner that had curved windows overlooking the lake. It was very well decorated, with blue carpeting, and yellow and blue wallpaper. There was a large king size bed.

"Now, this looks like a room fit for a queen," he told her.

"Yes, it is fun to watch the ferry come and go from the windows," she told him. "The other rooms here are just as nice."

Stan was impressed. "Thank you for the tour," he told them. They walked down the wooden staircase and out towards the car. "Well, what kind of food do you prefer?" he asked. "They told me about a great fish restaurant, a good steak house and an Italian place nearby."

"How about fish," Barbara answered glancing to see that her Mother approved.

The fish restaurant was along the road that cut in front of the city ferry dock. It had a good view of the harbor. As they got out of the car and started walking towards the restaurant, Stan mentioned to Barbara, "Too bad we can't get take out and eat on one of those boats" – pointing to a couple fancy boats in the slips.

"Well, maybe we could," Vivian mentioned. "I hate restaurants where tourists shout so loud that you cannot talk to the person next to you. Barbara, why don't you take your guest and pick up some take-out. I'll make sure there is a bottle cooled on board."

With that, Barbara pointed to a large black and white boat in the far slip. "Actually, that one is ours – the 'Deceptive Views.' We just preferred to have a few nights on land after being out on the water."

Stan was taken by surprise. One more coincidence? They picked up three fish dinners at the restaurant and brought it back to their boat. They went back to the 45-foot Sea Ray Sundancer – "Deceptive Views," parked in the last slip in the marina.

"Wow! Fancy!" Stan exclaimed. "I was just joking, when I suggested eating on board. However, I sure cannot argue about the view. You have a beautiful view of the lake from here. And, the only other diners to disturb you are the sea gulls."

The three had a great dinner. Vivian had a bottle of white wine on board that they shared, along with the Lake Superior lake trout they had picked up at the restaurant. It was a great way to end the day. Stan was really feeling nervous. He still felt like he had invited himself to a dinner on their yacht.

After dinner, Vivian suggested that they take the boat for a short trip out in the lake, to watch the sunset. She had enjoyed dinner, and was feeling better and better about their new guest. Whatever she was worried about, she appeared to have left it behind. Barbara agreed. It would be a good finish to the evening. She was also starting to enjoy the company. He had not mentioned his family once and she was curious. However, she did not want to bring it up.

Barbara told her mother that she was going to untie all the ropes, except the stern line. She would leave a loop on the cleat that she could release from the back of the boat. The boat was well tied. It had lines all over the dock. If a big wind had come up, it would not have moved an inch.

As Barbara climbed down the stairs to the dock, she untied the bow and mid-ship lines. Then, as she started to release the stern line and loop it over the cleat, she slipped on the edge of a dock plank that was slightly higher than the rest. Lunging forward, she quickly reached for the dock.

She did not want to fall into the water. That would put a serious end to a great evening. Reaching to catch her balance, she lost her grasp of the stern line, as she grabbed the dock. Now, as if it was in slow motion, she watched as it fell into the water – just out of her reach.

The brisk breeze was blowing in the wrong direction. Barbara watched as the boat was now floating out – away from the dock and backwards toward the open water. The end slip, where the boat had been moored, was a double-wide slip, and the other boat was not in the harbor. As a result, the swift breeze quickly moved the boat out of reach from the dock from either side. The direction of the boat's drift was another problem. It was definitely toward the large opening in the break-water and the open bay, rather than towards the other side of the slip.

Vivian was noticeably upset. Even though she had been on the boat many times, she had never operated it anywhere near a dock. She turned quickly and told Stan, "Hand me the cell phone. I'll call 911 and ask them to send a boat to get us back to the dock."

Barbara looked like a deer in a headlight. She froze in astonishment, realizing the boat was out of her control.

Stan turned to Vivian, "You know where the keys are for the ignition?"

"Yes, do you know how to drive a boat?"

"I think I can handle it OK," he answered.

Vivian rushed to the helm and dug the spare keys out of a lifejacket bin. "Here they are," she told him.

Stan put them in the ignitions and fired up the twin engines. "OK, you watch the wind direction for me and I'll put us back on the dock," he told her. The wind was blowing over 10-miles per hour from the northwest. To put the boat back on the dock the first time without knowing how it handled would be tricky, but Stan figured he could handle it OK.

There was no time to figure out the bow thruster controls. He would just bring it up within 10-feet of the final spot and turn the helm away from the dock. Then, by putting one engine in forward and one in reverse, he could use the rudder to move the stern towards the dock, while using the reverse engine to crab the bow into the dock.

Barbara was trying to shout directions from the dock – figuring that if a novice could get the nose into the dock, she could board the boat and catch it before it hit anything else. By the time she realized Stan knew how to run a boat, he was gently nuzzling the boat into the slip.

Barbara quickly jumped aboard. Feeling like a klutz, she asked, "Where did you learn how to run a boat?"

"A few years ago, a friend of mine and I lived on an old 50-foot houseboat on the river that a relative of my friend rented out to us for the summer, when he could not sell it," he replied. "It was a great boat for a couple of guys to have all summer. The agreement was that we would fix it up for him, and if he found a buyer, we would move out in two weeks. He had a problem finding a buyer for an old boat when the economy was bad.

"To bring it into the slip, I learned how to steer it, fighting the wind and current, and turning 90-degrees, while hitting a slip that was six inches wider than the boat on each side. It made you learn how to run twin engines in a hurry. A bow thruster would have been a real luxury on that boat."

"You are full of surprises. I had visions of having to call the Coast Guard to tow everyone in. Thank you again," Barbara said.

He handed off the controls to Barbara, who gently pulled it back out of the slip and trolled gently down the bay. It took a while before the two ladies started to relax and enjoy the evening. It had definitely been a tension breaker and it allowed them to talk more freely the rest of the cruise as they joked about what "could have been."

They trolled out to the area near the northwestern end of Madeline Island and watched the sunset over the hills behind Bayfield.

.

Barbara was starting to warm up to Stan and enjoyed talking about the books he had written. She had not read any of them. However, she thought she might look them up in the Bayfield library after her run the next morning.

Vivian was still a little apprehensive, and when Stan needed to use the restroom, she turned to Barbara. "Don't get too comfortable with him," she told her. "We still don't know anything about him. He's not wearing a wedding ring in case you missed it. I haven't heard him mention his family once."

"OK! Well we can check him out on the internet when we get back. If he is a writer, his books and his photograph should be all over the place."

"Just remember what I said," Vivian reminded her. "Don't trust anyone you don't know."

When Stan returned, Vivian's curiosity got the better of her. "Stan, I noticed you seem to be here on your own. Is your wife not with you in Bayfield?"

Barbara gave her a stare. She did not want to be "that" bold.

"No! I'm not married," he answered. "I spent all my time working my way through graduate school. Most women do not appreciate going out with guys that spend all their time in the lab and working.

"I just haven't had the time to settle down, I guess," he answered.

Barbara was glad to know, but also disappointed. It would have been nice if Stan were married. Things would be easier. At the same time, one more piece of the puzzle was put to rest, even though her Mother would probably keep reminding her, "You, are married."

As they headed back into the harbor, the sunset was all but gone. There was still a slight glimmer of light showing in the sky, which provided the light needed to put the boat back in the slip.

With the wind dying down at sunset, Barbara glided the Deceptive Views through the breakwater and gently into the dock, where she tied it up. She was careful not to trip on the board that stuck up near the back cleat, as she did earlier in the evening.

Stan drove them back to the Chateau and thanked the ladies for the wonderful evening.

As he was going to leave, he wondered to himself. *If he had that boat, would he be staying at the Chateau or staying on the boat?* The boat would have probably been his first choice.

* * * * *

When Barbara and Vivian got to Vivian's room, the first thing Vivian did was open the laptop and Google – Stan Moline. If he were what he said he was, they would find out quickly.

His name popped up right away. There were a number of links, including links to several bookstores and a website. When she clicked on a couple of them, the titles of his books and his picture showed up immediately under the fiction and mystery categories. "Well, I guess we know that part of his story was real," she said.

Barbara gave her one of those looks. "Someday you will have to believe your gut feelings," she told her.

"I've done that before. Didn't get me anywhere. You know, he handled that boat real well. He might be the one to help you steer the boat on a windy day," Vivian told her. "I'm just not going to be much good for you on the big lake, when the wind is more than a few miles per hour. Maybe Stan might be willing to take a few days off from his writing and help you with the boat, if the price was right. Besides, he likes mysteries. I do not like any of the other people we have looked at for skippering the boat."

Barbara sat down and thought about it. Her mother was right. On the cruise up from Chicago, Vivian got seasick whenever the waves were more than five feet, and was terrified by the sight of large clouds on the horizon. She was great comfort and company. However, she was definitely not a good sailor.

They had gotten to Bayfield on Thursday and had talked to several people about finding a dependable captain that could help with running the boat and following charts. So far, the two leads they pursued had been gruff old fisherman that only did odd jobs since giving up charter fishing a few years ago.

Barbara and Vivian had hoped to spend the next two to three weeks, if needed, out in the waters around the Apostle Islands, and if Vivian could not handle the waves, they needed someone they could trust.

Barbara pulled up the weather report on the computer. She had noticed the past few days that the reports for Bayfield were not especially accurate.

The big lake affected the weather, and what was forecasted for Duluth/Superior or Ashland, was not always the same as what might be expected for Bayfield. On top of that, storms along the Canadian side of the lake could cause large waves to travel all the way to Bayfield – even when there was little wind.

The report was for a cold front to move through over-night bringing thundershowers at night and strong winds and a chance of rain tomorrow. The rest of the week looked sunny. That meant that the boat would probably stay in the harbor for one more day.

Chapter 7

The Proposal

Tuesday

The next morning Stan put on his hiking shorts and came down to breakfast – Belgian waffles with fresh strawberries.

Jean took one look at him and laughed. "Didn't read the sign I see." She was looking at his shorts.

"OK, what did I miss," Stan answered.

"Cold front last night. We have a northeast breeze this morning. Temperature is 48-degrees. It is supposed to warm up as the wind shifts back towards the north. May even hit 65 by afternoon. The lake temperature affects our weather up here. When the winds are off the lake, find your coat. If it changes to the south by afternoon, put on your shorts."

"Good advice. However, if you think I am going upstairs and change clothes so someone else can have my waffle, better guess again." Stan was enjoying Jean and her cooking. She had warmed up quite a bit since the first greeting at the front desk.

"Oh, I almost forgot, Jean said. "Got a message for you this morning. Didn't take you long to find a gal. Someone named Barbara called at 7:00 am. this morning and asked if you could call her this morning before 9:00 am. I told her you would be down for breakfast at 7:30."

"Thanks," Stan answered. "I probably left something with her yesterday. Think I can get some more of your information about the area later in the day? All the information you seem to have gets me started in the right direction for figuring out where to set the book."

"Sure, just let me know when you want to talk."

Stan went up to his room after breakfast to change into his jeans. Then, he called Barbara to see what she wanted. It had been a fun evening; however, he was surprised that she would be bold enough to call him first thing the next morning. He must have left something on the boat or something!

Picking up his phone, he called the number that Jean had written down for him. Barbara answered.

"Thanks for calling," she said. I have a special request I need to ask you, which I do not want to ask over the phone. Is there a chance that you might be able to meet me at the boat this morning? I realize this sounds a little strange, but I really need to talk to you."

"Little strange? First, you accuse me of stalking you, and now you want to meet with me on your boat? I can't wait to see what comes next. OK! What time would you like to meet?" Stan answered in bewilderment.

"Thanks! I'll explain everything later. Can you meet me at 10:00 am?"

"No problem! Put your life-jacket on so I can spot you," Stan joked.

There was a moment of silence on the phone, then Barbara answered, "OK, I get it. I deserved that one. Thanks, I'll see you at 10:00." Then she hung up.

Stan sat in the chair in the corner of the room, looking out the window at the harbor – puzzled. What was going on? Had he missed some clues last night? Vivian seemed to be a little inquisitive. However, that is standard behavior for mothers. They are either trying to marry off their daughter or chase away any guy that comes close.

It was a fun evening; however, this really was coming out of the blue. Well, the only thing he could do was show up at the boat and find out what the mystery was all about.

* * * * *

At 10:00, Barbara was already at the boat along with her mother. "Thanks for coming," Barbara greeted him as he stepped aboard.

"I'll get some glasses of wine," Vivian said as she disappeared below deck.

Barbara motioned for Stan to follow Vivian to the salon below. She had three glasses and a bottle of a sweet red wine all set out on the table, by the time they got below deck.

Stan had a puzzled look on his face as they sat down at the table. First, he was not used to being served wine this early in the morning and second – well, he just could not figure out what was going on.

"OK! I surrender. You can keep me hostage on this boat the rest of the week," he told them.

Barbara laughed. "I'll bet you think we're a bit nuts. Actually, we wanted to see if you would be willing to help us with the boat for a couple weeks. Before you answer, let me explain the secrecy and why we wanted to ask you on the boat."

Stan was all ears at that point. So far, this was more of a mystery than anything he had found to write about.

Barbara decided to tell Stan the whole story.

"Do you remember hearing on the news or reading in the paper, about a sailboat that was lost in a storm up here, in May?"

"I often hear about boaters that are missing on the news in Minnesota, near the start of fishing season. Usually, they are reports of fishermen falling overboard and the cold water getting them. However, I don't recall anything about the Bayfield area," Stan replied.

"Well, the last week in April, my husband – Anthony, came up here to meet someone he was going to work with, on a boat. They had rented a 40-foot motor-sailor and the two of them were going to test some equipment on Lake Superior. It was something he had worked on for over a year. I think he was hoping to find some sunken ships that were not on the charts that had gone down in storms in the area.

"They apparently were working out of the harbor, just north of town. The people there told us that they would go out early in the morning and usually return later that night. One day they stayed out all night, tied up near Sand Island due to a storm. They had called the people on shore to let them know where they were and that they were safe. They came back the next day.

"Well, on the third of May, they went out in the morning and never returned. There were no messages and no warning EPIRB. The boat was equipped with an EPIRB 'distress warning' device that was required by the Coast Guard. They simply disappeared.

"When I did not get a cell call from him, I checked with the harbormaster and he called the Coast Guard. There had been strong, gale force winds that day. However, no one saw a boat in trouble. Two weeks later, the Coast Guard reported finding a small amount of debris near Isle Royal State Park – a life ring, and some pieces of wood – nothing else. They searched, but were unable to find anything. If the boat went down, the EPIRB should have automatically sent a signal. It was never found.

"We flew up here and hoped for some sign of them. After a week, the Coast Guard started asking me questions – as if I had something to do with it. I suppose they figured that since my husband was 13-years older than I was, and we had only been married less than 6-months, maybe I did him in for the money.

"Apparently, they ruled me out fairly quickly. Probably due to the fact that the boat trip was scheduled before we got married, and I was at our house with my mother the whole time he was gone.

"After another six weeks, we decided to take Anthony's boat up here and see if we could find something. He had taught me how to run this boat while we were dating last fall. I had used several boats in conjunction with my work in oceanography, and this one was just a little more deluxe – it actually had comfortable cabins in it.

"Unfortunately, my mother is not very seaworthy – she gets seasick. The trip up here taught us that if I was going to look for signs of the boat, I needed someone 'else' to help run the boat, if there was any sign of waves."

"So, why the secrecy?" Stan asked.

Barbara continued, "You see the equipment they were testing was something he was planning on selling to the Navy, or to people that do treasure hunting. When everything, including the equipment, disappeared, I started to wonder if something else was happening. He was an excellent sailor and an excellent swimmer. In fact, he had been a Navy seal when he was younger. How can they disappear without a sign – with an EPIRB onboard?

"That is why we were looking for someone to run the boat. In addition, when we did not find anyone – and this mysterious person showed up that knew how to run a boat, we were real cautious. We checked you out last night on the internet. At least you put a picture on a website."

"Thanks – I think. I have a feeling there is more to the story."

"Well, before I go on, we need to know if you are interested, and can keep it a secret."

"That's like shooting yourself in the foot, before you can ask if the gun is loaded. Can I say perhaps, and let you know for sure when I know what I'm getting into?" Stan said.

"Fair enough," Vivian replied. "Just promise that things stay on the boat if you want to say no."

"OK! Tell me the bad part first."

Barbara went on. "Well, the thing they were testing was secret. I mean real secret. No one was to know about it until the final testing was done and the results shown to the Navy. I did some of the testing with Anthony down in Key West, in January. Other than my husband and myself, no one else knew how to use it. That is no one except for the person he had out in the boat with him, the day he disappeared. I'm not sure where Anthony met him, but he doesn't seem to have any record."

"Well, not everyone has been in jail or has a DWI," Stan replied.

"No, that's not what I had in mind. He simply has no record – he doesn't exist. That was why the Coast Guard stopped looking at me. They found no link between this guy and me, and when they found no record of his existence, it raised a red flag."

"What did the Coast Guard say about the project?"

"Nothing," Barbara responded. "No one at the marina knew about it, and no one knew he was testing anything. I think the Coast Guard just blew it off as another depth finder."

"Can I assume it was something else?" Stan asked.

"Yes!" Barbara answered. "Remember, I assisted my husband on some of the testing. He could find a dollar coin on the bottom – at 100-feet in clear water. I don't think that's a normal depth finder."

"OK! So where do I come into this puzzle," Stan asked.

"I need help finding the boat and hopefully my husband," Barbara answered. "I didn't dare tell anyone, since I didn't trust – well, Vivian didn't want to trust most of the captains we ran into, which could help skipper my boat for me. You see, Anthony did not have the only model. There was a very crude prototype that was in the locker of this boat. He built a fancy one for actual testing that could be photographed. No one knew the other one existed – except for me. This one is homemade."

Stan stopped her. "OK! I'm starting to get the picture. You think you can spot the boat, if it is actually out there, with the prototype. Any idea how big Lake Superior is? It is over 1,330-feet deep in spots. Where was the debris found?"

Barbara took out a map. "Here is the location of the debris finds. I did a tracing based on the winds that day and projected them back in a cone of probability. The center of the cone is the direct path. The edges mark the probabilities based on different times of the day and slight wind shifts."

"Whoa! That's pretty significant work. You did all that? Where did you learn how to do projections?"

"Remember, I told you we traveled on the boat before we were married. I have a degree in oceanography. That's how we met. He was teaching a session at a graduate seminar that I attended. When I was interested in ocean charting, he asked me if I wanted to look into an internship. I married the boss. He was 38 and I was only 25-years old. Mother was not very happy about it. Now, she is all that I have.

"If you can help me even for a week, I think we can cover most of the high probability zone where the boat may have gone down."

"What then? What if we find it," Stan asked.

"Then the Coast Guard will have some work on their hands to find his body and retrieve the boat," Vivian stated.

"Well, I was writing a mystery. This sounds just as mysterious. It also sounds like hours of staying on course. Maybe I can do some writing while we watch the sun move from horizon to horizon."

"Thank you!" Barbara whispered. "I was running out of options. Now you can see why I wanted to talk to you on the boat and not in a restaurant where someone could hear us."

Stan sat quietly – thinking. *Hope someone hasn't put a bug on the boat. A restaurant might have been safer.*

"When do we start?" he asked.

"You haven't even asked about the pay," Vivian inserted. "This is not a charity job."

"Let's see what the week brings," Stan answered. "You can decide later if I was any help or not. The way I look at it, I get a week on a great boat without paying for a rental." Stan figured that he probably would not mind a week with Barbara either. This was like being paid to go out with someone's sister who just happened to be good looking.

Barbara looked over to Vivian. "Mother, could you order in a pizza? Stan, if you do not mind, we can go over some of the equipment and methods I want to use this afternoon, while the weather is still poor. Tomorrow looks good. I am hoping we can get several days in a row. If we can, we can cover a lot of territory."

Barbara opened the front salon door and showed Stan the electronics that were stowed on the floor in the corner. "That's the equipment we need to set up once we get out of the harbor, and re-stow before we return. In that location, anyone that looks inside will think it is just some computer parts and not realize it is exactly what we are going to use. We will be towing a small sled behind the boat about 300-feet."

"How fast can we go?" Stan asked.

"That's what makes this interesting. I have a cable that looks like a tow cable, which comes out of the stern. With a twisted steel cable, it can take a lot of force. We can travel at 25-knots and get good readings. With this gear, we should be able to cover 150-square miles in a day."

"You will be lucky to cover 15-square miles in a day, if you are looking for a needle in a haystack," Stan replied. "That's a lot of territory and you have a huge amount of territory on that map to cover. Where are you planning to start?"

"That is the million dollar question," Vivian quipped. "Barbara doesn't exactly like the debris map."

Barbara looked puzzled. "Yes! She is right. If you were going to look for sunken ships, where would you look?" She opened up a map of Lake Superior showing all the sunken ships in the past 250-years.

"There is about 31,698 Square miles of water out there. Most of the sunken ships are along the shoreline with a few along the reefs and islands.

"I do not think Anthony would go looking at the middle of the lake unless he wanted to test the ability to see the bottom. If he did, (pointing to the map) you might as well map the deepest point – the 1,330-foot area. However, that is not in the debris map.

"So, let's go back to the original assumption and work it backward. Shipwreaks are along the shoreline and reefs. We start there. Fifty miles each way from Sand Island – shoreline to ten miles out. That's our 1,000 square miles and hopefully, eight days to cover it weather permitting. If it is not there, we pound the deep on the ninth day."

"And then? What if you still come up empty?" Stan asked.

"Then Gitche Gumee's story might be right after all. Once again, it may not give up its dead. At least I will know I gave it the best try technology could give. That is what Anthony would have wanted.

"We will need to start early each morning," Barbara suggested

"One more question? You buying breakfast?" he asked.

Vivian spoke up, "If I can stay on shore, I'll buy breakfast, lunch and dinner."

"Six-thirty too early?" Barbara asked.
"See you then," Stan replied.

He exited the boat and headed over to a shop, to buy a couple tubes of suntan lotion, and a wide-brim hat with a tie down. He had not packed for a week or so of sun and wind.

Hopefully, they would find something – sooner rather than later.

Chapter 8

Preparation

Stan went back to the inn and checked his clothes. He needed to fill a backpack with everything he required for the day. Extra set of clothes, swimsuit (*for Lake Superior?*, he jested to himself), laptop, rain jacket, and well, if he needed more, he would buy it for the second day.

That meant one more trip out of the inn. He picked up a cheap backpack and swimsuit.

When he came back, Jean was just finishing a reservation for someone later in the week.

"Jean," he called. "It looks like I may make your work easier for the next couple days. I'm going to help skipper a boat, and will probably be gone for breakfast, while I'm helping."

Jean looked up in surprise. "That gal that called earlier?"

"How did you guess?"

"I'm not that old," she said. "That was a number for Bayfield. I do not know a Barbara that owns a boat. How did you find her?"

"Wow! You are good.

"What do you know about the report of a missing sailboat from around May 1st?"

"You mean the one, where two visitors took out a boat, and were never seen again?" she asked.

"That's the one."

"Well, Deputy Miller told me that two guys rented a sailboat. After a few day cruises, they think they may have hit some gales out beyond Sand Island. He said they had a report by the mail boat around noon, of a boat four-miles southwest of York Island heading northwest. That's the last anyone saw it. No bodies and no beacon. Strange!

"Is that the gal you are going out with? His wife? I heard she came in a couple days ago in a fancy boat."

"Yep! She needs a deck hand."

"You take care. Make sure you do not fall overboard. That water stays cold – even in the summer."

"Thanks! You think I can take a rain check for a day or two on that information on Bayfield you were going to tell me? I really want to hear all the information you have on the area."

"No problem! I'm not going anywhere soon," she answered.

Stan went up to his room. At least someone would know where he was. If he did not come back at night, he could bet that Jean would have the Coast Guard on the phone one minute after 10:00 pm.

He really wanted to start on his book. Well, he could start it in a couple days.

He decided that he better get to sleep earlier than normal tonight. The morning would come real early, and a full day in the sun and wind would tire him out quickly. It had been a long time since he had spent that much time on the water.

Chapter 9

Sea Legs

<u>Wednesday</u>

The alarm went off at 5:30 am. Stan jumped out of bed, shaved and got dressed. He grabbed his backpack as he was heading out the door of his room. When he hit the landing at the bottom of the steps, Jean handed him a bag. "Thought you might get hungry," she said. Inside were a couple warm rolls and some apple butter.

The weather was perfect; partly cloudy with a 5-mph wind. It was a good day for a shake down cruise. Stan still questioned Barbara's estimate that they could scan 125-square miles. That was way too high, even at that boat speed of 25-knots. By noon, he should be able to calculate whether she was right or not.

* * * * *

When he got to the boat, Barbara was waiting. She had the camper top folded up and the boat ready to sail.

"Welcome aboard," she said. "I scanned the harbor and did not see anyone that appeared to be watching us. Keep an eye out for people that look overly curious today as we head past the islands."

60

Stan was caught by surprise. Obviously, Barbara still thought foul play was involved and was not taking chances. They untied the ropes and quietly slipped out, heading along Basswood Island.

"Would you like a snack?" he asked her. "My inn-keeper sent along a couple rolls."

Vivian had purchased some donuts. However, these smelled a lot better and would be a lot less fattening.

"Thanks! You will have to thank her. I have some orange juice in the refrigerator below." She went below and came back with a container of juice, and two glasses.

When they reached the north end of Basswood Island, Barbara attached the tow to the end of the cable, and then released it the 300-feet. "It is set to maintain 10-feet in depth," she told him. "The power cords are wrapped into the cable. We can set up the monitors and check it from inside."

Barbara went inside and set up the computer and twin monitors on the floor. That way they would not fall if they hit a big wave. They were set up in the aft cabin, where the boat would be the smoothest.

She gave Stan a set of GPS coordinates to follow. Once they cleared the islands, they would cruise a grid pattern down the Wisconsin coast. She figured that six passes would cover the distance out to ten miles. They would have to make a few alterations around the islands.

The sonar skid had side-scan ability. It would not just look down. The angle to the side was adjusted to fit the depth, so that it made maximum use of the strong signal it generated.

As they sat drifting in the water, Barbara showed him the image on the screens. It was amazing. The detail was almost as good as watching the shoreline above water. Now he knew why her husband had named the boat "Deceptive Views."

"How do you watch it at that speed?" he asked. "That's a lot like watching the weeds go by next to the car at 60-mph."

"It has several modes," she answered. It will show real time scans or interval scans. It will also record all the data, which is why the computer has three large hard drives. Best of all, it has differential software. You can set it to spot anomalies. It can spot color changes, bottom changes, and even look for magnetic changes. This way I can watch only the things the computer spots, and then go back and look at them in real detail.

"If we pick up lots of anomalies, mother agreed to look at all the spikes with the 'Deceptive Views' tied up in the harbor, while we are sleeping. Actually, I will probably sleep on the boat this week. If she has a problem with the software, I can help her. If my husband's sailboat is there, we'll see it."

"OK! Let's give it a try. I'll take it out one mile from here and then stop. Let's make sure it works, before we burn all that gas," Stan told Barbara. "How wide is the scan at this depth?"

"At this shallow depth, it is only ¼ mile - each side. As we work deeper, we will be working a ¾ mile, per side, scan. If we go to real deep water, we can go out to nearly a full mile each way. This water is so clear that there is very little resistance to the signal. The biggest problem is cutting down the clutter from an overpowered signal as it hits the bottom. We can adjust the strength of signal generated."

"Wow! I see your numbers for square miles per day. Good job!" Stan told Barbara. "It would be nice to have some sort of monitor on top for the driver to see. How fast can you scream that you found something?"

"Well, I have the chart of known wrecks in Lake Superior over by the monitors. If anything else pops up, I will reach through the vent window and tickle your feet with a feather. Let's see if we can find it in the first hour, when we are testing the system."

"We might," Stan replied. "I have it from reliable sources that the boat was last seen four miles southwest of York Island, about noon that day. Figuring an 8-knot speed with that wind, a boat should have stayed within a 30-mile circle of that spot before the storm.

"If we figure they might have headed for shelter; that would make that circle even smaller. Our current course out to open water and back covers 25% of that area."

Barbara sat and stared at Stan.

"Physics major," he told her. "Just couldn't find a job in my field. I was always good at writing proposals."

With that, he headed back topside and ran the programmed course they set on the GPS for one hour. At the end of the hour, he brought the boat to a stop and went back down to see the results. So far, he had not seen any other boats paying attention to their boat.

Barbara was sitting on the bed, in the rear salon, looking at GPS points where the computer suggested that there was something that did not fit the surrounding noise signals.

"Nothing so far," she said. "The system is working great. You would think we had the final version of probes. I have spotted things that divers would love. Unfortunately, I did not see anything resembling a modern sailboat, or any part of one.

"Time to start running our grid pattern down past Cornucopia to Port Wing and back. I do not remember too many reefs on the chart, but remember, the probe is set for ten feet. We do not want to ground it at 25-mph. There are a few major points that jut out into the lake and at least two shoals that are less than 20-feet deep. We'll have to be especially careful of them when we head down the lake."

Stan headed back topside and set the coordinates for the first of the grid lines. His job was easy. He would run the boat watching out for other boaters and hidden sunken islands.

By noon, they had covered half of the area they had proposed to cover the first day. When they stopped for lunch, Barbara showed Stan that they had actually spotted six boats on the bottom. Unfortunately, none were the boat they were looking for. Most of them were on her chart, with the exception of two old fishing boats.

There were also several blips that needed further examination later. She had not taken the time to see what the numerous small targets were that the computer had spotted. They could have been anything from a beer can to a fishing rod that was left on the bottom of Lake Superior. Barbara was looking for something that made a significant blip.

After lunch, they would pick up the search from the spot they stopped, and run as long as they could.

They ran all afternoon – quitting at 6:00 pm, at the north end of Basswood Island. The tow was reeled in, and then disconnected from the cable.

By 7:00 pm, they were back in the slip.

Vivian was on the dock waiting for them.

"Any luck," she asked after looking around to see if anyone was watching.

"No!" Barbara answered. "Stan did a great job of driving and we covered a lot of territory. Unfortunately, we did not see any debris on the shoreline. We'll have to look again tomorrow."

Barbara figured that answer would satisfy the curious listener.

Vivian brought supper on board for the three of them. Barbara looked like a person that spent the day at the casino. Her eyes had the look of someone who had been watching the fruit rotate on the one-arm-bandit all day, hoping for a match.

They discussed all the good and bad hits they had seen that day. When they finished eating, Stan got up to head back to the inn.

"Thanks for all the help today," Barbara told him. "Without you, we would have never accomplished what we did."

"Thanks! Wish we had found something. I'll see you bright and early."

He headed back to the inn exhausted. The sun and wind felt like he had spent a week in the desert.

As he entered the inn, Jean caught sight of him. "Long day? Any luck?"

"Lots of water and sea gulls," he replied.

"Want a roll again tomorrow?" she asked.

"Could I get two?" he responded.

That night, Stan was really tired. He went straight to sleep. In the middle of the night he woke up. Something was bothering him. He was not sure, but knew something needed further thought.

He had similar thoughts when he was in college. He would often wake up in the middle of the night, thinking over a physics problem that he could not solve. In the middle of his dreams, he would wake up and realize the method needed to solve the problem. If he did not get up quickly, he would forget part of the solution by morning. As a result, he always kept an open notebook on the desk and a pen next to it.

Now, in the middle of the night, something was bothering Stan about the search. As he lay there thinking about it, it occurred to him. The EPIRB! These devices are designed to trigger an emergency signal to a satellite, whether or not the trigger was pulled, if they were submerged by water. Why didn't it trigger? Did the boat go down that fast that it sank to the bottom immediately? The signal device was designed to float. If it sank, it would have still given off a signal that the Coast Guard would have been able to pick up. Did the Coast Guard search for a submerged signal, or just a surface signal? He would have to ask the Coast Guard tomorrow. He would also ask how long the signal would remain active before it ran out of batteries. Maybe the submerged signal life was too short to be picked up by the time a search boat got to the right area. Still, no signal was a sign that something was definitely not normal. Maybe Barbara was right. Maybe there was more to the disappearance.

Secondly, what materials are on a sailboat – aluminum mast, a fiberglass and lead keel, some stainless steel hardware, and the test sonar device. Barbara was looking for a large blip. The only thing on the list that could do that would be a large color change or the magnetometer in the sonar device. That was the only thing that was magnetic. It could pick up the signature of metals. Was she looking for the boat, or mainly the sonar device?

Tomorrow was another day. He had time to think about it.

Chapter 10

Waves

Thursday morning wakeup was a little slower than Wednesday's. The long day they put in yesterday took its toll. Stan got out of bed and looked at the sky.

The sun was starting to appear over the eastern horizon. The sky looked good. That meant he needed to get ready for another day at sea.

As he rushed down the stairs, Jean met him at the bottom step.

"Got your snack," she told him. "Good luck, and stay out of the sun. You don't need a bad sunburn."

Just what every boy needs, he thought, *an innkeeper that keeps track of him like his mother.* He grabbed the bag with some fresh rolls, gave her a "thanks," and ran to the car.

* * * * *

Vivian was just leaving the boat when he arrived.

"Were you here all night?" he asked her.

"Yes, a good video movie to watch," she told him. "I must have fallen asleep in the middle of <u>Gone with the Wind</u>. Have a good day."

Barbara was waiting for Stan. She did not look as perfect as she had in the past. It was obvious she had not received the good sleep she had gotten used to at the Chateau. She had reviewed most of the hits Vivian had viewed and dismissed all of them as non-conforming debris.

Barbara was glad to have Stan back onboard. Even though they were working on different levels of the boat, it was company. Besides, Stan caught her by surprise yesterday. She had no idea he had a physics degree. She had been so one-dimensional that she only concentrated on making sure he was not a spy or crook. Today, she told herself she would try to do better.

"Good morning," she greeted him. "Do I smell food?"

"Yes! My innkeeper watches over me like my mother. She packed snacks for both of us again this morning. Hungry?"

They sat at the table below, and ate the croissants with strawberry and orange preserves. Vivian had picked up some apple juice for them for breakfast. As they sat there enjoying the breakfast, it gave them a chance to talk instead of just worrying about how they were going to cover the territory.

Stan had noticed that Barbara had green eyes. Yesterday, in the haste of work, he could not even remember what color clothes she was wearing. Today she had tan shorts and a red and white top. Best of all, he noticed the smile on her face when he arrived at the boat.

When they finished eating, Stan untied the boat and Barbara pulled it out of the slip, heading toward Basswood Island. The new starting point was one mile east of where they started yesterday. When they arrived at their destination, they checked for boats. Not a boat in sight. Then, they laid the tow and let out the cable.

"Today we cover another 25% of your predicted area," Barbara commented to Stan. "Think we can get lucky?"

"Hope so," he answered. "One question, did you check to see if they actually had an EPIRB onboard?"

"Yes, it is required of all rental units on international water by the Coast Guard," she told him. "They also require flares, life jackets, and a throwable life ring. They told me that none of the required items were found except for the life ring."

"Strange, with other boats in the area, someone didn't see some signal or hear something on the VHS radio," Stan commented.

"That's exactly what I said. Let's get going on the search. I want today to be our lucky day."

They started up where they left off yesterday, covering deeper water along the southwest shore of the search area. Try as they might, it appeared that the only thing they were going to find was sun and waves.

The waves were a little higher today and Barbara was glad when they hit the stopping point at noon. Her eyes were still blood-shot from yesterday, and the extra waves today made her a little woozy. She was starting to sense what Vivian felt like on the trip from Chicago.

At lunch, Barbara suggested they eat on deck. She needed time to watch the horizon and settle her stomach.

"You OK?" Stan asked. "You look a little under the weather."

Barbara looked at him and said, "Thanks! I'll be OK. It reminds me of reading a book while you travel down the highway. When you get out of the car, you can hardly walk straight."

"We can adjust the pattern this afternoon to cover the island areas if you want," Stan suggested. "We will have to do it today or tomorrow anyway. It might give you a break."

"Thanks! That might be a good idea. Wish I could just spend the time up here with you, instead of sitting below."

Barbara thought about that statement a moment. The way it came out was not the way she meant it to come out. She looked flustered.

"I know what you meant," Stan responded. "Let's take another 15-minutes before we get started. You need the break."

When they started the afternoon search grid, they covered the circles around the western islands. That gave Barbara a break while they were on the protected sides of each of the islands. By mid-afternoon, instead of a collared blouse, she had her swimming suit top on to try and stay cool.

Stan was caught by surprise when she came on deck. Barbara looked good in a jogging suit. However, in a swimming top, she looked even better. The bright yellow suit caught his eye the second she came into sight.

By 4:00, she felt good enough for one last run down the grid before heading back to the harbor.

Stan took a break to head down to the restroom while Barbara inserted the next "legs" into the computer.

For Barbara, the fresh air was a welcome break. Even though the boat had air-conditioning, her husband had always instructed her not to use it when the boat was up on plane. Air being sucked into the water intake, for the reverse-circulation heating/air-conditioning unit, might cause damage to the system. When the boat was running fast, up on plane, the hull caused a lot of trapped air from the waves to pass the water intake tubes. Sucking them into the unit could cause damage. At trolling speed or at the dock, this was not a problem and the unit was always used.

After the last pass, they stopped again near the top of Basswood Island.

"Still nothing on the screen," Barbara stated as she came back on top. "Mother will have another night of watching movies, looking for anything that makes sense."

Stan needed to take one more restroom break before they broke down the system. Barbara enjoyed sitting on deck in the calm protected area of the channel.

When Stan returned to the deck, they reeled in the tow, stashed it and headed back to the harbor.

Vivian was waiting with supper. The ability to call her when they were 30-minutes out, gave her the opportunity to have an order ready at the local restaurant so that it was still hot by the time they tied up the boat.

Supper was served on deck that night. Barbara preferred to see the setting sun rather than sitting below deck. Stan understood. It had been a long two days for her and she was holding up better than he thought she might.

"Did you know that our inn was used by bootleggers during prohibition?" Vivain asked Stan. "I just found out a ton of information about the Chateau after my long nap. Apparently, one of the first millionaires of the area built it around 1908. He sold it in 1912 and moved to the Pacific Northwest. In the 1920's, liquor was brought from the many stills in the islands and taken to the basement of the Chateau. Apparently, the carport on the side of the building was used for more than just letting guests in and out. From there, they supplied a number of hidden watering holes.

"Also, I found out that the nuns from the Catholic church right behind the Chateau, lived in the Chateau for a number of years. They were so worried about epidemics, that they bleached everything. After a few years, all the woodwork turned white. They had to oil it for years to get the natural wood colors back. You could probably put that in your book," she told Stan.

71

"That is really interesting," Stan told her. "Thanks for the detective work."

After dinner, he thanked Vivian for the food and the history lesson. Then he wished both of them a good night's sleep. Actually, he meant it for Barbara since Vivian had work to do.

When he left, Stan stopped at the marina. He wanted to know about the operation of the EPIRB.

The salesperson told him it activated at a depth of three-feet. The bracket that came with them released the floatable device that made contact with a satellite and instantly gave the coordinates of the vessel. Within a minute, it would be relayed to the Coast Guard. The only way it could have failed would have been that it was stuck and did not surface.

Stan thought about that all the way back to the inn. As he opened the door, he received a cheerful greeting – it was Jean.

"You survived another day. Look at all the money you have saved in rental fees for that vacation you are getting every day."

She was right. However, it just did not seem like a vacation. He was too tired.

Tomorrow's forecast was 85-degrees and a south wind. That will make it tougher than today.

He hit the bed and was out. He had forgot all about turning on his cell phone and talking to his sister.

Chapter 11

Sea Caves

Friday was just as predicted – warm and breezy.

Jean met Stan at the door once again and handed him a snack for two for breakfast. Stan was really starting to like her.

"Jean, did you know the Chateau was used by bootleggers in the 1920's?" he asked her.

"Yes! It was a growing business for over 12 years. This area has a lot of history. If you ever get off the boat, I can tell you a lot more. There was a big epidemic in 1934 that was really interesting. The nuns took care of a lot of kids."

"Keep your memory sharp," Stan told her. "My day job won't last for ever."

* * * * *

At the boat, Vivian was glad to see Stan. "I was worried you wouldn't show and I would have to go out in the waves," she told him. "Barbara is still a little off balance from yesterday, so see if you can go easy on her today."

"Me? She is the one that pushes. I'll see if I can get her to slow down a tiny bit if we get into too many waves," he told her.

As he opened the door to the cabin, Barbara was sprawled out on the cushions. She sat up startled, realizing that she must have fallen asleep. "Sorry, I must have dozed. Did you get rolls again?"

"Well, Jean must feel sorry for both of us. Today she packed scrambled eggs and bacon. I guess I will have to pick up something for her when we get back tonight."

"I can't believe you are that considerate," Barbara said. "Most guys would just take the food and run. Thanks for changing the grid pattern yesterday. I did not realize how badly the waves were getting to me. You kept us on schedule even though you changed the order of which area we scanned next."

"Well it was either that or clean the deck after you chummed the fish," Stan joked. "Got to protect the boss you know."

"Thanks!"

They sat down and ate breakfast. This time they both paid a little more attention to the other person's habits. Barbara noticed that Stan did not put salt on his eggs.

Stan noticed that Barbara did not eat bacon. She had also changed to a lightweight shorts and sleeveless top. Obviously, she had also seen the forecast and was expecting it to be warmer in the aft cabin than yesterday.

On the way to Basswood Island, Barbara let Stan drive and she sat next to him. They discussed the grid they would scan, and Stan suggested that it might be better if they took a break every two hours to get Barbara up on deck. That sounded good to her. She really wanted to get out of the cabin.

The forecast for Saturday was strong winds, up to 25-mph, from the west. Stan suggested that Barbara needed a break. The forecast for Sunday was rain. Two quiet days might help her get her land legs back, and give her a new lease on life by Monday.

Besides, Stan could use the days to do some research. He could finally sit down with Jean and see what she knew. With all the sun and wind, he realized the first day that he was not going to get any writing done on the boat. In fact, he hadn't even brought his laptop along after that first day.

Barbara agreed. She was looking forward to sleeping back on that soft bed at the Chateau. She might not even get out of bed until noon.

The forecast for Monday was back to a cool 73-degrees.

At the first break, Stan took the boat in near the sea-caves along the National Scenic Shoreline. They stayed about a couple blocks out to keep away from sightseers. They could still see the waves splashing against the backs of the caves. It was early enough that the normal kayak explorers were just heading out from the landing.

After the break, they took their last run down toward Port Wing and back – completing that portion of the grid. Still no sign of the missing boat. They had scanned out past the ten miles mark from shore. If it had been there, they should have seen signs of the boat.

Lunch was a turkey sandwich and bottled water. They sat in the calm water – protected by Eagle Island a quarter mile away. Stan asked Barbara, "What are you planning on doing after the search is over?"

"She sat there a few moments and the said, "I'm not sure. I really have not thought that far ahead. This whole thing happened so fast that I really haven't had a chance to do any planning. How about you? What about your book that I am preventing you from starting?"

Stan chuckled. "It will still be there when this is over. Besides, I am starting to enjoy having lunch with a good-looking girl everyday. It will be kind of boring all by myself with just my laptop trying to invent a story."

They had stopped for almost an hour today. Barbara was definitely not pushing the schedule. They had actually covered slightly more territory than she had calculated the first few days. The days off would give them both the rest they needed.

The afternoon search was as productive as the past afternoon. It was starting to become routine. At least the conversation was becoming more enjoyable. The breaks were getting longer and longer each time. They were making up for it by coming in slightly later each day.

Today, it was almost 7:30 pm before they reached the harbor. By the time they finished dinner, it was dark. The clouds had already announced the arrival of the fronts expected for the next day, and the darkened western sky brought sunset to the area earlier than normal. They agreed that they would wait until Monday to resume the search.

Stan headed back to the inn.

* * * * *

Once again, Jean greeted him at the door.

"Hey, you're getting later and later. You must be having more fun on those cruises than I thought." She was trying to get a rise out of Stan.

"Wind with rain late tomorrow! Probably a thunderstorm," she told him. "I've got two more guests for the night. Are you going to join us for breakfast tomorrow?"

Stan glanced over at her. He had forgotten to stop and get something for her to thank her for all the morning food.

"Jean, I don't know where this place would be without you," he told her. "Thanks for the heads up. Yes, if I can wake up in time I think I'll join you for a regular breakfast tomorrow and Sunday. That sun and wind really tires me out. I think we'll wait til Monday when the weather is better."

"No luck again today?" she asked.

"None! I think I'll work on my book tomorrow – if it doesn't put me to sleep. Maybe we can get a chance to talk then."

"OK, I'll bang on your door every time I walk by your room, when I'm making up the other rooms. Keep you alert. Drop you a new fact every time I go by."

"Thanks," he said, as he headed up to bed.

Chapter 12

Shore Time

Saturday

Stan showed up for breakfast at 7:30 am sharp. Except for a couple circles under his eyes, Jean thought he looked pretty good for a city boy, after a week on the water.

* * * * *

The day off could not have come at a better time. Barbara was exhausted from the heat and waves. She and her mother spent a relaxing day wandering around town. Any thoughts of scanning the lake could wait until Monday. Besides, Stan was working on his book today, and Vivian wanted no part of a full day of high waves.

* * * * *

For Stan, it took a little effort to get back to writing. By noon, he was back into the swing, looking at his notes about the area. Jean was doing her part to keep him on track. She had stopped by his room three times in the morning as she worked on the other rooms.

"Ever wonder why the Bayfield County Courthouse is in Washburn?" she asked.

"No! Why?"

"Well, Bayfield was established in 1857. The county courthouse was built in Bayfield in 1875. Later, when Washburn was established in 1884, 12 miles south of Bayfield, they wanted the courthouse. The citizens of Washburn lobbied the Capital in Madison for the courthouse. They claimed they were much closer to Madison than Bayfield.

"The law at the time was that all land owners could vote. It appeared that someone developed an interesting scheme. To get the courthouse, they sold lots. They were one square foot in size. In 1895, when the issue was pushed at the Capital that Washburn was closer to Madison, they had a vote to see who would retain the courthouse.

"Washburn won.

"When Bayfield figured it out, they complained to Madison about the vote. People from Washburn came up in eight wagons, tied up the workers at the courthouse and stole the files.

"The people of Bayfield went down to retrieve them by train. They were met with shotguns. As a result, Washburn won.

"Interesting isn't it?

"Also, during WWII, the basement of the Bayfield Courthouse was used to house prisoners. They were used for help in the orchards and farms.

"That ought to keep you intrigued until the sheets are dry," she told him.

Stan thanked Jean for the information. He looked on the internet for more information about the items Jean had mentioned.

There was a Big Top event tonight. That intrigued Stan especially since Jean said they told stories about the area. He had never been to anything like it. He decided to call Barbara and see if she and her mother might be interested in going that night. The weather forecast had indicated the wind would die down in the evening and the rain would hold off until late at night. There was no answer at her room at the Chateau, so he left a message.

About 4:30, Barbara called back. "Sure, we would love to go to it," she said. "Do you have to dress up for it?"

Stan laughed. "No, I think this is real casual. Jeans should do. They seem to run late so you might want a sweater before it is over," he told her. "I'll pick you up about 7:00 pm."

The Big Top Chautauqua was about three miles south of town, at the base of a ski hill. They had tents all set up that held up to 900 guests. Stan was impressed. He expected something a fraction of that size – something on the order of a small band shell in a park.

They did not leave the Big Top Chautauqua until 1:00 am. After the show was over, they stayed and listened to some story telling, and some impromptu music sessions by some of the musicians. It had been a fun night for all three of them
.

By 2:15 am, Stan had brought the ladies back to the Chateau, and found his own bed. He figured it took almost as long to take off his shoes as it took to fall asleep. He forgot how exhausted he was.

About 4 am, a loud clap of thunder awakened Stan and shook his bed. It was loud enough that he sat up in bed wondering what was happening. As he laid back in bed listening to the rain hitting the roof, he wondered what it would be like, to be out in the middle of Lake Superior in a big storm.

The big boat he had been travelling in for several days would be like a toy in a bathtub, out on the big lake. He had heard stories of waves between 20 and 30-feet high battering the big ships. It was not something that Stan wanted to experience for himself.

Chapter 13

Tidbits

<u>Sunday</u>

Breakfast at 7:30 am sharp. Four new guests were at the breakfast table for a meal of pancakes, peaches, and fresh rolls.

There were two couples that came up together for the weekend. At breakfast, they talked about all the sightseeing they had done the day before, and it sounded like they were enjoying themselves.

They thought the rainy day might put a damper on their morning and cause them to drive back home early. When they asked Stan what he did, and if he was enjoying himself, Stan decided that he would let them know he was a writer. However, he held back any talk about what he had been doing all week. They were excited enough to hear they had a writer joining them for breakfast.

After breakfast, Stan decided he had time to go back to the local church before writing, since it was Sunday.

A couple of the ladies he had seen the week before stopped him after the service and asked him how is writing was coming. They wanted to know if they were in the book. Stan gave them some polite answers about how he was still researching the book and he would not decide until later in the fall what would make the final cut in the book.

After church, he stopped at a shop and brought Jean some flowers for everything she had done for him. He put them on her front desk with a note, "Thanks for all the help!" Then, it was up to his room for a few hours of actual work. It took an hour just to get his weary eyes back, so he could start working on the book.

He worked for four hours straight. On the way back from church, he had picked up a couple of diet cokes and a brownie to keep his attention span working. As a result, he was content to sit and work – and perhaps dream a little, as he looked out the window at the rain hitting the boats in the harbor.

The view from his curved window reminded him of a widow's watch, just like the houses along the ocean used to have. There, wives used to sit and watch for their husband's boats to return.

Jean stopped by and thanked him for the flowers. Every once and a while she would feed him some tidbits about Bayfield.

"Have you heard about Hermit Island?" she asked. "The story told is that two men lived on Madeline Island. One day they had a fight while gambling. As a result, the final bet was that the loser had to move off the island.

"A man named Wilson lost and was forced off Madeline Island. He ended up on Hermit Island – named after his characteristic of living alone, with a garden on the island to sustain himself, making barrels from the trees to make money. He stayed there from 1847 to 1861. Rumor has it that he buried all his money, and to date, no one has found it

"Bet you can work that into your book," she told him.

He had counted at least four ferries that crossed to the island, before Jean banged on the door with another history tidbit.

"Thanks Jean – still awake," he shouted to her. "Can't wait for this one."

"Can I come in?" she gently asked.

"Sure!" Stan answered. "Still got my pants on."

Jean opened the door. The look on her face was not the smiling, jesting innkeeper Stan was expecting. She had a much more solemn look about her.

"What's up?" Stan asked her.

"I just got a call from Deputy Miller. He said that a whitefish trawler had snagged its net this afternoon. When he pulled it up to clear it, he found a body. Just thought you would like to know. I don't know if it is the one you were looking for, but we don't get many drownings up here."

"Thanks! Did he say where or when they were taking the body?"

"He said it was two miles northwest of Sand Island. They were going to bring the body into the boat launch at Little Sand Bay, after the Coast Guard was done interviewing the fishermen."

Stan shut down his computer and decided he would stop off at the Chateau and see if Barbara had heard about it, before driving up to the Little Sand Bay launch. Whether it was Barbara's husband or not, he wanted to see what he could find out about this person that was in their search area.

"Thanks Jean. I'll let you know if this means my cruising days might be coming to an end or not."

* * * * *

By the time Stan made the short drive over to the Chateau, he saw a police cruiser in front of the inn. Obviously, they decided to inform Barbara of the findings. She would have to view the body to determine if it was her husband or not.

Stan decided to go in and see if there was anything Barbara or Vivian needed.

When he got to the lobby, Barbara called over to him. They were all standing in the music room, just off the lobby and had seen Stan come up the sidewalk – Barbara, Vivian, and a deputy sheriff.

"Stan, please join us," she asked. "Deputy Miller has told us that a fisherman had picked up a body in his catch today. We do not know if it is Anthony, however, it may be another hour or more before they bring it to shore. The Coast Guard is heading to the area now."

"I heard," he told her. "Jean seems to get the scoop quicker than anyone." He glanced over at the deputy. He just nodded.

Stan figured that the Deputy had intentionally called Jean to let Stan know.

They moved back to the kitchen so they could talk away from the other guests. After the deputy told them about what he knew, he suggested that they head up to Sand Point.

"Would you like me to drive both of you up to Sand Point?" Stan asked. "My mind is off writing and it might be more comfortable than in a sheriff's cruiser."

"That might be a good idea," Deputy Miller replied. "I might be stuck up there for a few hours depending on what we find."

Barbara went back to her room and put on a pair of designer jeans and a sweatshirt. She figured she would be cold standing in the rain and wind. If it was her husband, she might feel even colder on the way back.

When she returned, Barbara, Vivian, and Stan followed Deputy Miller's car up to Little Sand Bay, where several cars had already gathered. There was another sheriff's car, a Coast Guard pickup truck, and the county coroner's car.

Deputy Miller suggested that they wait in the car – out of the rain, until they brought the body in, and he had a chance to determine the situation. He asked Stan if he would join him in his cruiser for a couple moments, so they could talk.

In the sheriff's cruiser, Deputy Miller asked Stan a few questions about his relationship with Barbara and Vivian. He had already heard most of the story from Jean and was aware that Stan had been out searching for Barbara's husband and boat for several days.

"Did you know either of the ladies before you came up here?" he asked.

"No! I came up to research a mystery novel, and ran into them in town. Think it is her husband?" he asked.

"Well, that's what I wanted to talk to you about. The word I got was that the body was dumped overboard. Someone weighted it down. That's why I called Jean. I figured you might be able to assist the ladies, if it is the missing husband. You know, bodies are not very good looking after they have been in the water for some length of time. The coroner will have to determine how long it has been in the water and cause of death."

"Thanks for the heads up," Stan replied. "I was wondering how this whole thing was going to resolve. In a way, I am glad they found the body out there and not us on one of our searches. That would have been something I was not sure how to handle."

"I'll let you know when I think they can view the body," Deputy Miller told him. "It might be a little while, due to the circumstances."

Stan went back to his car and sat with Barbara and Vivian. So far, the Coast Guard had not brought the body in. They could barely make out a couple boats just to the northwest of Sand Island.

About an hour later, the Coast Guard boat came into the harbor and tied off near the landing. Deputy Miller, the coroner, and the Coast Guard officers met the boat as they were tying off its lines, and went aboard. The body was covered in a tarp and they examined it for almost 20-minutes before Deputy Miller came back to the car.

"I'm sorry madam," Deputy Miller said to Barbara. "You will have to confirm it; however the body appears to fit the description you gave us a couple months ago. There is no identification on it so you will have to let us know for certain.

Stan, I'd like you to take a look before we show the ladies if you would."

Barbara was noticeably grief stricken as Stan exited the car.

"Stan, we may need your help on this one," Deputy Miller told him as they walked over to the dock. "I read your last book, yesterday, when I was sitting on the county road waiting for speeders. Got it out of the library. Good read. Good imagination.

"I want you to see what we found, before the ladies get emotional, and you need to get them back. Your mystery writing might help us figure this one out. It is definitely not the normal drowning."

Deputy Miller led Stan over to the body, and showed him what they caught in the nets.

Stan saw a slightly bloated bluish-gray body in a tan work shirt and tan trousers. Its hands were tied with three plastic ties, and around his legs was a gunnysack tied just above his knees.

"We found four large rocks in the gunnysack," the Coast Guard officer told him. "It was just luck that the weights on a fisherman's net caught the gunnysack. If it hadn't, he might have stayed that way for another 50-years at that temperature. I'm sure who ever put him there did not intend that anyone would find him. It was fairly deep water – over 60-feet. Another couple hundred feet further out and it would have been over 160-feet. We got lucky. The fishermen were fishing the drop-off.

"The coroner is going to want to keep the body for a full week to run tests. It is a lot harder to do a full job after this long in the water – that is, if he has been there all the time."

Stan looked at the body and at the rocks that were in the gunnysack. Then, Deputy Miller suggested it was probably time to let Barbara determine if it was her missing husband.

When she was escorted to the boat, they pulled the cover, exposing the face. Even though it was deformed from being in the water, Barbara recognized her husband's face immediately.

Deputy Miller escorted her back to the car, and sat and talked to her for 15-minutes, while Vivian went with Stan to his car.

"She's going to be taking this hard," Vivian told Stan.

"I suspect you are correct," he answered. "Are you going to stay here until they release the body, or head on back to Chicago?"

"I think she will want to stay for a few days while they determine what happened," she replied. "I'm not sure they ever will."

"Well, at least you will not have to stay up watching movies all night. Did you spot anything the other night? We were in this area."

"No! I saw pieces of an old wreck near the reef. Other than that, we missed it," Vivian replied.

"Yes, I saw that too on the screen when we changed GPS coordinates," Stan told her. "I'll stop by later tomorrow when everything settles down."

"I'm sure Barbara would appreciate it," Vivian replied.

The deputy escorted Barbara back to the car. "I probably will not know anything for some time, and I might want to ask a few questions later, when we start to get the whole picture," he told them.

Then he suggested that they head back to town and get some rest.

* * * * *

The ride back to town was a quiet one. For all the searching, the reality was still hard to see. He was dead. Not only that, it appeared that someone had murdered him. Who? When? Why? These were answers that the sheriff's office would be trying to figure out. It was a question for Stan as well.

* * * * *

He dropped Barbara and Vivian at the Chateau and told them he would call them tomorrow afternoon, after they had a chance to rest. They thanked him for all the help. Then, he went back to the inn. When he got there, he had company waiting for him. This time it was not Jean.

Deputy Miller was waiting for Stan at the inn. As he walked in the door, the Deputy suggested that they spend a moment together in Stan's room. He wanted to talk to him. Jean was at the desk. For the first time she did not say a word.

When they got to the room, they sat down at the table overlooking the harbor.

"Stan, you write fiction novels, what's your impression of this? We do not get very many murders in the Bayfield County area. Occasionally we might get an errant gunshot from a hunter, but this is different. I talked to the city police chief, and he agreed that we had jurisdiction on this one. Stan, you worked with the ladies. Did you see or feel anything that seemed strange?"

"Well, this is a strange one," Stan replied. "I doubt that either of them are connected with his death. They worked too hard to find him...or at least his boat. We hunted all over the shoreline for that boat. In fact, we were in that area where he was found Friday. The scanner was looking for a boat – not someone in cement shoes standing on the bottom.

"I woke up the other night wondering about the whole thing. I could not put a finger on it, but something was bothering me. It still is. Were you aware of the scanner they had for searching the water?"

"Lots of boats out here use them. Most of the big names in fish locators have side scanners now," Deputy Miller responded.

"That's what I thought. That is what is bothering me. Can you put a watch on that boat overnight to make sure no one touches it – including the ladies?"

"Sure, what's up?" he replied.

"I think this hunch of mine is getting closer to reality. There is some proprietary electronics involved in this case, and it may be tied to his disappearance. There are a lot of loose ends here that may be nothing, or might be the key to the whole mystery.

"I need another favor. You need to involve the FBI. Can you use your channels to have Special Agent Mark Lawson call me 'tonight.' He might not remember my name, but tell him it is urgent."

"Want to let me in on this?" Deputy Miller asked.

"Sorry, Agent Lawson may have some CIA contacts that might lend a hand in solving this. I need his permission to even tell you about it."

Deputy Miller thought about it for a minute.

"OK! On one condition; if you do find something, I want to be included."

"Deputy, that is one thing I can promise. I'm not a detective and I'll let the pros do that work. For now, I might be able to use some of my physics background to help you."

With that, Deputy Miller shook his hand and said, "Talk to you at breakfast. Jean said everyone else has checked out." He turned and headed back to his cruiser.

Chapter 14

Connections

Stan laid awake for what seemed to be hours thinking about the day.

About midnight, the phone rang. Stan picked it up and said, "Hello!"

The man at the other end of the phone said, "Damn, this better be good, you got me up out of a wonderful sleep. This is Agent Mark Lawson., what can I do for you."

"You told me to tell you if I caught any fish up in the Boundary Waters Canoe Area didn't you? Well, 'I did,'" Stan told him.

"Now I remember your name. You were that bushy haired guy that thought I was raiding your fishing camp a few years ago. You cost me a night's sleep that night too.

"What can I do for you?" Agent Mark Lawson was starting to wake up. "Tell me that you didn't call to give me a fishing report."

"Did Deputy Miller tell you anything?" Stan asked.

"He said he had a murder and you would only talk to me. That's what suspects always say. Are you a suspect in this one too?"

"No! However, you remember the picture you liked so well that showed the bottom of the Mississippi River? This is déjà vu. You need to be here now. Did you ever figure out if Dr. Harris's system for photographing underwater was a hoax or not? Last thing I heard at the University was that you were chasing him all over the country looking for it."

"Well, that's classified," Agent Lawson told him. "Why?"

"Because, if he is not hidden in prison for whatever you were chasing him for, and if it worked, I need to talk to him. There is a system here that is just as powerful, and it is at risk."

"You know, I can't talk about this over a phone," Agent Lawson told him. "Is that what this is all about?"

"Yes!" Stan told him. "And this time I checked it out. I didn't want to be used as a sucker twice."

"I have a feeling that I might need another fishing trip. Any good spots in your area? How soon are the fish biting?" Agent Lawson asked.

"Breakfast at the inn is really good," Stan answered. "Deputy Miller will be here also. They even have a few rooms open." Stan figured that Agent Mark Lawson was starting to understand what they were talking about, and Stan understood the need for secrecy.

"Oh well, it's only a four hour drive. I had nothing else to do tonight. Breakfast better be good. I guess I owe you one for suspecting you for that missing lens. We'll talk later."

* * * * *

Stan had met Agent Mark Lawson while he was working on his Masters of Physics at the University of Minnesota. Agent Lawson was investigating the theft of a high tech system for aerial surveillance.

Stan had helped the developer take some photographs of the bottom of the Mississippi River from the shoreline. The high-tech equipment was reported to be able to shoot pictures through the water.

After the project was completed, some of the equipment turned up missing.

While looking for the missing equipment, Agent Lawson thought that Stan had stolen the lens, while cleaning up the test lab. After chasing him all the way to a lake in the Boundary Waters between Minnesota and Canada, he found that Stan had only returned the telephoto lens to the professor it belonged to.

Agent Lawson had stayed up all night trying to get to the spot Stan was fishing, and had flown in at the crack of dawn, only to realize he was on the wrong track.

Nevertheless, Stan did not forget the software that had been developed at the University. It was even more powerful than the system on the boat in the harbor. It could see through water – perhaps from space. The question was – was it real, and did they actually get it to work?

Chapter 15

Meetings

Monday

By 7:30 am, Jean had a full house at the inn – at least for breakfast. When Stan came down from his room, Deputy Miller, Agent Mark Lawson, and Sheriff Wayne Bradley were all at the table discussing the case, waiting for Stan.

"Well young man, you look a little more rested that the last time I saw you," Agent Lawson greeted him.

"Well, you look the same to me," he joked. "You look just as tired now as you looked up on Basswood Lake."

Deputy Miller introduced Sheriff Bradley to Stan.

"Now, whatever you told Agent Lawson last night must have been good, Deputy Miller said. "I've never seen someone drive all the way up to Bayfield for breakfast before."

Jean brought out some scrambled eggs, sausages, biscuits, and some fruit. When she had it all in place, Agent Lawson turned to her and said, "Thank you for the great breakfast on such short notice. If you don't mind, we will need a little privacy for the next hour or so, while we discuss some important matters."

Jean politely nodded and told them she would get some work done in the kitchen. Just call her if they needed anything. With that, she left the room.

As she left, Sheriff Bradley spoke first. "I have a feeling that all of us are on different pages in this case. If you don't mind, would you – Deputy Miller, and your buddy Stan, please bring the rest of us up to speed as to what is really going on here, and why Agent Mark Lawson was called in, in the middle of the night?"

Deputy Miller smiled and said, "Well, I can only tell you what we have seen. I think Stan has some information that none of us is aware of, and may be important to the case. Let me give you the 10-minute overview and we can let Stan fill in any blanks that he might have observed.

"On approximately, April 22nd, two people rented a 40-foot Nauticat – NC40, motor-sailor from the Roy's Point Marina just north of town near Red Cliff. They went out on daily trips and returned each evening. On April 30th, they were forced to stay in a sheltered cove overnight because of a storm. They contacted the marina and informed them of their situation and moored out at an island. They returned to the marina the next day. On May 3rd, the boat was last seen southwest of York Island heading north. It never returned to port.

"On May 6th, upon receiving a call from Mrs. Barbara Fontaine, stating that she had not heard from her husband in three days, the Coast Guard started a search for the missing boat.

"On May 9th, possible debris from the boat was discovered along the shoreline near Isle Royal State Park, Michigan. A life-ring and some planking were found.

"Subsequent checks on the missing sailors came up with a person with no background history. The person sailing with Mrs. Fontaine's husband did not have a correct driver's license or social security number, and his home address was non-existent. Mr. Fontaine was employed at the Chicago Marine Institute. They reported that he was on extended leave – testing some equipment he had developed.

"A week ago, Mrs. Fontaine and her mother Vivian Jacobs arrived in their boat. They hired Stan here, to go out with them each day and search for the missing boat and her husband with their sonar.

"Yesterday, on July 11th, Mr. Fontaine's body was recovered in 65-feet of water northwest of Sand Island. His arms were bound with plastic ties and legs were bound with a gunnysack loaded with rocks.

"Last night when I talked to Stan about whether or not he noticed anything strange, he asked me to call Agent Mark Lawson, and ask him to give him an immediate call. That about sums it up."

"Well Stan, what is so important you couldn't tell Deputy Miller?" Agent Lawson asked.

Stan began with addressing Agent Lawson. "Let me know if I get too far into national security and you don't want to discuss things," he told Agent Lawson.

"First and most important, there is some equipment on Barbara Fontaine's boat that I have never seen before. It is private, non-patented, and unless they want to show you, they probably do not have to, since no government money was spent on it as far as I can tell.

"This much I can tell you, if you drop a silver dollar a quarter mile from the boat in 60-feet of water, it could tell you if it was a 'peace dollar' or a 'standing liberty dollar.' In fact, you could tell if it landed heads or tails. Agent Lawson, that's why I wanted you here. I remembered your work on that espionage case at the University.

"Second, as a mystery writer, this is probably the best mystery I have ever seen. The only problem is that I'll probably never be able to write about it. I woke up the other night with some real questions that I cannot answer. As I dig deeper, more questions arise.

"Here is a few of my observations.

"According to Barbara, his wife, Anthony Fontaine was testing a new underwater surveillance system. They had tested it together off the Florida Keys. That is where the 38-year old guy proposed to his 25-year old wife. Five months after they were married, he comes up here with a phantom person to do testing in Bayfield. Why here? Why the end of April when it is colder than hell on the lake? Why not Lake Michigan, where he has this beautiful boat complete with heat and all the comforts of home?

"His wife claims he was looking for undiscovered sunken ships. Most of them in this area are well mapped. Apparently, only his wife knew that the sonar unit he was using is not the only unit. An older prototype is on her boat.

"His wife maps the cone of significant probability from the debris field and wind directions. Unless the boat sank in the middle of Lake Superior in a gale in May, I'm not sure it matches his daily routine for looking for ships. Why didn't a search plane spot a sunken boat? The boat had a 1300-pound keel. If it sank, it would be sitting on the bottom with the mast sticking up. A 30+-foot aluminum mast is easy to spot in water you can see down 40-feet, even in 65-feet of water.

"I plotted a probability area of the search area, based on the known last sighting. We covered 80% of it before the body was discovered. We saw no sign of the boat."

"You missed the body, didn't you?" Deputy Miller inserted.

"Yes! I'll get to that. The software allows her scans for objects to be recorded. It records picture feed, GPS reading, bottom anomalies, color deviations, and magnetic disturbances. Our Navy should have equipment like this. Did you have it anywhere in your report what Mr. Fontaine was wearing when he went out the last day?"

Deputy Miller looked at his reports. "No! I don't see any mention by the marina as to what the men were wearing."

"That's why we didn't find him," Stan answered. "The tan clothes

98

would have been hard to pick up against a sandy bottom. Against the Lake Superior rock, my guess is, if we can get the GPS reading from the fishing boat, we can look at the scan from Saturday and see her husband directing traffic for the fish on the bottom of Lake Superior. I am not sure if it is sandy or rocky in that spot, however, with the exact color of his clothes, I think we can spot him.

"I tested it the other day when we were stopped at the end of our day's search. I wanted to make sure that I was not being faked out by a video made to look real.

"One evening I pulled the coordinates of the Fedora – the 282-foot wooden steamer that sunk in 1901, on my computer in my room. I knew it sank just west of Basswood Island along the shoreline near Red Cliff. I found the exact GPS location. When we were finished mapping the island area, I stopped the boat ½-mile from that coordinate. When Barbara came up to get fresh air before packing up the equipment, I went below to use the restroom.

"When I did, I stopped and looked at the computer. When I hit the live feed button on the software, the boat was in the far background. If I had time to zoom in on it, I could have probably counted the ribs connected to its keel.

"Getting back to your question, I'm still wondering exactly what she was looking for. Agent Lawson, that's where we need to talk later.

"Now, Deputy Miller, did you get a good look at those rocks in the sack yesterday? I do not remember ever seeing rocks like that along the shoreline of Wisconsin or Minnesota. How about you?"

"Correct!" he answered. "I sent samples to the state crime-lab after looking at them along with the gunnysack."

"The only place I have ever seen round and egg-shaped white rocks on a beach was northeast of here in a small town in Canada," Stan observed. "The only reason I remember it, was the sign – 'Do not remove rocks from beach.' I have never seen a sign on a beach asking people not to take rocks.

"I'm still puzzled by the experimental sonar. Why didn't Barbara tell you about it? Surely, it was a key to the missing theory.

"So we have a dead body, a missing body with no real name, a missing boat, missing electronics, rocks that might be from Canada, and what might be the best sonar made, which no one is being told is missing, and one sonar that is on the boat. I think that sums up my list of mysteries. Oh, did they kill Anthony for the electronics or for something they found on the bottom?" Stan concluded.

"Gee, I am glad I just came here for breakfast, and to go on a fishing trip," Agent Lawson told the others. "You boys look like you are going to be real busy."

Sheriff Bradley sat quietly as long as he could. "This one is getting way out of our league. I'm glad the FBI's involved. We need to run the grunt work and let you do the 'who,' 'what,' 'when' and 'where.' I'll stay in contact with the local police so they don't feel left out. We work together pretty well. They may know something we don't.

"Deputy, lets get a push on the crime-lab. See if we can match the rocks, and see if the sack has anything traceable. In the meanwhile, let's do some calling on hardware and feed stores from this side of Superior to the other side of Ashland, and see if any of them sold five or less bags to anyone since May 1st. It's a long shot, but that's all we have so far."

Agent Lawson turned to Deputy Miller. "Can you put a tight ring on her boat until we figure out some excuse to look at it? This may not be easy. Looks like I might be staying for a few days. I'll probably need a couple of my people up here as well. You think there is room at the inn for all of us?

"I'll ask," he answered. "Jean!"

She popped her head out from the kitchen, "Sure, I'll keep the other three rooms open for you."

Agent Lawson looked at Deputy Miller and rolled his eyes.

"It's OK, Jean's an old friend. She helps me out a lot up here," he told Agent Lawson.

"Make sure she keeps a lid on this," Agent Lawson replied. "Gentlemen, I think we need to meet later in the day and find a course of action. How about 2:00 pm at the city police station? No sense all of us driving to Washburn to the Sheriff's office.

"Stan, we need to take a walk."

* * * * *

The two walked a short distance to the historic steel bridge and sat on one of the benches overlooking the harbor.

"OK! What else is on your mind?" Agent Lawson asked.

"Did that spy software at the University ever work?" Stan asked.

"You know I can't tell you that," he replied.

"Well, if it did. A LANSAT satellite passes over this area daily. If it was programmed, it could scan Lake Superior in probably two passes."

"Whoa! I'm not saying it exists or not, but even if it did, that's a lot of pictures and a huge amount of area to look for a needle in a haystack. You don't even know where to look."

"If it did exist, and my guess is I know who might know how to address the satellite, you could scan the results for a 30-foot piece of aluminum color. That mast should be visible on the bottom on a sunny day. That might narrow your search to 20 or 30 locations. With the sonar on that boat, we could check it out, even if it was on the bottom of the 1,330-foot level."

Agent Lawson replied, "If that software did exist, it would be classified. They would never let anyone see the pictures."

"We don't need the pictures – just the GPS coordinates. If we can find the boat, we can tell if the sonar is still there or if it has gone missing; perhaps to Canada."

Agent Lawson got up from the bench. "Beautiful day. Too bad we're not out on that boat cruising the bay. Let's talk later. I'll find you when I need you," he told Stan.

Agent Lawson headed back to the inn to talk to his other agents at the office, while Stan took a walk down to the harbor trying to decide how to approach Barbara. He had told her that he would come by in the afternoon. He was still torn trying to figure out what her involvement was in the whole thing.

Was she really the new wife that did not know anything other than his testing of a new piece of equipment, or was there more to it?

* * * * *

Stan was having a sandwich at the shop near the marina when Agent Lawson walked in and sat down next to him.

"Are the sandwiches any good here?" he asked. "I hear there might be some good bird watching tomorrow. I would really like to see Mrs. Fontaine's boat. Think you can convince her to let us have a peek at it?

"The thought of her husband directing fish traffic has me intrigued. If necessary, we could probably get a warrant for the boat, claiming evidence on that computer, since we think it may have a picture of the dead man undisturbed on the bottom. However, I would really rather have her working on our side than have to serve a warrant. What do you think?"

102

"It sounds like a lot of work for me," said Stan. "You want me to convince a grieving wife and a suspicious mother that it will help them in the long run. Remember, I'm up here to write a book."

"I saw the widow this morning going on a run," Agent Lawson replied. "I think I know why you have enjoyed delaying your book. If I pick up your bill at the inn, how about helping us for another week?"

"OK! I guess I am hooked for two reasons. I would really like to know the outcome, and I really hope we do not find a connection between Barbara and the disappearance. She just doesn't seem like that type of person."

"Trust me, they never do." Agent Lawson said.

They sat there for almost an hour discussing how Stan might be able to get Barbara to cooperate fully with the FBI.

Whatever was holding Barbara up from telling the sheriff in the past would be hard to figure out. Without that knowledge, cooperation might be hard to get.

Chapter 16

Arrangements

Stan went over to the Chateau about 2:30 pm. Barbara and her mother were up in their room making funeral arrangements.

"Stan, thanks for coming by," Barbara said in a sad tone. "We were trying to talk to the funeral director back in Chicago. You would not believe the mess this is to make arrangements out of state."

"Yes, I can imagine. Especially, when you do not know when the coroner will release the body. Did Anthony have any relatives that need to be involved?"

"No! He was an only child and his parents died years ago. I never met them. In fact, I have not met any of his relatives. We were married in Las Vegas and it was just the two of us. Mother was not real happy about my getting married that quickly.

"The two of us were there at a convention. One thing – it saved a lot of money compared to a large wedding."

Vivian put a frown on her face. "I wasn't invited," she said.

"Mother, you know you would have been if there had been more time. We just decided to do it and not wait."

"So, there are no other relatives?" Stan said.

"Well, none that are close. I suppose I will find some popping out of the woodwork, now that he is dead. Too bad I couldn't have met them, when he was alive. Do you come from a big family?" she asked Stan.

"One sister and a brother that is somewhere in England. Rarely hear from him. My parents try and keep us in contact. Which reminds me, I keep missing a call from my sister. I'm probably in deep trouble by now. I was supposed to talk to Jane last Thursday."

"I'm an only daughter so my mother keeps an eye on me," Barbara said.

"Now, I have to find all our financial information. We had a number of loans, and I'm not sure how much is still owed. Anthony also had some insurance. I do not think it will even cover the loan on the boat. What a mess.

"That reminds me, we still owe you money for all your help. I haven't even had time to figure out what we owe you."

"Well, that can wait a day or two. Right now, it sounds like you need a break. How about, if I take the two of you for dinner, someplace away from all of this?"

"I think we are supposed to stay in town in case the sheriff needs something," she replied.

"Well, Deputy Miller told me it would be OK if we went to Ashland for dinner. It is only 30-minutes away, and the break will do both of you good. I'll treat."

Barbara looked up at Stan with her slightly bloodshot blue eyes. "Thanks! You are sweet. We do need to get away from Bayfield, even if it is only for an hour or two."

"OK! I will make reservations. Pick you up at 5:30."

He turned and headed out of the Chateau. When Stan reached the car, he called Agent Lawson. "How quickly can you get that warrant? I am taking both of them to dinner in Ashland tonight.

"If you have a computer geek look at the computer in the boat, you can be copying the three, two-terabyte drives before I get back. I will talk to them at dinner. In the meanwhile, you can copy the program and files. You and I can search them after dinner, and see if this device is what the government needs."

"Whoa!" Agent Lawson jested. "I am still in slow mode from no sleep thanks to you last night. You're moving quicker than I am.

"I do have an agent on the way up from the cities right now that should be in town by 4:30 pm. I will see if the local computer shop has some backup drives.

"I'm sure Sheriff Bradley has a judge where he can get a paper signed, since you witnessed recording the location of the body. Can you keep them out until 9:00? That should allow us time to copy the drives."

"Sorry, I guess this is more my specialty than yours," Stan replied. "Those drives will take hours to copy. I was thinking of you removing the computer and getting it back in the boat by morning. I do not think either lady will want to be on the boat after dark. Meanwhile, we can look at the data while it is copying."

"Do all the University of Minnesota graduates move this fast?" Agent Lawson asked Stan. "Sounds like a plan. I will let you know if there are any problems. See you at the inn."

* * * * *

Stan stopped off and bought a good pair of pants and a new shirt. Jeans probably would not do for this evening.

When he got back to the inn, Jean met him at the door. "Hand me those clothes," she insisted. "No guest of mine is going to go to dinner in clothes that look like they just came off the shelf."

Stan just stood there in amazement. How did she know? Were there any secrets in town that she did not know? He handed the new pants and shirt to Jean. In 15-minutes, she knocked at his door with some neatly pressed clothes. "Thanks!" he said.

He sat there wondering – *was he that obvious for what he was doing? Or, was someone following him and letting Jean know? Was it Deputy Miller?*

* * * * *

Dinner was fantastic. Barbara had dressed up in a red dress that she had brought along and except for the circles under her eyes, she looked great.

When Stan went to pick her up, he took one look at her in the dress and said, "Impressive!" For the first time, she had her long blond hair down instead of a ponytail.

Vivian, who was dressed in a sharp looking dark dress said, "I told her to wear black. She is in mourning, and I told her black."

Stan took another look at Barbara. "I think you look fine. No one in Ashland will even know who you are. The important thing is to get you out, and get time to relax."

They had taken their time driving to Ashland. Instead of 30-minutes, it took 45-minutes. Stan was trying to be the perfect host and kept the discussion light and all about Barbara. They discussed the oceanography that she had done, and where she went to school. By the time they reached the edges of Ashland, she sounded like a weight had been lifted from her, even if it was only for a few hours.

They ate at the Platter Restaurant. It was a historic restaurant in town, with an old tradition of good food and good service. The building was built in 1880, and was one of the oldest restaurants in Ashland.

Tonight was no exception. Even Vivian was starting to take a liking to Stan. She always hated the "me, myself and I" attitude that Barbara's husband seemed to show. Anthony was always trying to sell a new idea, and sometimes he forgot to turn off the salesman attitude once he got home.

Stan ordered a prime rib, while Barbara and Vivian ordered walleye dinners.

When the waiter brought them, they could tell why the place had been a local favorite for years. Everything looked like it was cooked perfectly. Even the presentation on the plate looked fantastic. Vivian ordered a bottle of wine for the table just to add to the atmosphere. It was a time to relax, enjoy the good food, and forget the rest of the day. That's exactly what they did for the next two hours.

Since they had no reason to get back quickly, they just ate slowly and talked. They even had dessert. Vivian and Barbara shared a piece of German chocolate cake, which was definitely not on Barbara's normal diet. Stan had a hot fudge sundae.

After they finished eating, they saw some pictures on the wall about the history of the restaurant, and asked the waitress about it.

The waitress told them, "The mansion was built as a bordello. The second floor had many small rooms, with doorways to the hallway. It was built next to the sanitarium where people went for clear air to recover from tuberculosis. There were three buildings to the sanitarium.

"The customers would park behind the establishment and enter away from peering eyes. Later the basement became a gaming casino and probably a speak-easy liquor location. The basement had several rooms with brick walls and signs of finished baseboards along the floor.

"In the center of the building, was an open airway that led to the roof. In the summer, it acted like air-conditioning letting the warm air lift from the basement to the roof area, where it was open to each floor. In the winter, the vent on top was closed to hold the heat in the building.

"We are in the process of re-doing the whole building – bringing it back to the stately building it once was."

On the way back to Bayfield, they joked about eating at a bordello. It definitely gave them a different light on the restaurant. Vivian wished that they would restore a room upstairs, complete with mannequins, to show the history. It was part of the history of the house, and would only add to its intrigue and ambiance, since the stories in the dining room had already disclosed its past.

Stan hated to break the atmosphere he had created, but decided that he would have to bring up the subject.

"Barbara, I am concerned about your sonar device," he told her. "The sheriff knows we have been searching the bay. Pretty soon, he is going to ask how we were doing it. Since it is now a murder investigation, they may start asking questions. I think you should tell them about the missing unit. If you don't, and they find out, it could be a real problem."

"You are right," she said quietly. "I have been worried about the same thing. I am surprised they have not asked before now. They must know that we are not just looking for floating debris after all this time. Besides, they used Coast Guard scanners right after he went missing. My work must sound like over-kill. I just don't know how to tell them, without looking like I hid something."

Stan paused a moment and suggested, "Maybe I could let it out when they talk to me. If they ask why we did not tell them before, I could just say – you did not ask. Then, if they come and talk to you, you can show them how you have been looking for the sailboat. I think you can ask them to keep the technology secret – if that's your wish."

"You think they will?" she asked.

"I think so. However, I am not sure you should. I think the sonar's level of ability is something that the Navy should be using. They would definitely keep it secret. If you try to use it very often for your work, someone is going to find out. Then, you will have to make some decisions that would have been a lot easier before anyone else knew what you had. Besides, what if the person that killed your husband, did it to steal the only copy? He may come back after yours."

Barbara thought a minute. "I hadn't even thought about that possibility." She stared at her mother as they drove down the road past Washburn toward Bayfield. The sun was setting and they had to start watching for deer near the road.

* * * * *

Agent Lawson's team had been very busy while Stan and the ladies were gone. He had requested that his agent stop at a computer store in Duluth on the way up and purchase a fast desktop, three two-terabyte drives, and two monitors. They arrived in Bayfield at 6:00 pm. He set up shop in the one extra bedroom at the inn – with the assistance of Jean.

The judge had signed the search warrant to search the boat, and without knowing whether Barbara would cooperate in looking at the software, Sheriff Bradley and Agent Lawson had cautiously removed the computer from the boat and had it back at the inn where they could examine it. Fortunately, Stan had given them the password to access the system. He had watched Barbara put it in one morning. She had no idea about hiding passwords. It had surprised Stan.

Meanwhile, Deputy Miller was burning up the phone lines between Superior and Ashland asking about customers purchasing gunnysacks. It was a real long shot, as almost all the farmers had a stack of them for selling apples, corn, and other goods to the stores, and along the highway in the fall. So far, the best he had was the general store up in Cornucopia whose owner thought that someone had bought two bags a month or so ago. He could not remember anything about the person or exactly when it was.

* * * * *

When Stan pulled up in front of the Chateau, Vivian got out first and thanked him for a delightful evening.

Barbara waited a few moments and turned to Stan, "I'll let you talk to the deputy about the software. I am tired of secrets. It's too stressful." She gave him a kiss and thanked him for the evening.

"I'll talk to you tomorrow," she said as she got out of the car and walked up to the Chateau with her mother.

* * * * *

When Stan pulled up at the inn, he was pleased at how well the evening went. He even had a glimmer of hope that his intuition was correct, and maybe Barbara was not connected with the murder.

Still, the statement about "secrets" lingered in his mind.

As he opened the door to the inn, Jean smiled and said, "Norwegian room. They are waiting for you."

Chapter 17

Copies

When Stan opened the door, Agent Lawson and Sheriff Bradley were sitting in the room, along with two other FBI agents, who were looking at the computer monitor. "I'll never doubt you again," Agent Mark Lawson told Stan.

They had gotten the program running. When they looked at a sampling of one of the scans, they were amazed. It was just as Stan told them. The detail was exact – with a long depth of field.

Mark decided at that point it was imperative that they start copying the drives – immediately. Fortunately, his agents had picked up a boosted, quad core computer running the latest operating system. They used some "Y" connectors and were able to copy the original drives as if they were all internal drives to the FBI's computer. This saved them hours that it would have required had they used a USB connection.

When Stan walked in, they were almost finished copying the first of the three data drives.

Agent Mark Lawson had already installed mini GPS tracking devices on the three original hard drives and another in the power supply of the computer. If anyone tried to steal it, they could follow their trail.

When he showed it to Stan, Stan had another suggestion, "What if they steal your computer from the inn? Got that protected?"

Mark looked like one of those deer Stan saw on the highway earlier in the evening. The ones that stood there frozen in the headlights. "Put trackers in these too," he told his crew.

Then Stan reminded him of the sonar device. "Since it is sealed shut, can you put a tracker on the fins that is unnoticeable? You would have to put one on each side to keep it balanced."

"We'll work on that when we return the computer, before dawn. The deputy has the boat watched 24/7. How would you like to show us your sunken freighter?" Agent Lawson asked.

Stan took the notepaper from his pocket with the GPS coordinates of the old schooner Fedora, in Lake Superior. Then, he searched for that coordinate on the computer program. When he had a match, it displayed what looked like the hull of an old wood schooner sitting on the bottom.

Mark took one look and stated, "You didn't tell me whether they used nails or pegs to build the hull. How did they do this?"

Stan answered, "That's my question as well. It is one thing to display this in black and white. How did they do it in color?"

Then Stan searched for the coordinates where the fishing trawler triggered its MOB (man overboard) signal on their GPS fish finder. The Coast Guard had said that the fishermen triggered it immediately after seeing the body coming up from the bottom.

Everyone stared at the monitor. Nothing there!

Stan moved the search a few points each way until – "There! I see him," the Sheriff shouted.

If Jean was listening in, she could have heard him down the block.

Stan zoomed the software in. Sure enough, there was Anthony – upright standing on the bottom. The resolution was amazing. They scanned around for the other sailor to no avail. There was no one else down there.

The software was amazing. What a tool it would be in the right hands. They all sat in amazement.

Agent Lawson asked Stan, "Any luck at dinner?"
Everyone turned and looked at Mark Lawson.

"OK! You know what I meant," he replied.
"Yes! Better than you thought," Stan answered. "Barbara agreed that I should tell you about the sonar. She was worried about what you would think when you found out about it. I suggested that since it was a murder investigation, the sooner Barbara told you everything the better. She told me that I could tell you that she would be glad to talk to you if you could keep it secret."

Mark Lawson sat back in his chair. "That's the first good thing I have heard today that seems to be heading the right way. I'll let you arrange a meeting with her tomorrow. Everything we do tonight, never happened. Everyone understand? Let's not spook her now.

"For now, Stan, what other scans do you think we should look at tonight, before we hit phase two, tomorrow?"
Stan suggested running some of the hits that Vivian looked at, plus running another filter for any color variation from the bedrock color.

At midnight, they decided to call it a night. They had looked at several pieces of junk on the bottom. However, there was nothing that should raise a lot of interest. Mark Lawson's team would put the computer back, while the others got some sleep.

"Breakfast at 7:30 am," Mark said. "We'll run a wish list at that time."

Chapter 18

Deception Revealed

The alarm came early that **Tuesday** morning

Jean prepared waffles for the crew, and then left the room as they discussed the wish list for determining clues. Mark Lawson joked, "You know, I think Radar O'Riley on MASH was Jean's brother. She seems to know everything as we say it."

Deputy Miller laughed. "Yeah! The best thing is; she keeps me up to date on everything going on in town. If you have a question, ask her."

They put together a list for the day.

Deputy Miller was assigned talking to the marina operator who rented the sailboat to the pair. "Find out the clothes they wore, any accents, what they took onboard, even what beer they drank," Mark told him.

Stan was to set up a meeting with Barbara and Mark Lawson. "Let's make sure it is informal and we keep her willing to work with us," he said. "Remember, she knows nothing about the fact that we have the software and have marked the disks."

Sheriff Bradley was to contact the crime-lab. "They may not have the cause of death and time line yet, but they should have the info on the rocks by now. Let's find out where they came from. Oh, ask them if they have anything on the gunnysack," Mark suggested.

"I'm going to be busy the next hour. I'm going to talk to a man about an eagle," Mark said. "If you need me, give me a call."

As he said that, his phone rang. "Our blond is on the run," he said. "She just left the Chateau on a jog. Stan, you set up the timing."
With that, they broke up and each started working on their tasks.

* * * * *

Deputy Miller spent much of the day up at the Roy's Point marina trying to get information on two men that disappeared three months earlier. It was not an easy task.
As he talked to the manager, a few items did show up that were not in the original report.

The manager told him, "The sailboat was not one of the regular boats he rented all summer. This one belonged to a person from Milwaukee. It was a lot more deluxe than the standard summer rentals, which varied from 28 to 42-feet in length. This boat was a 40-foot motor/ day sailor that could operate just as well as a motor or sail propelled boat. Instead of a very small motor, it had a good size diesel engine on board and was equipped with heat and air-conditioning.
"The helm had a partial enclosure. By using the camper-back canvas, the occupants could be completely sheltered from the wind and rain or could head inside to operate the boat in case of bad weather. That was why the renters had requested this boat. They had called late last fall and requested a list of boats available for rental the end of April.

Because of the temperatures, most renters do not even think of starting the season until closer to June.

"The boat sat higher in the water than a standard sailboat and had a hefty 30+-foot mast. It could generally handle anything Lake Superior dished out, as long as it was not a freezing storm."

When asked about the renters and shown a picture of Anthony Fontaine, the manager remembered, "That was one of the people that was still missing, who rented the boat. The other person gave me a $1,000 cash deposit. Never, did get the rest of the money. I did get a copy of his driver's license and credit card. After the boat disappeared, the sheriff told me they were fakes. Even the copy of the captain's certificate for renting the sailboat was a fake. I tried contacting Fontaine's family to collect on the rental, but I did not get too far. Once his wife found out that the other guy had made the rental agreement, she was not too excited about covering the bill. I really hated to contact the owner and let him know the boat was gone."

"Can you tell me anything about the two men?" Deputy Miller asked.

"Don't remember much about them. I remember that they would head out about nine in the morning, after the sun started to warm it up, and be back around 4:30 pm, before it started to get cold for the night. I do remember them bringing two coolers with them each day – you know those blue and white coolers that have wheels. I remember hearing it rumble down the ramp the first day thinking it was too cold to go out and drink beer all day. It must have been in the low to mid-50's for highs back then. That's about it. I did help them with the generator the first morning. Figured they would need it for heat.

"Still can't figure out how a boat that size could disappear without a trace. I've had one boat sink in my 15-years here, and it hit a reef. That's it over at the dock. It took six weeks to get it fixed and refitted."

"Anyone else talk to them that you can remember?" the deputy asked.

"In April? No one here but my crew working on the docks, trying to get the boats in the water. Oh, I do remember something. They said they were staying at a bed and breakfast on the lake. One with cabins. Wonder if 'they' ever got paid?"

"Let me know if you remember anything else," Deputy Miller told him. When he got back to the cruiser, he compared notes with the original report. Copies of the driver's license and VISA card were in the report. When he checked back in, the sheriff was talking to the crime-lab.

* * * * *

Sheriff Bradley had gotten a hold of the state's crime-lab and was trying to get some preliminary information on the crime scene.

"Well, there is not a lot to tell you," the crime-lab assistant told him. "We ran tests for fingerprints, even though we doubted there would be any after all that time. There weren't any.

"The rocks were not from Wisconsin. We think the only place around the lake that they are plentiful is Marathon, Ontario, Canada.

"The gunnysack is a puzzle. There is a brand name on it, but we are having a problem reading it. It is really faded. Our guess is that it was not new.

"We're still working on the time and method of death. It is a lot harder with these Lake Superior drownings. You have to take in account the water temperature at the depth the body was found, and whether or not there was any alcohol in the person's system. So far, the alcohol test came back with a trace. However, there was evidence that your body may have been dead before he was dumped in the lake. Still running tests to determine the cause of death. Other than that, looks like your 38-year old was in good shape."

"Thanks," Sheriff Bradley told her. "Let me know when you have more information. The FBI is hot on this one now, and I'm sure they will be barking at me and looking for answers."

He hung up the phone and called Deputy Miller. "Hi, any luck at the marina?" he asked.

"Some small tidbits. Nothing earthshaking. I'll be back in town in a few minutes," he told the sheriff.

* * * * *

Stan arranged to have lunch with Barbara and Vivian at the Rittenhouse.

"Wow, this is a fancy place," he told Barbara. "I peeked in the door last week, but did not have dinner here."

"Yes, it is part of the Chateau. We can get reduced price meals here because we are staying at the Chateau. Did you talk to Deputy Miller this morning?"

"He stopped over at breakfast. I think he gets free meals occasionally from Jean, for watching over the place. I told him that you would like to talk to them about the boat.

"I told him it had some special equipment onboard, and that he needed to make sure it was in a private report and not something distributed to the media. He said, 'No problem.'

"Would 3:00 pm be OK?" Stan asked. "He also asked if it would be OK if I came along as well, so that he did not have to re-interview me again. Sort of save some time."

"That sounds fine Barbara answered. Where did he want to meet?"

"He suggested the police chief's office, if we were worried about people hearing us talk about equipment. I can pick you up if you would like."

"That would be wonderful," Vivian responded. "I'll be glad when all this is over."

"I think mother and I are going to have soup and salad for lunch. What are you interested in...?"

Lunch was very good. Stan headed back to the inn and informed Deputy Miller about the discussions.

Somehow, he just could not concentrate on working on his book. Too many distractions.

* * * * *

At 3:00 pm, Stan and the two ladies drove up to the Bayfield Police Chief's office.

When they got inside, they were introduced to the Sheriff, the Bayfield Police Chief, and Agent Lawson of the FBI. All of them were careful not to let on that they had met with Stan several times this week.

The meeting was very informal and everyone tried to keep it from feeling threatening. Barbara explained to them, "My husband had an experimental sonar device up here that he was using on the sailboat. I know I did not mention it. Now that it appears he was murdered, I figured you should know about it. I don't know if it has a bearing on the case, but if it does, you need to know."

Agent Lawson asked her about the technology, and whether or not she knew about its operation.

"Well, yes and no," she answered. "I helped test it last fall off the Florida coast. I can run the software, but as for how it works, I am afraid I am not an engineer. The other thing you need to know, I have the only prototype on my boat. We have been using it to try to find the sailboat.

"I'm worried now, after finding Anthony's body that someone might try and steal it if they knew it existed."

"Deputy, can you put some surveillance on the boat while she is here?" Agent Lawson asked.

"I'm sure we can work out a schedule," the sheriff answered.

"Would it be possible to see how it works?" Agent Lawson asked.

"Oh, yes!" Barbara answered. "When would you like to do it?"

"I'm really busy on a couple problems with eagle hunters lately," Mark said. "Can I let you know tomorrow or the next day?" Mark figured that answer would allow Barbara to feel relaxed that he was not pushing for immediate answers.

He also knew that Stan would get the message.

The rest of the meeting they discussed the reason her husband came to Bayfield, and where he met the other person that was on the boat.

Apparently, her husband had met him at a trade show in Chicago. He was discussing underwater mapping and the other man asked him to meet at the bar later in the evening. He had a project and he wanted a partner.

Anthony told her that the man had found some files in an old document at a library. It indicated that a ship, with 1,000 twenty-dollar gold pieces and other trade went down in a storm in Lake Superior. He was an experienced diver, and he needed an expert in underwater locating to find the ship. If he were willing to do it, they would split the treasure.

They arranged to do the locating in late April, to keep others from seeing what they were doing. Her husband had a loan for $200,000 on the boat and slip, loans on the cars, and house. He hoped that this might be a quick way to pay it off. He was always looking for an idea that would have a quick return. She never met the other man. She was only aware of what her husband had told her.

When her husband did not return her call three days in a row, she was worried about the storms and called the sheriff.

He checked and found that their sailboat had failed to return for the three days. They had told the marina manager that they would not be staying out at night. After one more night, the Coast Guard went out looking the next day.

"I assume his life insurance paid off your loans." Agent Lawson asked.

"No, I did," Vivian volunteered. "Barbara may have been a farm girl before she went to college, but our farm is one of the largest orchards in eastern Illinois. I decided that Barbara needed some help until she got her feet back under her.

"When everything is settled, then she can decide if she wants to stay with her job, or come help me manage the orchard. My husband died a few years ago and the work is getting harder each year."

Mark Lawson leaned back in his chair. So much for the idea that the wife had her husband killed for the money. He could scratch that one off his list.

As he sat there listening, his phone rang. He excused himself, answered it and walked out of the room, only to return a few minutes later.

"Barbara, I just checked the weather report for tomorrow. Looks like a great day with little wind. Do you think we can do a test of your sonar tomorrow afternoon? Say 1:00 pm?" Agent Lawson asked her.

"Yes! That would be fine," she answered. "Stan, could you help us with the boat tomorrow? It would make it a lot easier to show them how it works."

Stan agreed. He knew that Mark Lawson must have found something and he really wanted to see what it was.

The short meeting was quickly adjourned, and Stan took Barbara and Vivian back to the Chateau. "See you tomorrow," Barbara told him. "I'm glad we finally told them about the sonar."

Stan could hardly wait to get back to the inn and see what Mark Lawson had found.

* * * * *

When Stan returned to the inn, Mark Lawson was waiting for him in the lobby.

"What kind of Subway sandwich do you like?" he asked. Mark suggested that they take a drive and get some food.

In the car, Stan asked, "Did you find the sailboat? That was really quick."

"Don't know a thing about a sailboat," he said. "I was just wondering if you could lead us to this GPS location tomorrow. I always wanted to see Stockton Island. By the way, what's your take on the hidden treasure?"

"That was the first I had heard of it," Stan answered. "Almost makes sense. I can tell you that she was looking for a boat harder than a body in the water.

"I just thought it was the sailboat he rented. Maybe it was a different boat? Does gold show up on a magnetometer? Probably does since people use them to search the beaches in Florida – don't they," Stan questioned.

"Keep up the good work my boy. This may end up being a great book after all. I might even buy a copy," Mark told him.

They picked up Subways and headed back to the inn.

Chapter 19

Bird's Eye View

Wednesday was as pleasant as Mark Lawson said it was going to be – sunny, low wind and a high of 78-degrees.

The morning breakfast had the same participants. You would think someone would figure it out and go rob a bank, or go speeding down the main street. Between the officers at the table and police watching the boat, the town was almost on its own.

Jean had omelets, rolls, and apples ready for the gang. She knew the routine, set out breakfast and then become scarce.

Deputy Miller reported on his conversations with the marina manager. "The only thing that stood out was the two coolers they brought on board every day."

Everyone had a guess what was in them, but that was all it was – a guess.

Agent Lawson suggested, "This afternoon, Stan, myself and one of my agents will take the cruise with Barbara. Sheriff Bradley, you talk to the Coast Guard. You should be ready if we call you around 2:30 pm.

Sheriff Bradley asked, "Are you that confident?"
Mark just nodded his head.

"Everyone go back to checking out your leads. Hopefully, after this afternoon, we will have a little more direction," Mark told them.

* * * * *

At 12:30 pm, Stan picked up Barbara and they headed down to the boat. Vivian decided to stay at the Chateau. She did not want to see any more waves until they had to leave for Chicago. The trip back was something she was already dreading, and would not look forward to, when it would happen.

Agent Lawson and another agent met them at the boat at 1:00 pm sharp. Mark prided himself on being on time.

After he introduced his assistant, Barbara suggested that they move away from the harbor where she could give them a demonstration of the equipment.

Mark Lawson turned to Stan, "Think you can point this thing towards Stockton Island? I always wanted to see that island, and every time I get up here, the ferry always goes the other way."

"As long as it's OK with Barbara," he answered.

"Sure, that's just on the other side of Madeline Island. We can head that way," she told Stan.

It took 15-minutes to get far enough away from the harbor to release the tow. Then, Barbara gave the agents a look at the bottom that would make the best of fishermen envious.

"With this unit, you can adjust the gain and the angle of view. In close channels, if you don't drop the gain, you get a lot of feedback. In open water with the gain all the way up, we can see almost ¾ mile each way and down to the bottom. The tow is pulled from ten to twenty-feet below the water and 300-feet behind the boat, to reduce clutter."

"How are you powering the unit?" Mark's assistant asked. "That much gain must require a lot of power."

"You are correct. It needs 36-volts at the tow. There is a low loss power cable woven into the tow cable for the 36-volts, and another shielded cable for sending the signal back to the boat," Barbara answered. "As for what it does inside that metal bullet, I'm sorry; I really don't understand that part."

"What else can it do?" Mark asked knowing it had more capabilities.

Barbara answered, "There is a GPS built into the software that pulls off the boat antenna. The information from the tow is linked to it, so that all the information can be stored – including the video. We can look at it later.

"As you can see, it picks up black and white like other sonar. If I switch it over, it picks up full spectrum color. Using the software, my late husband showed me how to filter for changes in structure, changes in color, and search for a specific color. Finally, there is a magnetometer in the unit that will sense metals. That's why it is 300-feet behind the boat."

"So your husband could use this to find gold coins?" Mark asked.

"I suppose," she answered. "However, he didn't take the main computer with him. This one has a huge set of hard drives and is very fast. He only had his laptop with him. It had a 500-gigabyte hard drive and a standard processor.

"He probably had to reduce the scan rate instead of doing constant live feeds like I'm showing you, and he couldn't store a lot of data. He needed to watch the screen for what he wanted. I think he believed that they knew where they needed to scan."

That was something that caught Mark Lawson by surprise. He did not have the full system with him on the sailboat. "Anything else different?" he asked.

"The tow was newer and he had a wireless link to the computer from the tow harness. Other than that, this older unit has the same capability," she told him.

As they were watching the screen, a large object came into view on the port side. Mark's assistant interrupted, "Is that what I think it is?"

Out about 200-yards from the boat, was a large sailboat sitting on the bottom. It was listing at about 20-degrees, as the keel was touching the rocks on the bottom. It sat in 75-feet of water. The shiny mast stuck out like a sore thumb.

"My, my!" Mark stated. "It looks like we may have something to record. We can do that, right? Stan, can you make a circle towards the left with about a 500-yard diameter?"

"What do you see," Stan asked.

"Well, I'm trying to make out the name on the stern of the boat, but it looks like it might be our missing sailboat," Agent Lawson said.

Barbara was in tears. There it was. It was almost as much of a shock as when they called and said they had found her husband. Finding the boat was like putting the final chapter on a book. She excused herself and went to the restroom in the forward cabin. A few minutes later she returned, "Sorry about that. I think everything is settling in at the same time."

Mark Lawson asked Stan to call the Coast Guard.

After taking a series of scans of the boat from different angles, Mark told Stan that he could take the boat back, as soon as the Coast Guard arrived.

It did not take more than a few minutes. The summer station for the National Park Service was only a mile away and around the corner of the island. Whoever scuttled the boat must have figured that no one would look right next to the National Park Service visitor station.

When the Park Service boat arrived, they dropped a buoy marking the location of the boat. The Coast Guard arrived a few minutes later after heading out from Bayfield.

When they looked straight down in the clear water, they could just barely make out the shiny mast. Once again, if they had scuttled it a few hundred yards further from shore, it would have been in over a hundred-feet of water. Obviously, whoever did it did not have a working depth finder on their boat.

Several patrol boats arrived within the next hour to secure the area and start the process of determining how it sank. If they had only looked at the video on the computer, they could have determined that the two holes in the hull were probably caused by shaped explosives that put the boat down in a matter of minutes.

Barbara shut down the system and packed up the tow. She did not think she would need it again on this trip.

The return trip back to Bayfield was a quiet one. She sat next to Stan on the driver's seat. Stan put his arm around her, and held her most of the way back.

At the marina, Agent Lawson asked Barbara if he could have a meeting with her the next morning. "I have a few odds and ends that need your attention," he told her. "Can we meet at the Chief's office about 9:00?"

"Whatever you like," she answered. She was in no mood to argue or discuss things at that point. She closed up the boat and asked Stan if he would take her back to the Chateau.

When they got to the Chateau, she thanked Stan for all the help, and went to her room. There, when her mother joined her, she explained everything that had happened.

Chapter 20

The Raising

Sheriff Bradley worked closely with the Coast Guard to gather any information about the sinking of the boat, before giving the OK for a salvage crew to come in and refloat the boat. They would attach floatable buoys on each side of the vessel with straps running under it. Then, they would start the slow task of gently inflating the buoys and raising the vessel to the surface. At that point, they could tow it to the marina where a lifting hoist would bring it out of the water and set it on platforms in the lot. All of this was planned for Thursday. However, it was contingent upon divers finding nothing new around the boat.

* * * * *

Thursday morning, things went as planned. The vessel was raised, inspected and towed to port.

By 3:00 pm, it was sitting high and dry in the marina. The insurance company had been notified and had a representative already on site to determine if it could be salvaged or not.

* * * * *

Barbara and Vivian met with Agent Lawson at the Police Chief's office earlier that morning. The meeting was light and informal. Agent Lawson was still looking for any clue about the mystery sailor that was still unaccounted for. However, most of all, he was worried about the equipment that was on the sailboat.

Initial reports from the divers at the scene, reported no sign of the sonar tow or electronics onboard. That was concerning to Agent Lawson who now faced a couple of problems. Who killed Barbara's husband, who sank the boat, and who is in possession of a very valuable piece of electronics. That was what he wanted to speak to Barbara about this morning.

"Mrs. Fontaine," he said, "Relax, I'm not here to question you. I have a few things to talk to you about. Please think them through before you give me an answer. I am concerned about who killed your husband. I am also concerned that they may have killed him to get the sonar device he designed. If they did, you may be in danger as well.

"Finally, I have just finished talking to my colleagues in Washington, and they would like to purchase the rights to your device for national security. You may want to listen to their offer. It's better than the pieces of gold."

He paused a few moments before continuing. "I was hoping you might consider selling the unit to the Navy. Whether you do or not, I would like to have it removed from your boat, while allowing us to let the word out that you have a duplicate unit – a newer and improved unit on the boat.

"If we did, we would put a fake unit onboard and have your boat watched continuously for three weeks. If someone stole the other unit, they might come back for the improved version. It would give us a chance to catch the killer. The only problem with that would be that you could not take the boat back to Chicago for a few weeks. We would pick up the dockage fees."

Barbara looked at her mother and asked, "How much are they willing to pay?"

Agent Lawson replied, "The number they were talking about to me was 1.3."

"One hundred thirty thousand is a lot of money. However, I think it is worth more than that," she replied.

"No! They were talking 1.3 million dollars," Agent Lawson calmly stated.

Barbara looked again at her mother. "That would cover all my loans and then some. What would you do?" she asked her.

Vivian looked her in the eye. "Your decision. Are you going to pursue oceanography or the apple business? What if it stops working? You have someone that can fix it? You don't even know how it works."

Barbara thought for a minute. Her mother was absolutely correct. It was a great device, but she had no idea how it worked. In fact, she wondered how her husband even knew how to make it. He was not an electrical engineer. How did he put it together in the first place?

"Can I let you know about that offer tomorrow?" she asked Agent Lawson.

"Yes, but how about the other part – using your boat?" he asked.

"If it would find the killer, do it," she told him. "Make sure you take the sonar device off the boat and my computers."

"Thanks! We will have a metal tube made by tomorrow morning and put a laptop on the boat. No one will know the difference besides you and us." He thanked them for coming in and helping with the investigation.

As soon as they left the office, Agent Lawson contacted an agent in Duluth. The agent had already been sent a drawing. Within

30-minutes, the agent had a shop in Duluth making a stainless steel tow almost identical to the one they were using, except it had some lead in it for neutral buoyancy.

Later in the afternoon, he brought it directly to Mark Lawson along with a laptop computer. When it got dark, Mark's people could switch out the devices, making sure they had GPS tracking devices on them. If they got lucky, they might be able to catch the killer.

* * * * *

That night, Stan finally called his sister. He took a lot of static from her for not talking to her for a full week after they agreed to talk. Jane was getting worried.

If he did not return on Saturday, she was planning on sending out the blood-hounds. Somehow, she figured that Stan had gotten lost in his new book and forgot all about his sister.

Stan tried to reassure her that he really was tied up in something important and did not have time to call. He told her he would explain everything when he saw her.

Chapter 21

Rumors

Friday morning, when he joined the others at breakfast, Mark had a favor to ask Jean.

When she brought out an egg bake, with sausages and apples baked into it, Mark asked her to sit down.

"I would like to ask a favor," he told her. "We are attempting to set a trap. I know that you know just about everyone in town. Do you think you could spread a rumor for us? We need to get it out quickly, and get it to a lot of people."

"You want me to spread gossip?" she asked. "Normally, my job is to get the gossip."

"Well, think of it as a job in reverse," Mark said. "You know the case we've been working on? I need you to let people know that there is something special on Mrs. Barbara Fontaine's boat. She brought some high tech equipment on it for searching for her husband and the missing boat. It was the newest version of a project her husband was working on, and that's how we found the missing boat. Think you can get the word out?"

"I get you," she answered. "You think the crooks will come back looking for the new and improved version. Sure, I'll make sure all of Bayfield knows about it by noon. I'll start with the hairdresser. That will get the ball rolling."

Mark looked at Deputy Miller.

"I told you she was the best with information," Deputy Miller told him.

The group sat and discussed the events that happened the past two days. The sailboat was up on blocks and a crew had gone over it with a fine-tooth comb. There were a number of fingerprints recovered.

No sign of any coolers, computer, or the tow. However, the batteries were left on board. Someone must not have realized that the modem was attached to the battery charger box. It was still attached to the battery. In their haste to scuttle the boat, they must have figured that they could buy new batteries somewhere else and not haul the heavy marine batteries out of the boat. The marks showed where the three large batteries and the main battery sat, before it was scuttled. They had shifted slightly as the boat settled.

"OK!" Mark said, "Deputy, lets go over that list of candidates. Let's see if we can add or subtract anyone."

Deputy Miller read the list they had been working on:

"Wife – low probability. No links to the accident so far. Insurance is the only motive. Family has plenty of money.

"Mother-in-law – low probability. Didn't care for the deceased. No obvious motive.

"Marina manager – low probability. Worked there for 12 years. May have known about the sonar. May have heard them talking about treasure hunting.

"Someone at the deceased work place – may have heard about the treasure hunt.

"An outside engineer who designed the unit and was jealous – this has a higher probability, especially after a few comments by his wife, Barbara yesterday. She questioned whether or not Anthony had the ability to assemble the equipment. Someone else had to have actually put it together and perhaps designed it. We need to explore this a little more."

"That's all the leads so far. I think we are still missing the major clues we need."

"Anything new with the crime-lab?" Mark asked.

"Looks like Anthony might have been alive longer than we thought. He disappeared on May 3rd. Coroner puts the time of death at approximately May 10th. We were looking for him on the 6th. In addition, he did not drown. Coroner said he thought it was chloroform."

"OK! Keep the pieces coming. Maybe we will get lucky with the decoy.

"Stan, I'm not sure we'll need you from here. We appreciate all the work you have done. If we get lucky, it will probably be thanks to all the work you have done for us," Mark said. "I'll keep in touch with you. I think I'll stay on for just today. I'll let the sheriff let me know if any leads show up. My work is stacking up on my desk back at the office."

With that, Mark shook Stan's hand and said good-bye. Somehow, Mark knew that they would be back in touch sometime soon.

Around 10:30 am, Mark got a call from Barbara. She wanted a better deal – $1.5 million and wanted to keep the prototype. Mark argued that if it were ever stolen, the technology would be worthless to the government.

They finally agreed on a compromise – 1.5 million, the prototype would be duplicated at a government lab, and returned with some modifications. It would have a tracking device installed permanently inside the unit, and it would be modified to only scan in black and white, and at up to 500-feet.

It was still a valuable tool for oceanography. Any changes or repairs had to be done through his office. Barbara agreed to the terms.

* * * * *

Stan felt as though it had been an exciting two weeks in Bayfield, but he still had nothing to show for his time. Tomorrow, he would have to leave for the cities.

His opportunity to spend quiet time researching was almost gone and although he did have a good set of historical facts and places, it was still not enough to establish the story line around.

At 11:30 am, Jean said she had a call from Barbara. She wanted to talk to Stan. Stan thanked her and called her back on his cell phone. He realized that he had not given her his cell number in the past.

"Stan, thanks for calling back. Mother reminded me that we still owe you money for all the work you did for us. Would you like to join us for lunch? It would be nice to see you before you head back tomorrow. We're going to be staying for another week."

"Sure, I would love to," Stan replied. "Where do you want to go?"

"You can join us at the Rittenhouse," she replied. "How about 12:30? Is that OK?"

* * * * *

Stan drove over to the Rittenhouse and met them. They had a nice lunch in the green dining room, and Barbara told Stan, "I decided to sell the sonar."

Stan was not too surprised. He figured the technology was too sophisticated for Barbara to figure out if anything went wrong. "Good choice," he told her.

The sandwiches were more than they could eat. Vivian gave Stan a check for $1,000 to cover all the time spent on the boat, and thanked him for letting her stay ashore.

She had determined that she really was not cut out to be a sailor.

Stan felt bad taking the check. If they had just batted their eyes at him, he would have probably done it for free. Besides, he did get to see a lot of the Apostle Islands that he would have normally missed. It was probably a better cruise than taking the excursion boat.

Stan asked Barbara, "Have you completed the plans for your husband's funeral?"

"Yes, the coroner has released the body. He will be shipped back to Chicago and we will have a memorial service for him next month," she told him. "That will give us time to get the boat back to Chicago and finish any other arrangements that are necessary."

"I hope the investigation ends soon, so you can start to get back to a normal life," Stan told her.

"Thanks! I am also looking forward to that time. I have decided to help my mother manage the orchard. I need a break from the water," she told him.

"I understand" Stan replied. If you ever head up to Minneapolis, I'd love to show you around."

Barbara appreciated the offer. For now, her life was going to be occupied by wrapping up the loose ends and managing the fall harvest, all at the same time.

After lunch, Barbara gave Stan a big hug and a kiss on the cheek, for all the support he had given her. Then, she and her mother hiked back to the Chateau. They needed the fresh air.

Stan wandered the town looking for ideas. So far, the only idea that kept going through his mind was that he wished he had another week he could spend up here with Barbara.

That evening brought showers to the lake. Stan spent the evening in his room looking at the few ideas he had generated during his stay in Bayfield. There really was not enough to center a book on. Well, maybe some great ideas might come to him as he drove home late in the morning.

Chapter 22

Heading Home

Saturday morning breakfast was back to one – Stan. Mark Lawson and his assistants had pulled out the evening before.

Jean told him that she had two people call about reservations for tonight. Along with the two reservations she had from weeks ago, that meant a full house. She was going to miss Stan.

She told him to come back up, later in the fall, when all the tourists are gone, "that's when you can see the real town."

"I may have to," he told her. "I still do not have enough information to even start my book. Besides, I might miss your great breakfasts."

* * * * *

It was still drizzling at 11:30 am, when Stan packed up and headed for Minneapolis.

Twenty-five miles south of the lake, it was sunny. Stan stopped at a small town on the road between Ashland and Duluth for lunch. In the small restaurant, he listened in to several conversations at adjoining tables, hoping to hear some tidbits that he could use. To his surprise, he heard two fishermen talking about the sonar unit that was used in

Bayfield to find a missing sailboat. They were wondering if they could purchase one for fishing. Jean must have really gotten the word out.

Stan wished that he had spent a couple days just talking to Jean. He had a feeling that there was a lot of knowledge in her head that he missed by being out on the lake.

* * * * *

When Stan got back to his apartment in Minneapolis about 4:00 pm, he called his sister Jane. They spent an hour talking about all the events that happened in Bayfield.

"You going to write about it?" she asked.

"Can't right now," he answered. "The investigation is still going on. No way of telling when or how it will end. I do have the inside track on what they were doing. Maybe by next spring they will have it wrapped up. I still may not be able to write about it though. I think that the FBI might censor some of the critical information in the case."

"Sounds like you enjoyed being with the young lady up there."

"Yeah! I guess you're right. She's got too much going on to get distracted," he told her.

"Where have I heard that before?" she asked. "Isn't that your line, when I ask you about taking some girl out on a date?"

"Perhaps! You're right again. Think I'll change?"

"Maybe both of you can change," Jane answered.

Stan told Jane that he would tell her more about the events of the week the next time they got together for supper.

Then, he hung up the phone and started looking through his emails, hoping for a response to some of his writing applications. What he needed was another short assignment for a month or two to get his bank account to the level he wanted. It would be nice to be able to head back to Bayfield later in the fall and try one more time to write that book.

$$* \quad * \quad * \quad * \quad *$$

Three weeks had gone by, and no one attempted to get on the boat. Mark Lawson's hope for a speedy ending was fading into the Lake Superior sunsets.

Barbara and her Mother untied the "Deceptive Views" from the dock and took the long cruise back – through the locks at Sioux St. Marie, and then down Lake Michigan to Chicago. Vivian endured the voyage. She just did not enjoy it.

It was the second week in August and the summer sun was very hot on the water. After the first couple days, they decided to take long breaks at noon so that they could run slow and use the air-conditioner. Vivian would take a short nap as they slowed down. It helped her cope with all the wind and sun. She also found a shower at the end of the day helped to refresh her.

Barbara was much quieter on the way back. Vivian figured that everything had caught up to her, and she was thinking about the funeral and having to get their house ready to sell.

She had told her mother that she wanted to be at the orchard the first week in September. Vivian told her to take her time. However, she knew that her daughter would do whatever she felt was right, for her.

The next few weeks went by, as if they were run by remote control. Barbara was back in a northern suburb of Chicago preparing for a funeral and getting her house ready to sell.

She received a few offers for her boat from friends at the marina. However, she was not ready to sell the boat at this point. She still loved the water and she decided that she would keep it for at least another season before deciding if she had time to use it.

* * * * *

Mark Lawson's team was busy looking at the sonar unit. The team informed him that they had made a good purchase. After four weeks of concentrated effort, they were still trying to figure out how it worked. The technology was extremely complex. It would probably cost them millions of dollars if anyone tried to build this thing from scratch, with only the knowledge of the technology used.

They doubted that Anthony developed or even built it. That raised a lot more questions than it answered. Where did the technology come from? Who built it? Where did they build it? Who paid for it?

Mark's team looked through the finances of Anthony Fontaine with a fine-tooth comb. There was no outlay of cash appropriate to the cost of building this thing or purchasing it. The deeper they dug into his past, the bigger the questions that surfaced.

In fact, two agents were assigned just to look into Anthony's past. This was evolving from a murder investigation into an investigation into technology theft on the national security level.

Mark had talked to Sheriff Bradley and informed him that the priority was elevated on the case. Unfortunately, Sheriff Bradley was still looking for clues and had not made any breakthroughs at his end either.

There was one clue that they were still trying to figure out. The boat was scuttled in a different location than the body. Which came first? Probably the boat since it was too easy to spot. Why didn't they send Anthony down with the ship? If they could solve this part of the puzzle, it might shed enough light to start to put the rest in place.

145

One thing was coming into the sheriff's head. There had to have been a second boat. Where did it come from? Was it local, rented, or did it come from another location? One more job for Deputy Miller to check on.

Could they find a second boat that was used in the same time period? It would take a lot of work to try to eliminate every boat owner in the area.

Chapter 23

The Shoot

Stan found a couple of short jobs; writing an article for a magazine, and another assisting a person who wanted to write his life history. They were really make-work projects for Stan.

They gave him the extra income to allow him to get back to his own book later in the fall.

The magazine wanted him to write an article for the November issue about the re-vitalization of a small town along Lake Minnetonka. He needed to take a few pictures and interview three selected business people to write the article.

The autobiography was a favor to a friend. He had convinced Stan to help a friend of his to organize and get his book started. So far, it meant he had to sit down with the writer one evening a week. It would be months before the person had enough written to even assist him in editing his thoughts.

As the second week in August approached, Stan did a search on the internet to see if he could find out anything on the funeral for Anthony Fontaine. He found a listing for an announcement at a funeral home in Evanston, Illinois, for August 23rd. It listed the funeral location at a local Methodist church. Stan figured that he had found the correct one. Since Barbara had to stay in Bayfield for a couple more weeks, and then bring the boat back to Chicago, she would have had to postpone any funeral at least until the end of August, or first part of September.

If Anthony did not have many relatives, Barbara might have decided to have just a small memorial funeral at her local church for their friends and co-workers. He copied the information into his laptop.

Since it was a beautiful sunny day, he decided to head out to Lake Minnetonka and see what pictures he could take that would make the sleepy little town look as though it had been reborn. If he searched the area in the afternoon, by evening, he might be able to take most of the pictures he needed making use of the warm setting sun. This always helped to add brilliance to the colors and make things look alive. It was amazing what a slightly redder sunlight and long shadows could do for a picture.

Stan found that the town had spent a lot of money making things look modern. They had installed new brick roads along the lake, with older style lampposts that gave the community the look of character.

The restaurants, shops and marina along the water reflected the new look for the area. A lot of money had been spent in making sure everything fit the new look that the city had decided it wanted to portray.

As Stan checked for camera angles, he kept thinking about Bayfield. The difference was distinct. One was modern – designed to look older. The other was old – designed to look like a quaint old town. It was interesting to see the differences that the town planners were trying to maintain.

Stan found many good angles for shots of the downtown and the marina. He also arranged to have the three individuals he needed to interview, available for pictures right after dinner. So far, this job was going to be an easy project for him.

Around 7:00 pm, Stan met with the business owners and took about 20-pictures with them in the shots, with their businesses in the background and with views of the town.

He still had time to shoot another 50-pictures after they were finished, which gave different angles of the town, marina and lake. By the time he headed back to his apartment, he was confident that he had most of the pictures he needed for the article. He anticipated using only six to eight of the pictures he had shot.

The next day, while he was looking at the marina pictures, it put him back in the frame of mind that included Bayfield – and Barbara.

He wondered if it would be appropriate if he showed up for Anthony's funeral. How would Barbara and Vivian take it? Would they be glad he came, or would they feel he was intruding?

Stan's publisher had been pushing him to get out and do some book signing at a number of bookstores. It was not Stan's favorite method of publicity. Usually, it meant that he would sit at a table for a few hours, smile, and sign 20 to 30-books.

If he was traveling to a big city, by the time he looked at the travel costs and lodging, he rarely broke even. His publicist would remind him that the articles about him in the papers would usually sell more books than he did in the evening.

Stan was wondering about setting up a couple book signings in the Chicago area, for a couple days before Anthony's funeral. If he did, he could write off the trip, and have an excuse for being in the area.

He called his publisher and set up one afternoon and two evening book signings at bookstores in Chicago.

* * * * *

Deputy Miller was busy the three weeks after Stan left Bayfield. When he was not busy writing tickets for speeders, checking on people illegally parked on county roads, answering calls for animals hit on the road, and checking on bad checks at the shops, he had set aside time each day to check with the local marinas, about boat usage from the last week in April, until the end of May. He was looking for anything that brought a link to the Fontaine murder.

He looked for transient slip rentals, first time boat renters, and anything that was out of the ordinary including any locals that needed their boat out of storage earlier than normal. It was a lot of paper work. However, if they were ever to catch the culprits, they would probably have to find several links during the same period of time to point to a single individual.

All the information was put in a database that they could scan for date, number of people, length of stay, etc.

One afternoon, when he was talking on the phone to the marina operator in Cornucopia, the manager told him, "I remember fueling up a boat from Canada about that time. It stuck in my memory because I rarely have visitors to the fuel dock from Canada, and especially that early in the year."

Deputy Miller decided that he should drive over and talk to him directly. He was at the point that any link, no matter how minor it was, might be the only link they had.

When he arrived at the marina, he met with the manager, John Morley, in his office.

"Yes, I remember waiting on the boat. I was trying to get all the boats back in the slips, when an older Chris Craft, I think it was a Constellation, came into the gas dock and wanted fuel. As much as I wanted to sell a full tank of gas, it interrupted my hoist work, and actually cost me over an hour of time.

"That time of the season, we are real busy trying to get our regular customers boats back in the water and get them operational. You have to hook up batteries, make sure the auto-bailer is working, and that the engines work without having leaks all over the place.

"Anyway, as I recall, it took almost a full load of fuel. Then he wanted to charge it on a Canadian credit card. That took another 15-minutes of hassle, making sure I could process it."

"Did you keep any receipts?" Deputy Miller asked.

"Probably! My filing system is not too great, so most of the papers end up in a file for months before I throw them away. Usually, I wait until I get paid from the credit card company, and then, unless I get stiffed, throw them away and use the credit card's statements for taxes," John Morley told him.

"I realize it has been a long time, since May. Do you remember anything else about the person or the boat?" Deputy Miller asked.

"Well, the only reason I remember it in the first place was the boat. Up here, I see a lot of boats, some new and some old. This was an old one. Usually, the old wood boats are in bad shape these days, cause people just don't like working on boats. They just want to show up on weekends and use them. If it doesn't run, they call me. Then, they expect it to be fixed by morn.

"Well, this was an old Chris Craft Constellation; you know the old wooden boat from back before they shifted to fiberglass.

"It was still in good condition. In fact, they showed me the boat after I commented that it was in really good shape. Except for a spot or two that needed touchup on the varnish, it was in as good of shape as I have seen them.

"I don't remember anything about the two guys that ran it except that I remember the Canadian accent. You know – ending their sentences with 'Aye.' Kind of jumps out and grabs you – the first Canadian you hear each year."

"So there were two guys?" Deputy Miller asked.

"Yeah! That's what I just said, two guys."

"Were they both Canadian?" the Deputy asked.

"Only talked to the one guy," he answered. "All I can tell you is that he had an accent. He might have been in the U.S. for 10-years for all I know."

"OK! It is still important. Can you dig up the receipt? We really need it. It might give us some way to track that person." Deputy Miller requested.

"Well, you can always track the boat's ID," he said. "I always write it down on credit card or check purchases. It's on both receipts."

"Both?" Deputy Miller asked.

"Yeah! He came back maybe a week later and topped off. That's the last I seen of the boat."

"You have a good memory," Deputy Miller told him.

"Well, in this business, you have to. People don't keep records of the maintenance anymore. I usually have to remind them when to have things checked.

"Take the tall guy over there. Had to tell him, last week, he'd better put new batteries in his boat next spring. He probably figured that they'd last as long as a car's battery. Just because you don't use the boat most of the summer, it don't matter. Couldn't start it last week.

"When I looked at his boat, he had three year old batteries. I'm amazed they still started the boat. Coarse, he's too cheap to change it this year. I had to take it in and charge it overnight to get him through the next couple weeks, before we pull the boat for winter.

"Now the guy that owned that Chris Craft, he knew about maintenance. You don't keep an old boat running if you don't do the little things before they become a problem.

"The only thing I could not figure, he wanted to buy a quarter sack of corn I had outside. I always keep some corn around to throw to the ducks. For some reason, he wanted to buy what I had."

"What was it in?" Deputy Miller asked.

"Oh, I keep the corn in an old sack. Usually fill it up at a friend's farm once a year. Kept it under the shelter so it didn't get wet and moldy – right next to the cases of oil," Morley replied.

"How long would it take to find the receipts for May?" Deputy Miller requested.

"Probably 20-minutes," Morley answered. "That important?"

"Could be," Deputy Miller responded. "See if you can find them, so I don't have to come back later."

In 15-minutes, the manager held out a box with all kinds of credit card receipts. It was labeled April/May.

"Told you I could find them," he told the deputy.

Deputy Miller looked at the box and realized that there were probably more than 250 slips.

"OK! Looks like one of us has a long night ahead of us. I need it for evidence. Let me take it and get back to you if I have any questions. If I find what I need, I'll get the rest back to you the next day," the deputy told him.

"Fine, as long as you are doing the looking and not me," the manager answered.

Deputy Miller put the box in his cruiser and headed back to Washburn.

On the way back, someone pulled right out in front of him, without stopping for a stop sign at a cross-road. This was the driver's lucky day. The deputy did not want to spend the time writing out a ticket. He wanted to get back and let the sheriff know what he had found.

* * * * *

It took Deputy Miller and the Sheriff almost four hours to go through John Morley's receipt box.

Sure enough, just as he told the deputy, there were two fuel receipts in the box with Canadian credit cards that matched each other about a week apart. One was dated for April 21st and the other May 1st.

Just as Morley had told Deputy Miller, he had written down the boats registration number on the slip. That would be valuable information for tracking the boat. The other piece of information that was valuable was a line on the slip; $2 – duck feed.

* * * * *

The next morning, Deputy Miller and the Sheriff drove out to Cornucopia Harbor to bring back the unneeded slips.

Sheriff Bradley wanted to go along to get a reaction to a photo that they wanted to show the manager. They brought a copy of the picture of the gunnysack.

It took only 20-minutes to drive the back road, over the hill from Washburn to Cornucopia.

The manager greeted them as they drove in, "Wow, you guys are fast. Did you find the card you were looking for?"

They showed him the two credit card receipts. "These the ones you remember?" the sheriff asked.

"Yup! That's it. See the Canadian card and the registration I wrote on the slip. He probably filled up the second time to dump his waste and fill up with water."

"Good, that is going to be a lot of help," Sheriff Bradley replied. "One more question, is this the sack you sold the corn in?" He showed him a picture of just the sack.

"Heck yeah! Where'd you find that?" the manager asked. "I had it for years and all the writing was almost gone from sitting in the sun. Had to get a new one from the farm after the Canadian wanted this one."

"I need to have you fill out a report for us. This might help us with some missing equipment we are looking for," he told him.

The Sheriff specifically did not mention the drowning. He did not want to let out any information that might put in question any evidence they might gather. So far, this was all they had.

"One more thing, we really need a description. Anything you can remember – a hat, height, weight, anything."

They sat and talked to the manager for the next hour. Unfortunately, since it had been months, he really could not remember anything about the two guys, other than one had an accent from Canada. When they finished, they headed back to Washburn to contact Agent Mark Lawson.

* * * * *

By the time they got half way to Washburn, the sheriff got a call from the state forensic specialists.

"Sheriff Bradley, I completed the work on your Mr. Fontaine today and thought I'd let you know the report will be in the mail as soon as possible."

"Thanks for the heads up," he replied. "Anything new pop-up?"

"A little, not too sure how much help it will be for you. Death was caused by formaldehyde inhaled into the lungs just as we suspected.

The deceased was dead maybe 12 to 24-hours before the body was dumped into the water. That's the best guess we can give you.

"Time of death is a tough one. We would estimate around May 4th to May 12th. That's as close as we can get with that cold water.

"There was numerous signs of body trauma, but these appear to have been years before his death. Your note about him being a Navy Seal might account for the injuries. We would not rule it out.

"We did find some partial fingerprints on some of the utensils you supplied from the boat. There is not enough for identification, but you might be able to use the partial for elimination.

"One more item, when we did some photographs of the boat interior, we did not see anything. However, when we scanned the images with filters cutting different colors, we found a couple shoe prints. We checked the boat again, and found the prints are light and made with red clay. You know, the clay that shows up along the shoreline in the area and is terrible to clean once it dries. Can't date it, but once again, it may help eliminate suspects. This one is of a Men's Nike running shoe – size 8.

"There was nothing to date the time of sinking of the boat. One more thing – the scuttling was a professional job. Someone knew exactly where to blow holes in the hull to eliminate all the air chambers."

"Good work," Sheriff Bradley told the examiner. "I'll be looking for the report."

* * * * *

When they got back to Washburn, they called Agent Lawson.

"Mark, Sheriff Bradley from Washburn. I think we might have gotten lucky today," he told him. "I told Deputy Miller, that I wanted to track every boater he could find during our dates.

"We found a boat from Canada that got gas twice around that time."

"Wow! You tracked every boat in Lake Superior and found one that got gas? We need a little more than that," he replied.

"Yes, I agree. However, this one bought a sack of corn and the harbor manager just ID'd the sack as his."

"Like I told you, Deputy Miller is a great blood hound. Give him a raise," Mark told the Sheriff. "Send me a copy over the wire along with your report. I'll look it over. Did we get an ID?"

"Just a credit card number, type of boat, boat registration number, and two guys on the boat."

"That's a great start. I'll track down the boat," Mark told them. "See if anyone else saw that boat or anyone on it."

Chapter 24

Mounties

Before the phone turned cold from hanging up, FBI Agent Mark Lawson was back on the phone to the Canadian Royal Mounties.

He told him that he had a murder and robbery he was investigating, and the only leads he had so far was a boat and a credit card. He needed their assistance to track the owners, and to make sure that the owners did not get spooked. He told them that they had used fake ID's in Bayfield and the only lead was a positive ID on the boat and credit card.

Captain George Morrissey told Agent Lawson to give him a few hours. He would have the registration checked, and see what leads he could find from the credit card. The card might still be another fake. However, if you have the registration number on the boat, we can track its location.

He would call Agent Lawson back as soon as they had any information. "I'll call you before we make contact with any individuals," he told him.

Mark put out a request to the Coast Guard, and all sheriffs in counties along the Great Lakes, to be on the lookout for the Chris Craft Constellation.

"Do not make contact" was on the request. "Contact FBI Agent Mark Lawson – ASAP."

After 3 hours, Mark got a call from Captain Morrissey of the Canadian Royal Mounties.

They ran a search on the credit card and had a hit. The name on the card was apparently real. It belonged to an individual about 5-km east of Marathon, Ontario. His name was Morley Cox, known as Buzz. Description: Age 47, 5-foot 9-inches, 185-pounds. Divorced. Worked for a dredging company.

The boat came up as registered to a different person – William O'Brian of Thunder Bay, Ontario. Description: Age 42, 6-foot 6-inches, 295-pounds. Married, Provincial Engineer. Current location of boat – undetermined. Confirmation of location of home berth by tomorrow. Will check to confirm if it is in harbor.

Along with the information, they sent drivers license photos to Mark.

Mark was impressed. For international cooperation, that was fast. Of course, in the US, he could have pulled that information on a suspect in 15-minutes. The Canadians said they would wait for direction before approaching either individual.

Now things were getting interesting. They had a match to the boat and the gunnysack, and now a name of a person that lived close to the rocks that were found in the sack.

He sent the photos to Sheriff Bradley, to have Deputy Miller confirm with the marina manager in Cornucopia. Mark could not believe it was getting this easy.

Chapter 25

Book Signings

Stan arranged for book signings on the 21st and 22nd of August in Chicago, at three different book stores. Two were downtown and one was in a suburb. He sold a total of 50 books between them.

Since they were hard copy books, he cleared $250 after the bookstore got their cut. It was a good thing that he was not counting on book signings for a living.

On the 23rd, Stan drove to Evanston for the funeral. The funeral announcement said there was to be a memorial service at 10:00 am, with a visitation one hour before.

Barbara had made all the plans for the funeral. She had informed the church that she expected only about 100 people for the funeral, and had a luncheon planned for after the service. She expected about 20 of her relatives and the rest being friends and co-workers of hers and Anthony's.

She still had no knowledge of any relatives on Anthony's side that might exist.

During the visitation, Vivian helped Barbara make sure she remembered the relative's names, and stayed close, in case she needed any thing.

Barbara did not think she needed help with names. However, when emotions run high, she was glad that Vivian was close. She found she had a problem remembering the names of some of the relative's children. She had only seen them a few times and with the stress, that part of her memory was on vacation.

Stan wandered into the receiving line with about 30 people between himself and Barbara. After 15-minutes, when he had moved up to within a couple people, Vivian spotted him, and gave him a smile.

She decided to wait until after Barbara saw him. Then she could go over and talk to him.

When Barbara finally made eye contact with Stan, she put a big smile on her face and shortened the discussions with the people in front of Stan.

Stan gave her a hug and said, "I hope you didn't mind, I was worried about how you were holding up with everything that happened, and thought I would come down and offer you some support."

"Oh! I'm so glad you came," she told him. "The past month has just been a blur, and I'm not sure if I have done everything or not.

"Thank you for everything you did for us up at Bayfield. Without you, I'm not sure what would have happened." She put her arms around Stan and gave him a long, strong hug.

"Can you stay for the luncheon after the funeral?" she asked. "I have to say hi to the others in line, and I would really like to sit down and talk."

"Sure, I came this far, I had hoped to be able to see you."

Stan walked over to the side and Vivian proceeded over to talk to him. He was still looking at Barbara. Her hair was down now, and she looked like a lady rather than the jogger with a ponytail.

She also looked tired, just like she had looked after a long hot day stuck in the aft cabin of the boat.

"I'm so glad to see you here," Vivian told him. "She has been so stressed out that when she saw you, and put that big smile on her face, that was the first time I had seen it, since we left Bayfield. Thank you for coming."

"I wasn't sure if she would want me here or not," he answered. "I figured the past few months would catch up to her as soon as she started to relax. How are you holding up?" he asked.

Vivian replied, "I'm a lot better now that the trip back from Bayfield was over. I think it took me at least a week before I got my land legs back. Next trip – I'm driving. Are you going to stay for the funeral and luncheon?"

"Yes! My schedule is flexible."

"Thank you. I'm sure she would like to sit down with you after this is over and just talk.

"Hope you don't mind, but I need to say hi to a friend that just walked in." With that, Vivian walked over and met two ladies that came for the funeral.

Stan went on into the church and took a seat in the back.

Just like the Lutheran church in Bayfield, the Methodist church filled up from the middle rows to the back. Stan was wondering why people never sit in the front, unless they are family members at a funeral. Maybe the churches should offer some special incentives. He was thinking; padded seats only in the first six rows, ushers could let the front rows exit first, and finally, heated front row seats for the wintertime. That might change the way people sat in church.

The church held about 500 people so with only 100 there; it did not seem very full. However, it was for friends and relatives. Sometimes a few close friends are worth more than a church full of people that know you by name. It was obvious that faith and friendship held them together.

The memorial service was short, a few songs, a short message, and a few prayers for the family. Barbara had Anthony's body cremated soon after it arrived in Illinois. His ashes were scattered into Lake Michigan. After the memorial service, everyone proceeded downstairs for a luncheon served by some of the women of the congregation.

Vivian caught Stan and asked, "Would you like to sit with me and my two friends? I figure you probably will not know anyone and Barbara will have to move around and thank people for coming."

"I would love to," he answered.

They went through the line to pick up their food and sat at a large round table.

The other two ladies, Marcella and Edna – long time friends of Vivian's, were interested in the young man that they had never met or heard of, who was joining them. When Stan told them he was a writer, they spent the entire time at the table asking him questions about his books, how he did research, how he picked his characters, etc.

Barbara looked over at Stan a few times and saw that Vivian had him under tow. She was glad to see that he was not by himself.

When she saw Vivian's friends talking to him, she knew that she did not have to worry whether he could find something to talk about or not. Barbara knew that these two ladies would tie him up in chit-chat for the entire time they were at the table. They had been friends of Vivian's since she was in school, and Barbara had been stuck sitting with them many times in the past. It was not that they were not interesting. It was just that they never quit talking.

163

Barbara decided that she should talk to her friends, and when people were starting to leave, hopefully, she could spend some time talking to Stan.

When about half of the people had left, Barbara walked over and sat next to Stan, "Do you have time to stay and talk for a while after everyone leaves?" she asked.

"I would love to," he answered, as the other ladies at the table looked at Vivian with one of those stares that only women can perfect.

The two ladies excused themselves from the table and thanked Stan for the lovely conversation. Then, they turned to Vivian and said, "We'll be talking to you tomorrow. You can fill us in on what we have missed." With that, they left the church and drove back to the town, which was close to the orchard Vivian owned.

With almost everyone gone, Vivian had a chance to talk to Stan. "Sorry about my friends," she said. "When you have been friends as long as we have, you start to feel like family and want to know everything that is going on."

"That's OK," Stan answered. "It gave us a chance to kill some time before everyone left. So you enjoyed your sea voyage, and have signed up for a cruise across the Atlantic next month I hear."

"If I did that, you would have to come back for another funeral the next month," she joked. "I'll settle for a small farm pond and a fishing pole. Better yet, I'll sit on the dock with that pole. Did you get your book finished?"

"No! I'm still back at square one. I am hoping to go back to Bayfield next month and see if I can get it going again," he answered. "How are things here? Is Barbara still planning on joining you at the orchard?"

"Yes, I think it will be good for her. I only wish it was not our busy season. However, it may take her mind off all of this. You know, the FBI has talked to most of their co-workers. Barbara has not said anything, but I think she is worried that they still think she had something to do with everything."

"Well, maybe we can talk about it, when everyone is gone," Stan suggested. "I'm just glad to see that both of you are holding up OK. It has to be stressful."

When everyone had left, Barbara came up to Stan and asked, "How is your schedule? Do you have to leave for home soon or can you come over to my house and we can sit and talk a while?"

"I'm here to make sure you are OK," he told her. "I can make all the time you would like. Vivian said that she would prefer talking out on your boat."

That got a chuckle out of both of them. "Mother, can you drive my car? Then, I can show Stan the way without getting him lost."

"I would be glad to," she answered.

They left the church and headed back to Barbara's house. Her house was only a mile from the church.

As they turned into Barbara's driveway, Stan looked at the house. It was a nice two-story, stone-fronted home, that fit nicely in a very up-scale neighborhood. In short, it was a well landscaped, beautiful home. It fit in perfectly with the boat that Barbara had up in Bayfield. Stan did notice the "For Sale" sign near the street.

"Any luck trying to sell the house?" he asked.

"Actually, I had a bid yesterday. I'm trying to decide if I should just take it, and not try to get my full asking price. They offered me $7,000 less than I'm asking. I would really like to move and forget everything that has happened this year," she told him.

"Sounds like a good idea. You don't need to worry about a house here and live near the orchard. Are you going to move in with your mother, or find a place there?"

"I think I will move in with mom for this fall. Then, I can decide what I want to do. Maybe a townhouse, or something with no maintenance."

They drove up and parked in front of the garage. Vivian was just getting out of Barbara's car. She had gotten there just before them, and they all went into the house together.

Chapter 26

Leg Work

FBI Agent Mark Lawson and Sheriff Bradley worked together trying to establish any links they had on their two Canadian people of interest, with any other activities in Bayfield where they might have been seen. If they were in town for over a week, someone had to have run into them somewhere. If not, they had hid on their boat without making any other contact, except for purchasing fuel.

Deputy Miller took their pictures to the Bed and Breakfast Inns and places that rented cabins. Since the Roy's Point Marina manager thought his two renters were staying at a B&B with a cabin, they hoped the picture and time frame would bring a match somewhere.

His earlier investigations had produced three locations that people were staying for a week or more during that period. At the time, it appeared that the mystery person might have rented the place. No one had recognized Anthony's picture; meaning either Anthony did not interact with the manager, or they had the wrong location.

Now, Deputy Miller could go back and see if they recognized the pictures of their two people of interest. If they did, they had one more piece to the puzzle.

* * * * *

At the Bed and Breakfast just north of town, which was on a small gravel, dead-end road off the main road, he got a hit.

The manager thought that the individual from Marathon, Ontario, looked familiar. He was not positive. It had been a long time. However, his face was familiar. The other picture did not look like anyone he had seen in Bayfield.

Deputy Miller tried to push the issue, "You think you rented to him, or just saw him in town? Take your time and look closely at the picture."

"No, I think this is the guy that rented the cabin at the beginning of the season. I remember that I had to open it special – just for him. We normally did not open the cabins for another couple weeks. He just didn't want to stay at our attached rooms. He wanted the cabin. Since it was for two weeks, I agreed."

"Did you get a name and address? How did he pay for the week?" he asked.

"I have a name and address in the register," he answered. "As I recall, he paid cash – up front."

He went over and grabbed the register. It listed a name and address from Duluth, Minnesota.

Once again, he showed the picture of Anthony to the manager. "How about this guy?"

"No! But, there were two people. I just never saw the other guy. For the cabins, we just drop off a cold breakfast at the door. Never saw the other guy."

"Did they stay the entire two weeks?" Deputy Miller asked.

"Sorry, too long back to remember. We get a lot of guests over the summer. Some stay for a day and some for a couple days. If they left a day early, I cannot remember. I just don't remember anything about them that stands out."

When Deputy Miller got back to the office he checked out the name and address he was given in Duluth. The name corresponded to the address. He passed the information on to Agent Mark Lawson.

* * * * *

Mark was starting to get enough information to be able to start the investigation into the people of interest, they had established. His first and easiest, was checking out the name from Duluth. Since the manager had matched him to the person from Canada, he figured it was a fake ID.

Mark asked one of his agents in Duluth to contact the individual and see if he had been in Bayfield the end of April. He also asked Deputy Miller to take that person's driver's license photo to the B&B's manager, to see if he recognized the photo.

By supper time, he had an answer on both inquires.

The person said he was working those two weeks, at a store in Duluth. It was confirmed by his boss. The manager at the B&B did not recognize that person's photo.

It was just what Mark had anticipated. The renter had used a name picked out of a phone book and paid cash so that there were no records.

Now it was time to link the Canadian Mounties to the case. They would have to do the investigations up there. One thing in their favor, they were very good at what they did.

Mark put in a call to Captain Morrissey of the Royal Canadian Mounties.

"Captain Morrissey, 'hi,' this is FBI Agent Mark Lawson. I think we are zeroing in on a couple of your people, with this murder case

I have been working on. We need your help putting them at the scene, and trying to establish a motive. So far, everything is circumstantial, but the links are strong. How's your work load?"

"Agent Lawson, I was wondering how long it would take for you to call and ask for assistance. So you think they are connected, aye?"

"Yes, I'll send you the file shortly.

"We have a positive on your man in Marathon linking him to purchasing part of the murder weapon using his credit card, and a positive by the marina manager to the photo that you sent. Here's what I need you to do."

Mark told him that they needed to be careful not to spook the individuals, as they still had to prove they were at the murder site. He asked them to check out the boat, check with the harbor manager to see if it was used, and then check to see if the owner was at work the last week in April and first week in May. "So far, we have no positive ID on him, only his boat."

"As for the other person, we have Morley Cox – Buzz, positively ID'd twice at a harbor 20-miles from the murder scene during the period. He bought the gunnysack used for the cement anchor of the individual, and the rocks in the sack matched rocks from the Marathon beach area.

"Unfortunately, we have no witness to the murder but we have a couple of possible motives:

"Possibility number one, is a missing high tech sonar unit the deceased was using with an unknown individual who has disappeared. He may have been killed for the unit.

"Possibility number two, they were reported to be looking for treasures on the bottom of Lake Superior. They may have killed him to keep whatever they found.

"Possibility number three, something went wrong, and he was killed to cover up whatever it was.

"I think our man in Marathon, Morley Cox – Buzz, knows what happened. You might want to watch him while you see if the other person of interest in Thunder Bay was involved. If we can place him at the scene, we may have some leverage between them to find out what happened.

"Oh, if you can get on the boat, look for a laptop and a metal tow that is a cylinder about 18-inches long and 6-inches wide. Sorry about not converting those numbers to metric ahead of time. I forgot about that one."

"No problem! We've got computers up here too, you know, aye. I'll get on it right away. We'll let you know when we make contact and if we find any information. I'll also pull the credit card information on both people for a few months to see if there are any connections to the case."

Agent Lawson thanked Captain Morrissey. "If you get anything positive, I'll fly up and buy you lunch."

Now, Mark Lawson had to sit and wait. It was not his favorite thing to do. He had three cases going on at the same time, and all were in the same state of limbo.

He called Sheriff Bradley and let him know that the Canadians were officially on the case.

Mark had a message to call Carl Harris. Mark had gotten Carl the director's job at the NSF (National Science Foundation) after Carl developed some "top-secret" classified surveillance software, and helped him track a foreign agent that was trying to steal the software.

171

Stan Moline had been one of the other graduate students who were involved in the project's development.

"Carl, to what do I owe the honor of this call?" Mark asked.

"Just calling to bring you up to date on that sonar unit we have been working on.

"I think we have the technology figured out, and the software that runs it. It took four engineers five weeks to crack it, and that was with the unit in front of us. I am not sure if I know any labs in the US that could have built this. I am glad we have a copy, but I would feel better if we had the other one. Better yet, I wish we had the designer. I saw your file on this guy – Anthony. You were right – not a chance he built this."

"That's what I was worried about," Mark replied. "The murder is just the tip of the iceberg. We have the Canadians checking into two people of interest. The bad news, neither of them could have designed this either.

"Someone else is involved. I'll let you know if we get any leads. I know this is bouncing all over the National Security boys. Tell them, we're working on it."

"I know you are Mark. I'm not trying to put pressure on you, just wanted you to know what we found.

"Say 'hi' to Stan for me. Tell him I still owe him for this one. Glad our photos found your boat. Talk to you later."

Mark leaned back in his chair. Now, he really hoped the Canadian was dumb enough to have been hired by someone to steal the sonar. It would make things a lot easier. So far, nothing was easy.

Shortly, his boss would be calling, trying to stay ahead of the National Security boys, wanting answers. Life was so much easier in the old days, when all the FBI had to do was chase bank robbers. Now, instead of J. Edgar Hoover and Eliot Ness's detectives, you needed Sherlock Holmes and a whole team of scientists.

Chapter 27

Time to Talk

Stan was glad he had taken the chance and gone to Chicago for the funeral. He knew that Barbara was going to feel swamped with everything that had happened and now she had to adjust to helping manage the family orchard. That was enough stress for several people to handle.

Barbara led Stan and Vivian into the family room. She had nice brown leather furniture with a large TV mounted on one wall, and a stereo system built into the room.

As Stan sunk into the soft leather recliner, he thought of the furniture in his apartment. No! He decided he really did not want to think about his apartment. Barbara and Vivian sat in the sofa.

They took a while talking about all the things that had happened since they were in Bayfield. It had been a lightning-fast roller coaster ride for Barbara. She had to complete the funeral arrangements, find a realtor, clean up the house, put it up for sale, and let them know at work that she would be quitting in a few days.

That meant that all of her work needed to be transferred to someone else who could follow up on what she had been working on.

All of that had to be completed in less than a month. No wonder she looked exhausted.

Vivian had been getting the orchard ready for the fall season. Apple picking was about to move into full speed. Displays, markets, and advertising had to be completed during the same time frame.

Fortunately, most of the people from last year were back to work this fall. That meant she did not have to do a lot of training. When Barbara moved in, she could finally come up for air.

Stan was not sure which of them needed a break the worst. For her age, Vivian was a great example of a woman who could handle the business and still keep the world in perspective.

Stan thought he had been busy since coming back. Now, he felt like he should never complain again about his schedule.

Stan talked to them about the times he spent on his magazine article and photo-shoot, and about working with a person writing their autobiography. The book on Lake Superior had a temporary hold attached to it, at least until he could head back to Bayfield.

After a while, Barbara brought up the subject of her husband.

"Stan, I'm really worried about what Anthony was doing. I thought I knew everything. Now, I'm not sure I knew him at all."

"What's happening?" he asked.

"Well, I told you I sold the sonar unit to the FBI. I was worried that someone would steal it or it would accidentally break. I had no idea how to fix it. Mother agreed with my decision.

"Apparently, the FBI has been checking into Anthony, and talking to his co-workers. From what I hear from my friends, the FBI does not think he could have made it either. They cannot even find any records of his hiring someone or buying it.

"I don't know what to think. I'm worried they will think it was stolen and want their money back. I thought that when the funeral was over and I moved to the orchard, I could re-start my life. Now, this might be chasing me for the next ten years.

"Have they talked to you?" Barbara asked Stan.

"Yes, several times up in Bayfield. I'm glad we told them about the sonar. It would have been worse if they found out while looking for the murderer.

"No one has implied to me that they think you are involved. I really hope that is the case. I think you have had enough."

"Thanks," she replied wiping a tear from her eye.

"As for the money, they bought the technology, right? My guess is that they are really cranking up the hunt to find the designer. Just help them out any way you can. If you know of anyone who your husband had done business with, let them know.

"Remember, to them, this is not personal. They are not out to get you. They are looking for someone involved with national security. You know they are going to turn over every stone, whether you are sitting on it or not."

"I guess so," Barbara said. "It's just that I feel like a fool. I had no idea that some of the things my husband claimed to be working on were fake, or worse. How could I have missed it?"

"Some times it is important to know someone a long time, before you get married," Vivian stuck into the conversation. "I'm not saying, I told you so. It is just a matter of fact. Sometimes you get surprises even with people you know for years."

Stan asked Barbara, "How bad is it? Have you found other things?"

"I don't know. You did not see many of his relatives today did you? What else am I going to find in the next year, or two, or three? I am worried about any bills he may have run up, or any contracts he might have signed. I just don't know."

They all sat and talked for almost the full afternoon. Stan could not find very much to say that would help Barbara's situation. He really felt helpless.

While Vivian took out some pasta and prepared supper, they took a walk out in the back lawn. Stan held her hand as they walked slowly and talked about what Barbara had been going through. Somehow, Barbara had held her emotions together for the past few weeks. Now, she told him she was afraid everything was going to come unglued.

Stan put his arm around her and held her tight. They just stood there holding on to each other for several minutes, until Vivian called out to them that the food was ready.

After eating supper, Stan explained to Barbara and Vivian that it was time for him to head back to Minneapolis. It would be a long drive and he probably would not be home until 2 am.

Both Vivian and Barbara thanked him for coming and for listening to their worries. Barbara gave him a note with her new address and phone number, "Please call me in a week. It is nice to have someone I can talk to."

Stan gave her a big hug and kiss. "Don't worry, things will clear up soon. They always do."

Then, Vivian gave him a hug. "Thanks for being here. You don't know how much it has meant to both of us."

Vivian really wished that Stan lived closer. Barbara needed someone other than herself to talk to.

They waved goodbye as Stan got back in his car and headed back home.

* * * * *

Stan had just gotten back on the freeway heading back to Minnesota when his cell phone rang.

"Hello!" he answered.

"Have a good visit," Mark Lawson asked.

It didn't take more than a second for Stan to realize who had called. "Still watching her?" Stan asked.

"No! Trying to protect her. Too much we don't know. Anyway, I was calling to let you know that Carl Harris said thanks. He said to tell you he still owes you one."

"So he still does exist," Stan joked. "Has he picked the hardware yet?"

"He thinks he has a handle on it. Did Barbara say if she had any idea of who designed it?"

"No! She is really scared. She doesn't know who she married. It is really bothering her. Any leads?"

"Working on one. No promises but we have a lead on the guy who bought the anchor. If you talk to her again, anything she can think of, no matter how stupid, we can use it," Mark requested.

"OK," Stan replied. "Oh, Mark, ask Carl how much radiation a 36-volt sonar unit might put out, if someone didn't know enough to run it deep under the surface."

"Damn! I wish you scientists would just talk to each other. Then again, I would be out of a job. I get your drift. It might be worth watching for. Talk to you later." Mark hung up.

Ten seconds later he was talking to Carl Harris and checking up on the suggestion Stan had made. That sonar packed a punch of electromagnetic energy. Stan knew that from his physics degree, if a novice had it on the surface, the government might be able to spot a disturbance from one of their satellites.

Chapter 28

'Aye'

On September 3rd, Mark Lawson got a call from Captain Morrissey in Canada.

"Mark, got some info for you. Our boys checked on the boat. She is sitting in the harbor in Thunder Bay. It has only been used three times this year according to the harbor manager. It was out for two days last week, a three day holiday on the 1st of July, and a couple of weeks right after they put it in the water around April 22nd.

"That puts it in your window."

"Great, that's what we need," Mark answered. "Any idea where it was the other days?"

"Yes, we know exactly. It was in Minnesota. The owner – William O'Brian, told us he took it down to the casino in Grand Portage. We confirmed his story with the Harbor Master in Grand Portage.

"Now the bad news. The owner was in town the whole time it was out in April. We checked him out. Looks clean. He gave the boat to a friend, a person that lives 10-km west of Marathon to use on a holiday. Apparently, they were old school buddies.

"O'Brian informed us that he had called him out of the blue, and asked if he could rent the boat. Said his job was hurting because of

179

the recession and he needed to just head out to the islands and relax. In exchange, he promised to get him some Chris Craft riggings he found for the boat, which were in prime condition.

"Apparently, the owner is a fanatic, about keeping the ship prime – just like you said in your report, aye."

"You got a lead on this new fellow? What's his name? Any word on the other person?"

"Whoa! His name is Jacques Laroche. I'll send you a picture with a description. Working on both your suspects. We may have a link between Laroche and Cox. If we can establish it, we may be able to put them both on the boat. We have both under observation.

"Now the good news, we took their pictures to the library in Marathon. Turns out the librarian recognized your first guy – Morley Cox or 'Buzz.' He spent a lot of time looking through reference books last winter."

"Bingo! I knew you guys were good," Mark shouted into the phone. "I'll schedule a flight up there if you have the time in your schedule to pick them up for questioning. Maybe we'll get lucky and one will squeal to get a deal."

"Good, how about if we meet on the fifth. I'll send you the details as to where we will pick you up at the airport."

Mark was feeling better all the time. Still, it did not account for the designer.

As soon as he received the information on the new person of interest, he sent it along to Sheriff Bradley.

Captain Morrissey sent the information to Agent Lawson from his office in Thunder Bay, along with the information on Jacques Laroche. From Thunder Bay, they could drive to Marathon. *Jacques Laroche of Marathon, Ontario. Description: Age 49, 5-foot 11-inches, 205-lbs. Married. Worked for road construction.*

After looking at the details, Mark griped, "Hell, I might as well rent a boat in Bayfield. I'd get there faster. The flight and drive along the lake would easily take up a full day."

* * * * *

Stan made it back to his apartment in Minneapolis late that night. He was glad that he did not have a job that required him to get up at 6:00 am.

At 7:30 am, his sister called on her way to work. "Just wanted to know how the trip went." Jane really wanted to call him the evening before, but had all she could do to wait until 7:30 am.

Stan growled. "What time is it? I didn't get in until 2:15 am."

"Sounds like you spent time with Barbara," his sister pushed on without losing a second. "Was she happy to see you?"

"How about calling me on your lunch break. I can fill you in then," he replied.

That was not what his sister wanted to hear. Jane wanted all the juicy gossip. Now, she had to wait, wondering all that time what happened.

"OK! Call you at 11:30," Jane said as she disconnected.

Stan hated morning calls. Try as he might, he rarely got back to sleep. He got up and made some breakfast. All the turmoil yesterday had given him an appetite.

Later in the morning, Stan called up to Bayfield and talked to Jean.

"Hi, got any rooms open the end of the month?" Stan asked her.

"Well Stan, I recognize that voice. I was wondering if you would head back up this fall. You know that September is our high season. It is close to the start of Apple Fest. Tell you what! I will hold a room for you the last week at the normal rate, if you want to come up.

"I was wondering how you and that fancy gal were doing. Have you talked to her lately?"

"You really are good," he told her. "Yes! I made it down to her husband's funeral this week. Remember, you promised me a wealth of information if I came back."

"OK! Only if you promise to write me into the book," Jean told him. "See you the end of the month."

Stan hung up. He wished it was already the end of September. He had just returned to town, and already his feet were itching to get back on the road.

At 11:30 am sharp, his phone rang. He didn't even look at the caller ID, he just answered, "Hi Jane."

They talked almost the whole lunch time Jane had available. She did not want to miss a single thing. Jane especially liked the discussion Stan had while sitting at the table at the reception. She could just imagine two little old ladies keeping him from talking to Barbara. He must have been squirming in his shoes.

"So when are you going to see her again?" she asked.

"She gave me her phone number and asked me to call her next week," Stan answered.

"Wow, this has to be a record for you, isn't it. I'm not sure you have ever spent that much time with anyone unless they were in the lab."

"OK! It's not to that point," he told her.

"Are we still on for pizza, tomorrow night?" he asked.

182

"You bet, back to the real dates," she joked. "See you then." She hung up.

Stan had made an effort to get over to Jane's apartment for pizza at least once every couple of weeks.

Actually, Jane set it up to keep track of her brother. Since he rarely called his parents, she felt it was her duty to watch over him and keep them informed.

Chapter 29

Confessions

FBI Agent Mark Lawson flew up to Thunder Bay, Ontario. Then, he and Captain Morrissey drove the 100 or so miles, along the northern side of Lake Superior to Marathon.

The numbers were in kilometers and Mark was never a fan of converting from one unit to another.

As they drove down the provincial highway, Mark asked Captain Morrissey, "Did you get a chance to check the boat for fingerprints? It would be real nice to get a solid link between these two individuals."

"We haven't yet. If we get a little closer on either of them, I think we can get a provincial judge to allow us to hold and print the boat.

"Actually, the boat owner has agreed not to use or even go on the boat for the next three days. I have held off getting the judge involved, because I think we will want warrants for both suspect's homes, cars, and financial records. I'd rather hit the judge once or twice rather than try for each individual request. With the evidence so far, I do not think we will have a problem.

"The first question the court will ask is, "Have you talked to the person of interest?" I am hoping we can get something out of Jacques Laroche, since we have evidence the boat was under his control, and the boat was in Bayfield. Add to it the cement anchor, and he might just roll over and tell the whole story.

"Everything we have seen in our investigation on Jacques does not lead to a habitual law breaker. I think we need to start with him.

"The other one is a little tougher person. Seamen are not always the easiest to break, you know, aye. They are used to a tough life on the water, aye. Besides, if we print the boat and do not find anything, we lose our leverage. If we do not know there aren't any prints, we can bluff our way. Lawyers hate that."

When they got to the Royal Canadian Mounties post in Marathon, they met with a local deputy in charge of the surveillance.

Deputy Francis Knudson brought them up to date. He had both people of interest under observation and had personally talked to the librarian who had identified Morley Cox – best known as Buzz.

Deputy Knudson asked the two officers, "Would you like me to bring both of them in for questioning?"

Captain Morrissey took the lead since it was his jurisdiction. "Deputy, I would like to talk to Jacques Laroche. Is there a place in his daily routine that we can talk to him without bringing him in for questioning? I would like to catch him so unaware that he does not have time to think about what he might say."

He glanced over to Agent Lawson to make sure it met his approval.

"Well, he usually heads down to the bar about 4:00 pm, for a quick snort before heading home for supper."

"That would be perfect," Captain Morrissey stated. "Let's catch him just before he goes in. That way he will have time to talk, and they cannot say he was drunk and did not know what he was saying."

At 3:55 pm, just like clockwork, Jacques parked his car and started to walk over to the bar. As he did, Captain Morrissey met him on the sidewalk, and asked him if he could ask a few questions.

The startled Laroche agreed and followed Captain Morrissey to his car where Agent Lawson was waiting as well.

"Mr. Laroche, my name is Captain Morrissey, and the other gentleman in the car is Agent Lawson, of the US, FBI. We have a few questions to ask you, and I would appreciate it if you think twice and answer only once – the real answer.

"It appears that you have been involved in some activities in the Bayfield area and we have evidence putting you at the scene. If you don't mind, I think at this point, the best thing you can do is to explain your side of what happened, before someone else convinces us they were the innocent party."

Agent Lawson looked Laroche in the eye. That was a rather blunt way of telling a suspect that they had the goods on him without even mentioning what he had done.

Laroche looked nervous. He looked like the cat that just got caught eating the canary.

"Look, I'm married, and I did just what that guy said we had to do, aye. He said that if we followed his instructions, they would drop the charges," Laroche answered.

Captain Morrissey and Agent Lawson looked at each other in amazement. What was Laroche talking about? This case was getting stranger and stranger.

"Please explain," Captain Morrissey replied.

"The guy – the guy with the Park Service. He told us that if we gave him the stuff we recovered, and went back to Canada promising not to come back, he would drop the charges of illegally recovering historic relics from the bottom of the lake.

"We did as he said. So, why are you here?"

Agent Lawson shook his head. Well, part of the story checked out. They were looking for relics. "And how about the ones you kept?" he baited him.

"I only kept the three things – honest. I forgot they were in the locker below, until we were heading back across the lake. Do I have to give them back too?" he asked.

This time it was Captain Morrissey that was surprised by Agent Lawson's question. "Where are they?" the Captain asked.

"They're at my place.

"Please, my wife does not know anything about it. Can we discuss it without involving her?"

After Laroche said he would cooperate with them fully, they agreed to let him drive home, pick up the "recovered goods," and then follow them to the post. He would tell his wife that he needed to meet someone for a meeting. He was told not to make any phone calls and to come back out immediately.

Captain Morrissey followed Jacques from a short distance and waited until he came back out of his house. Then, he followed him to the Post at Marathon.

Meanwhile, both Captain Morrissey and Agent Lawson discussed this strange case. Nothing was following the script they expected.

At the Post, Jacques Laroche sang like a canary. He told them about how he had run into Morley Cox – Buzz, at the bar one day. "Buzz was bragging about how someday he was going to go find this treasure in the lake, and not have to go back out on the noisy dredge and work in bad weather.

"Buzz told me that he had found a record of a ship that went missing back in the 1800's. It was carrying some gold coins, reported to be 1,000 according to the notes, and some items for the Catholic church.

"He said it was found in some old letters in the archive. He tried to trace it through other sources but did not find any information. For Buzz, that meant there was a chance that no one else knew about it either.

"Anyway, after talking to him a couple days, I asked why he hadn't gone and recovered the gold. He told him he was working on it.

"Buzz said that he had talked some guy into helping him find it, and now all he needed was a boat to haul it back. I told him I could get a boat.

"The next day he came to me and offered 10% plus expenses if I ran the boat across and back. He figured that no one would think twice about a pleasure boat going to the Apostle Islands and back.

"So, I contacted a friend and borrowed his Chris Craft. I stayed onboard it the whole time to make sure nothing happened to it. My friend is a big guy, and I knew if something happened to it, they'd find me in the rocks, aye."

"OK! Let's start this little adventure from the beginning. Tell us what happened over there," Captain Morrissey told him.

At this point, even Captain Morrissey was starting to get curious about the whole thing.

"Well, Buzz and I traveled over to Bayfield in the Chris and anchored off Oak Island. He said he had to meet this guy who was going to use a fancy sonar to locate the goods.

"Buzz had it down to about 8 locations. He said he had to give the guy 50%, so that left us with the other 50%, minus the expenses. We had gas, and Buzz had arranged a place to stay. He also rented a sailboat for them to use. My cut kept getting smaller and smaller. He needed to dive and I told him the Chris was not a diving boat. Beside, he said it was too noticeable out there. He needed to blend in."

"Go on," Agent Lawson told him.

"Well after a few tries at locating things, where they went out in the morning and back in the evening, Buzz called me and told me they would meet me near York Island. They had found the ship.

"I couldn't believe it. I thought it was unbelievable. We met up and sure enough, old Buzz was shouting like he had found the biggest treasure in the lake. When he and this other guy showed me the treasure, I was shocked. Sure enough, old Buzz had found the ship he was looking for and there was indeed a chest with a bunch of gold pieces in it. It also had a few gold crosses and things for a church. I put a couple of them in the boat to clean and look at later.

"Then, while we were so busy that we didn't even see him coming, this Park Service deputy shows up in a small cruiser.

"He came from around the island so we didn't even see him coming, aye. Well, don't you know, the first time we get lucky and find anything, he tells us it is against the law to remove historic relics. He's going to throw us in jail.

"Well, thank goodness Buzz is a fast talker. He gives him some line about involving the Canadian Consulate. Next thing I know, the deputy tells us that if we return all the goods, and leave the country, he would drop the charges since we did not know the laws.

"We handed over the coins and I guess the other guy – the American, ended up with a fine. We headed back to Canada as quickly as we could.

"You going to arrest me for keeping the cross?" Laroche asked. "Buzz doesn't know I still have it. I didn't tell him."

"Are you saying the American was left with the Park Deputy?" Agent Lawson asked.

"Oh, hell yes," he answered. "We figured we got off lucky."

Agent Lawson asked, "Did you and Buzz purchase a gunnysack when you got gas?"

"Yeah! Buzz ripped his dive bag and he needed a new one."

"And where is that bag now?" he asked.

"I think we left it in the sailboat along with the coins," he answered.

"And, do you know anything about some rocks that might have been in it?" Captain Morrissey asked.

"Yeah! Like I said, it was his dive bag. He used it to weigh himself down for the trip to the bottom. He put about four rocks in it to get him down in a hurry, aye. Then, when he came up, he would pull up the bag on a rope later. We had about 20 of the rocks in the Chris on the way over there. I think I ended up throwing away about five by the time we returned. He lost some in his first dive bag."

"And, you say the American was alive when you last saw him, aye?" Captain Morrissey asked.

"Yeah! That's what I said. Why?" Jacques asked.

"They found him with your bag around his knees on the bottom," Captain Morrissey told him. "So far, you are the chief suspect. You had the boat and bought the bag."

"Whoa! I'll pay a fine for the cross and return it, but you're not pinning that on me. He was alive, as we are here, when we left."

"Well, Captain, looks like we may have to talk to Buzz and see if he wants to pin it on his buddy," Agent Lawson told him. "One of them is bound to tell the truth."

"**I did!**" Jacques shouted. "I told you the truth, aye."

190

Captain Morrissey asked the Deputy to hold Jacques until they had a chance to talk to Buzz.

Captain Morrissey gave Jacques one last chance to change his story. He said it was the truth.

Captain Morrissey and Agent Lawson drove over to apprehend Buzz. As they did, Agent Lawson wondered aloud. "Think these two were dumb enough to get conn'd by Anthony and the other guy out of the treasure? If they did, who is the mystery person? If not, was Buzz in on it? Did he dupe Jacques?"

On the way, Agent Lawson got a phone call from his office.

They relayed the information from Sheriff Bradley, about the coroner's report. They also told him to check for a suspect with tiny feet.

So far, Jacques did not fit that role. The print was closer to a womans shoe size. When they were done, he replied, "Thanks! That might go along with what I'm starting to see here."

Buzz was just coming out of the local café when Captain Morrissey stopped him.

"Morley Cox, I'm Captain Morrissey, I need you to come with me. I have Agent Lawson of the FBI with me, and we have some questions for you."

Buzz looked around. He had nowhere to run. Reluctantly, he agreed to go with the constable.

He sat in the car, quietly, not saying a single word, until they reached the post. Once inside, they sat across a table. Buzz still had not even asked what this was all about.

Captain Morrissey and Agent Lawson played the game at its best.

Whatever Buzz was worried about them asking, he was obviously relieved when he was told it was regarding Bayfield. Relief was not what Agent Lawson had hoped to see.

After two-hours of bluffing that Jacques had told a different story, Buzz had stuck to the same story that Jacques had told them earlier. There was slight changes, but the story was essentially the same.

Buzz had met Anthony at a meeting in Chicago. He had waited for him in the bar at the hotel and asked him about joining his expedition looking for gold coins. He guaranteed Anthony that he had the information, but he needed something to scan several locations that were indicated in the references he had gotten at the library.

Anthony had claimed that he had a metal detector similar to those used on shore, which they used underwater.

Buzz met Anthony at the ferry dock in Bayfield and the two of them drove to the cabin. Buzz claimed that Anthony never even met Jacques until they found the treasure. Jacques had the boat tied up in a bay, and Buzz called Jacques on the cell phone to tell him it was time to meet up.

Once again, Buzz claimed the rocks were for diving ballast, and Anthony stayed with the Park Service Deputy. He was to return the boat to the marina.

Either these two people had totally rehearsed their excuses, or it was real.

For now, Agent Lawson was forced to let Jacques go. Captain Morrissey decided they had enough to hold Buzz for a couple days.

Captain Morrissey and Agent Lawson also decided to have a sketch artist brought in to get a drawing of the Park Service deputy that the suspects said they saw. If both decided on a person with the same characteristics, they may at least have a start for someone to look for. If not, well then they were not off the hook totally.

Besides, Buzz was definitely involved with something else that they had not uncovered, so far. This would give Captain Morrissey a little more time to shake out a story.

Bluff as he might, Agent Lawson could not get either of them to bite and accuse the other one of Anthony's death. He had definitely placed both individuals at the scene of the crime. However, he still had no proof that either was involved in murder.

So far, the best he could do was charge Buzz with bad checks and false identification at the marina, removing relics from national park land without a permit, carrying them across into Canada without paying duties, and possibly theft of the sailboat. That and another nickel would probably buy Agent Lawson a cup of coffee. He needed something to make the charges stick and get a confession out of Buzz.

Jacques was a different matter. So far, all they had on him was removing relics from national park land without a permit, and carrying them across into Canada without paying duties.

No, the trail had hit the fork in the road. Now it was time to find the other trail. He could still work with Captain Morrissey on the bad check charges, and possible stolen property charge on the sailboat rental. The other important clue he picked up on was the fact that Buzz thought they had a metal detector. No mention of other capabilities had been made by either suspect.

Chapter 30

Pizza Night

Stan showed up at his sister's apartment right on schedule for pizza night.

Nate Duncan, Jane's boyfriend was already there when he arrived. They had been going together for almost three years now. Nate was a regular for pizza night. Usually, they cooked a pepperoni, sausage and mushroom pizza in the oven, while having some cheap wine and talking about everything that happened in the past couple weeks.

Stan was all set to get grilled on his trip to Chicago. He did have something exciting to tell them though; his replacement bicycle was in at the shop. He could pick it up in a day or two.

On this night however, Jane had a different agenda. She wanted to tell Stan that Nate had proposed, and they were engaged to get married.

She had all she could do not to call Stan and tell him over the phone. Nate had requested that she tell him at pizza night.

Stan was excited for them when they finally told him. "Well, it's about time," he told her. "I was beginning to think you two had buried a piece of coal somewhere and were not getting married until it turned to diamond."

Jane told him all about how Nate finally asked her, and how she made him wait for two hours before she gave him an answer.

"That was kind of risky wasn't it? What if he changed his mind during that time?" Stan asked.

They spent the next couple of hours discussing Jane and Nate. When Nate was finally getting tired of the spotlight shining in his eyes, he turned to Stan and asked, "So, what about you? I have not heard anything about that 'work trip' you took to Chicago. If I'm correct, might I understand you were doing more than selling books?"

Jane looked at Stan. "I'm waiting to hear also," she told him.

Stan told them all about the funeral and going back to Barbara's house afterwards to talk.

"Does that mean you are planning on making a number of trips in the future?" Jane asked.

"Well, actually, I am," he told her. "I'm planning on going to Bayfield the end of the month to get back on track with that book."

She looked at him with that look of disappointment. "I was hoping you were going to say that you were going to see her again," she stated.

"Well, she did give me her phone number and asked me to call at the end of the week. Is that close enough for you?" Stan asked her.

Jane wanted to really grill Stan; however, she did not figure this was the time or place. She would get him on the phone later and have a long talk with her brother.

* * * * *

Agent Mark Lawson flew back from Canada with as many questions as he had acquired answers.

Time to call Sheriff Bradley and take another look at all the facts and characters involved. They had to be missing something that would give them some direction. This case had so many points of interest; someone had to have seen something.

When he got back to the office, he sat down with one of his agents and called Sheriff Bradley on the speaker phone. "Sheriff, this is Mark Lawson. I've got one of my crack agents with me. What's your take on the report I sent you from Canada, and the info the crime-lab came up with?"

"Well, I'm still waiting for those composite drawings. Can't wait to see our new mystery person.

"The fingerprints we lifted might have a partial match to your man Buzz. It's only a 40% match. However, considering everything, that's a good ratio. I'm not sure what percentage of a print they had to use. There is definitely prints from the deceased on the boat. Those we have accounted for. What we still do not have are links to a few other prints. May be important, may be someone else that was on the boat before this started – just can't say.

"Footprint! That's a small size shoe. Too small for your big Canadians. What size did you estimate Stan Moline had? How about the victims wife or mother-in-law? We need to throw all the variables back in the fire and pull them out one at a time."

"Good thoughts," Mark replied. "Let's dig out all the reports and see if we missed something or if we missed a question. Speaking of that, I was thinking while I was up in Canada, where's the car? Victim dies and I did not see any comments about a car. Did he drive from Chicago or have a rental car? He had a computer. What do we know about it? What brand was it, how old was it, where did he get it? And, one more thing, that motor/day sailor, did it need gas? Where did they get it?"

"I'm on it," Sheriff Bradley replied. "See if you can get that composite drawing."

"Working on it as we speak," Mark answered.

* * * * *

Towards the end of the week, Stan called Barbara to see how the move was working out.

She sounded totally exhausted, and was busy trying to catch up to all the changes at the orchard that had happened in the past couple years. New inventory systems, new accounting sheets, and many of the older workers she had known were no longer working the mad rush of the harvest season.

Vivian had things in very good condition. It was just different from what she remembered.

She was pleased to stop and spend a few moments talking to Stan. It seemed that Stan was the only person she would allow to discuss anything from her past. Now, she needed that outlet to help let go of her emotions.

They talked for almost an hour. Then Stan promised that he would call her in another week. He wanted to make sure she had started to relax.

* * * * *

Captain Morrissey had the two people of interest work with his sketch artist.

Jacques did it with grace, as he hoped it would keep his name out of any murder plot. Buzz was not too happy about doing it. He was sure they were cooking up some surprise for him and he reluctantly helped with the drawing.

When they were done, they sort-of resembled each other. This much was for sure; they both described a correct National Park Service hat with logo, and Jacques thought he had sandy-brown hair, where Buzz wanted it darker brown. Other than that, when it came to facial features, they really did not remember a lot.

For a less than two-hour encounter four months ago, it really was as expected – average face with no visible scars, a hat and a uniform.

He sent the information to Agent Lawson, who forwarded it to Sheriff Bradley.

Chapter 31

Second Attempt

Stan was anxious to get back to Bayfield. He really did not like the feeling of getting tied down to a long term job, but at the same time, when he started something, he wanted to complete it. He just hated to start something and leave it out there dangling in space.

This next book of his had to get finished.

* * * * *

After another week, he was heading back to Bayfield to see if Jean could fill in all the blanks he needed for the book.

When he opened the door to the inn, Jean shouted out, "How many are you inviting for breakfast this week?"

Stan was taken by surprise....well, not really. Jean always seemed to be a step ahead of him.

He laughed, "Well if no one else is staying in this place, I hope you'll join me." He signed the registry and Jean just pointed to the stairs. "Got your same room all set for you. Even put the literature on the table just like last time. Good to have you back."

When Stan got upstairs, Jean had left a box of chocolates on his pillow with a note, *"Thought you might need some energy to write late at night. Don't forget to turn off the lights."*

Stan came down for breakfast at 7:30 am – sharp. Jean did not even remind him of the breakfast time.

When he got there, he found he had company, or at least Jean had company – Deputy Miller was sitting at the table. "Wow, I did not expect to see you here," he told the deputy.

"Jean said you were coming back to town. Thought I would stop in for breakfast and see how you were doing," he replied. "How's that book coming?"

"Slow!" he answered. "That's why I came back. How's your investigation coming? Got it wrapped up by now?"

"Sheriff told me that if I grabbed you and threw you off a cliff, we could wrap up the paper work and claim to have solved the case." The deputy said it with a twinkle in his eye.

Just then Jean brought out breakfast – "Well, it is ham and eggs for your last meal," she said.

"No other guests for the inn?" Stan asked.

"Typical Monday. Everyone went home to work. We're booked full up for the weekend. Getting close to the busy season – Apple Fest. Deputy Miller came by to give me the county's financial report for the weekend. He wrote three speeding tickets, four parking tickets, and had to report to a hit-and-run by the ferry dock when the city chief was busy – someone hit a duck. That about it?" she jabbed at Deputy Miller.

"I just don't understand why you don't run for mayor," the deputy told her. "You already know everything that's happening in this town."

They had a good breakfast – just the three of them, and talked about everything that had happened in the past months. Bayfield had not changed very much.

Deputy Miller told Stan about the investigation. "We found the guys that rented the sailboat. Couple of Canadians.

"Unfortunately, they claimed they were back in Canada before Mr. Fontaine was murdered. Everything points to some other individual. It is still a mystery case. Got one shoe print – don't know if it is connected or not."

"Does that mean the foot is severed, or just not part of the case?" Stan joked.

"You must have gotten a good night's sleep," Deputy Miller replied. "No, it's just an old print made from the clay. Small shoe. What size you wear, Stan?"

Stan looked at his hiking boots.

"I guess they are a size 9 ½. I usually buy them a size larger than my shoes. They are size 9. Want to check?"

"No just trying to put an image in my mind. You are about 5'-10" aren't you? What do you weigh?"

"I'll tell if Jean tells," Stan answered. It got a good laugh.

"I am 5'-10 ½" and weigh 175-lbs. Deputy, I think you have me beat."

Deputy Miller laughed, "My left shoe weighs that much. I was trying to figure out the proportions of a person with a small shoe size – about size 8," he said.

"Looking at you, that would put the owner about 5 foot 4, to 5 foot 6, and about 150 pounds."

Jean laughed, "And you're the best we have? What if it wasn't a man? Ever think of that? A 110-pound female could have that foot size.

"I thought you were sharper than that."

Deputy Miller sat back. He had never even considered it. Neither had Sheriff Bradley.

The ladies they had dismissed were back in consideration along with everyone in town. Nevertheless, he had not tied the possibility of the shoe print to a female foot.

Breakfast was enjoyable. They had a good conversation, and then Deputy Miller asked Stan what his plans were for the day. "What are you going to try and research this trip?" he asked.

Stan told him, "I think I will take that trip out to the lighthouse and to the caves. Last time I was here, I managed to see them from about ½ mile. I would like to get a little closer.

"Also, Jean promised to spend a couple hours with me if I came back, giving me the history of every rock and hill in the area.

"So, you say you are going to sit and listen to her for the next month?" he joked.

"No, just a couple days. Wish I could stay longer. Let me know if you find anything on your mystery person," he told Deputy Miller.

After the deputy left, Stan and Jean sat and talked for almost three hours.

"Where can I start," she told him. "You stop me when you get bored.

"Did you hear about the great flood? There used to be a dam upstream from the iron bridge. They used hollow logs wrapped with iron to bring water to Bayfield. Well, in 1942, they had a flood under the bridge. Took out the dam and wiped out seven businesses – three by flood and four by fire. It was caused by all the clear cutting of the trees leaving nothing to stop the water on the hills. A huge rock went rolling through the bakery and into another store. The flood also took out the town's paper. All the old copies were stored down the basement and the town's history was lost.

"There was the house that they wanted to move from Pikes Bay to Madeline Island in 1977. They pulled it over the ice with a truck. Unfortunately, they miscalculated the weight. It broke through the ice. It took three weeks to sink. They had to weigh it down with sandbags until summer. When they tried to lift it by the rafters, the bottom broke out of the house and the top collapsed. Had to use divers to retrieve the pieces.

"There is a lot of history with the Ojibwe Indians. In the 1400's the Ojibwe made Madeline Island their home. They migrated there due to a prophecy known as the Seven Fires Prophecy. According to the prophecy, they would leave their lands in the east and they would follow to a land that would be the center of the universe. They would make seven stops along the way. The seventh stop was an island in the shape of a turtle that fulfilled the prophecy – Spiritual, Political, and Economic. It had food – white-tail deer and fish, birch trees for making canoes and baskets, wild rice grew along its water, and they could get their tobacco from the red willow trees for their religious ceremonies.

"As early as 1693, a trading post was established on the island. Many languages were spoken – French, English, and Native American.

"By the 1820's, the post had been English, French, English, French and then American.

"By the 1850's, two Frenchmen returned from the area with a load of pelts worth around $120,000. It was a lot of money in that day, and started the big push for trapping and lumbering in the area.

"As soon as the trees were cut and removed, farmers came in to make their fortunes. However, the severe lake conditions took their toll.

If they could survive the cold winters, bringing their harvest to market without being caught in a big storm on the lake was another adventure. Between the cold and the weather, many gave up.

"In 1854, a treaty split the Ojibwe into reservations on the mainland, Catholics - north to Red Cliff, Protestants - south to Bad River. Only the eastern tip of Madeline Island was offered to the Ojibwe. Chief Joseph Buffalo walked all the way to Washington, D.C. to keep their lands and not have to move to Minnesota like the government wanted. It took him three months. Senator Rice was involved in the settlement.

"Bet you didn't know that after your trip to Madeline Island. You have to dig to get the facts.

"Did you know that before the Wright Brothers flew at Kitty Hawk, we had a farmer who tried to fly? He was hoping to take his potatoes to town. He built a plane in the loft of his barn up by Red Cliff. When he went to test fly it, all the people from town came out to watch. It came out of the barn, took off and flew straight down into the ground. All the people turned and went back home.

"Here's another little known fact. In Bayfield, titles were handed out by townspeople to all newcomers. Apparently, they did not like people that bragged about a title they might have. As a result, they made up their own. One could be an Admiral, Major, or Count, just by showing up in town and staying."

Jean had given Stan the general story of many other unique places in town and those close by, including the information on several of the boats sunk nearby. By the time Jean stopped to answer a phone call for the inn, Stan figured that had enough information that he could check out several of the stories himself, for the next few days or so.

At noon, Stan took the excursion boat out to the lighthouse. It was a packed trip and he was fortunate to get a ticket at the last minute.

The restored lighthouse was interesting. The trip gave Stan a different perspective, looking at the islands and water from the boat. When he was on Barbara's boat, the "Deceptive Views," he was looking at the area for the first time. Since he had a few months to think about it, and had done more research from a different perspective, the view from the tour boat seemed different.

Now, he was looking for something to write about. At the same time, it was triggering thoughts about earlier in the summer.

* * * * *

Deputy Miller had a full day as well. He was searching for records of gas purchases by Buzz and Anthony.

There was no record of fuel purchased at the Roy's Point Marina. It was possible that it did not need fuel before it sank. However, the likelihood was that it was fueled, sometime, during the time it was out on its daily trips. As a result, the deputy was out checking the six locations in the area where the boat may have obtained fuel. Eliminating Roy's Point dropped it to five.

Once again, he had to ask the marina operators to pull receipts from months earlier. If they paid cash, they might never find it. The local marina in town was unlikely, as he doubted the sailors wanted to be seen in town. However, he checked with the local marina and the marina south of town. Three down, three to go.

Odds were that they got fuel close to the area they were searching. That meant Cornucopia and Port Wing. Since they had fueled up the Chris Craft in Cornucopia, he doubted that Buzz would head back another time to get fuel. If they went back too many times, someone might get suspicious and remember him.

Port Wing was a blank. The list was getting smaller and smaller. Deputy Miller stopped off at the Cornucopia Harbor on the way back to town.

John Morley was hoisting a boat out of the Lake and hauling it to its dry land perch.

"John," Deputy Miller called to him, "can you take a minute off when you get that cruiser over to its parking spot?"

John Morley glanced over and gave a nod. Then he finished his job of precision driving, by parking the boat perfectly between two large boats. His crew set the stands under the stern, mid-ship, and the bow of the boat. Then John gently set it down in place.

"OK, Deputy Miller, what can I do for you today?"

"Remember those guys from Canada we talked about earlier?"

"Yes! What now?" he asked.

"Any chance that either of them might have come by around the same time, in a 40-foot motor/day sailor and bought fuel? I did not see any other credit card slips when we looked earlier, but we were looking for the Chris Craft. How's that great memory?"

"Well, if you did not find any credit cards, he probably didn't use it," John Morley replied. "Same two guys in a different boat? Why didn't they just use the Chris?"

"Might have been one of the same guys and another guy." Deputy Miller took out a picture of Buzz and Anthony Fontaine. "Guess they wanted to use a smaller boat," he answered.

"That guy" – pointing to a picture of Fontaine, "he was in here. Cold rainy day. He wanted to leave a boat for an hour to go up to the café and warm up. Yeah, I remember his face."

"How about a receipt?" Deputy Miller asked. "If they used a credit card, it would be in the same box. If they paid cash, well sorry, the register receipt will not show anything other than gas purchased. You might want to check with the café."

"Thanks! That helped a lot," the deputy replied as he got back in the cruiser and headed up to the café about a block away.

The bar/café was one of three in town. The deputy figured they would head to the closest one if it was raining, and they were on foot. The first café' told him that they were closed that early in the spring. He parked in front of the general store and walked across the street to the next café.

Inside, he showed the pictures to the bartender and to the waitress. Neither one recognized either of them, but said that they might not have been working on the day they came in. Deputy Miller looked around and saw about six customers in the place.

He walked across the street and checked with the general store. There was always a chance they might have stopped there after eating. It was one of those "everything including the kitchen sink" stores. They knew everyone that came in by name, and if they did not have what they needed, they could either order it or tell them where to find it.

Unfortunately, the owner had not seen either of them, either. It looked like a dead end.

He tried the third cafe with the same results.

Deputy Miller drove back to town and reported his finding to the sheriff. At this point, he figured he probably did not need to check out the marina at Washburn, which was 12-miles south of Bayfield, and definitely out of the area the deceased was reported to be searching.

Everything looked like they had stayed in the area they were going to search. The two Canadians had left a good trail. The only exception was the bad check at the marina for the boat.

Why had these suspects used a fake identification, and later used a credit card for fuel?

Chapter 32

The Hike

Stan had enjoyed his trip out on the water. It was a lot cooler this time of year and it felt good to wear a light coat rather than bake in the sun. He decided to finish the day by walking along the cliffs of the Lake Superior National Shoreline that extended over the sea caves he had seen from the water that summer.

It was a great walk, and the leaves in the woods were all turning color. The hike took him almost a mile from the parking area, through the woods along the shoreline, and ended up high on the cliffs overlooking Lake Superior and the sea caves. He stood there watching the waves splash in and out of the caves 60 to 80-feet below him.

Stan could imagine 100-years earlier, some trapper canoeing along the shoreline and getting caught in a storm. If they tried to use the caves as shelter, as the wind shifted and the waves pounded the opening, they would have had a problem trying to get back out. Was that what Anthony Fontaine was looking for? Were they checking out the areas near the caves looking for treasures that someone had tried to save, when their boat started to sink? Lake Superior definitely had its secrets. Many of which will never be told.

When Stan got back to his car, he noticed all the mud on his hiking shoes. What a mess. A few spots on the trail that were full of leaves were also full of water and mud hidden below the leaves. With his hiking boots on, he had just walked through it. Now, when he got back, he would have to clean off his boots and the car mat.

He got back to the inn late that evening. Jean was wondering what had happened to him. She expected to see him right after dinner – heading up to the room to start writing.

"Hi, did you get lost?" she asked as he came through the door.

"Took the excursion to the light house you recommended last time. Then, I decided to take the walk along the Lake Superior National Shoreline you had also suggested. Wow! What a view. Would not want to fall off those cliffs into the water."

She looked down at his feet. "What happened to your boots," she asked. He was walking barefoot.

"Mud! Didn't think you would appreciate me tracking up the inn. Do you have a place I can wash them off?"

"Thanks! Most guests would rather track up the place. Sure, hand them to me and I'll take the chisel to them," she joked.

Stan was puzzled by the joke. "OK, thanks. He hiked back out to the car and picked up his boots from the trunk. Some of the mud was starting to harden. He saw what she meant. You could make bricks out of that stuff.

Jean probably worked about 45-minutes on his boots before she returned them to his room. "That's the best I can get them," she stated.

Stan looked at them. "Wow! They look new." She had scrubbed them until all the new and old dirt was gone. The only thing he saw was that one boot was slightly red and the other was not.

Jean saw him look at the color. "Red clay," she told him. "Acts like a dye and really gets into things. You might be able to bleach both boots to get them to match. Otherwise, you can just look like someone from the area. You must have stepped into a spot with clay. There are areas all over this place that have spots where it collects. Locals hate it. You can even walk along the beach and step into a two-foot spot that has clay just under the sand. You sink right into the sticky stuff."

"Thanks for all the work getting them clean," he told her. He decided that tomorrow morning he would probably stop and get some new running shoes. He could use them when he wanted to look more presentable.

The next morning at breakfast, Stan had company. Two people had rented a room for the night and had joined him for breakfast. They were commenting to Jean on how they really liked the Bayfield area and enjoyed the night's stay. They were heading back to the Chicago area that morning after spending a few days in Duluth, and now one in Bayfield.

Breakfast was scrambled eggs and some caramel sticky rolls, which were fresh out of the oven. Stan missed the breakfasts with Jean and Deputy Miller.

After breakfast, Stan headed down to the local store for a pair of shoes. They did not have the brand he liked, but he picked up a good pair of shoes for walking. He would just have to wait until he got home for his running shoes.

Then, he drove down to Washburn and took the back road over the hill to Cornucopia. He wanted to see every angle of the area, and hoped for a high view of the lake or some scenic hidden valley. When he got back to Bayfield, he felt he had a good understanding of the area and was ready to start actually putting the book to words on paper. He could collect the small paragraphs he had written about items he saw, and the stories Jean had told him, and start to weave it into a real story.

Later, he went over to Maggie's for dinner. As he was waiting for his order, he was listening to the people at the bar talking about the preparations for Apple Fest that was coming in a few days. It sounded like the whole town got into the act. They were preparing for tents in the park, a parade, banners, a scarecrow contest, everything.

As Stan got back to the inn, he told Jean that he would be heading out in the morning. He had something he needed to do, and had to leave a day early. He really appreciated all the help she had given him.

He went up to the room and wrote until midnight.

* * * * *

The next morning, Jean had breakfast for Stan and four new guests. People were heading into town for Apple Fest. "Going to miss you," she told him.

"I'm going to miss you," he replied. I'll send you a book when it's finished.

"Heading back to the cities?" she asked.

"Well, I thought I might check out the apples – in Illinois."

"I wondered as much," Jean answered. "Oh! Deputy Miller asked if you could wait until he stopped by. He had a question for you."

"Sure!" As Stan was finishing breakfast and the other guests had left the table, Deputy Miller stopped in.

"Wanted to stop by and wish you well on that book," he said. "One more favor, when you are in Illinois, can you check on Barbara Fontaine's and her mother's shoe size?"

"You think they did it?" he asked. "Is that why you asked me for my size too?"

"Well, the sheriff gave me a check list that included everyone we have talked to in the case, including Jean. We have to eliminate all possibilities even though we doubt they were involved – just like you. I think he is running out of clues and suspects. Anyway, Jean called me last night and said you might be heading to Chicago."

Stan just turned his head and looked for Jean. She was in the kitchen cleaning up. "I just told her this morning," he told Deputy Miller.

"Didn't I tell you she knows everything that's going on in Bayfield. She knew. Must have seen it in your eyes. Anyway, I would appreciate it if you could let me know."

"I will see what I can do," Stan answered.

.

Chapter 33

Orchards

Stan packed his car. As he threw his bags in the trunk, he looked at his boots and wondered – *how did Jean know he was going to Illinois?* He went back in, paid his bill, and thanked Jean for all the help.

The trip to Illinois was not too bad. Weather was nice and he had his music along to listen to as he headed to the small town just northwest of Chicago.

* * * * *

Five hours later, Stan was at the entrance to the orchard Vivian and Barbara owned. Just as Bayfield was preparing for Apple Fest, the orchard was decorated and primed for the fall harvest that had already begun a couple weeks earlier. With several types of apples, there would be a different apple ready for picking for the next few weeks.

As he drove into the orchard, there were signs all over directing customers where to park. As he soon found out, the place was packed with customers. Signs pointed to the "Apple Barn" where you could select the bags of apples you wanted, try some apple bars or even an apple pie. On the other side, they had an area for little kids to play. They made a small maze out of hay bales. There must have been 75 people wandering around picking out their favorite apples.

214

The smell of apples was everywhere you went. Stan smelled the apples on the trees, as he drove in from the main road. Once in the buildings, you could smell the sweet smell of apples in the Apple Barn, smell the even sweeter smell coming from the apple press that made fresh apple cider, and most of all, from the concession area where they sold fresh apple pie by the slice.

* * * * *

Agent Mark Lawson got a call on his cell phone at 8:30 am that morning on his way to the office.

"Mark, this is Carl Harris. Just wanted to let you know we may have a lead on the electronics used in that sonar. We won't know for a little bit, but there are some pieces that might lead to the manufacturer."

"Good to hear from you. Great, let me know if you get a match."

"One more thing," Carl told him, "We picked up a magnetic disturbance off Raspberry Island this morning. Small boat I'm told. We're monitoring to see a direction."

"On it!" Mark shouted. He hung up the phone and called Sheriff Bradley.

"Sheriff Bradley, Mark Lawson. I was just told that there was a magnetic blip sensed off Raspberry Island this morning. Can you get some manpower out to record any boat out in the area? If I get a lead as to direction, I'll let you know."

The sheriff was quick to answer, "OK, I'll ask the Coast Guard, Park Service, and excursion boat to report all boat sightings. Then we'll check the marinas from here to see if any boats are coming in or out. You think it's our sonar unit?"

"That's my hope. Let's see if we can track its movements," Mark answered.

* * * * *

Even though it was late in the season, there were still a few boats making use of the last few good days before the icy winds of winter took over the lake. Within the next four hours, the sheriff had a log on eight boats in the general area and 25 boats listed by the marinas as having gone out or still out from their slips. The sheriff had hoped it would only be two or three to keep track of. This meant he and Deputy Miller would have to drop everything else and concentrate on elimination to find the boat. It was hard to keep up the observation of that many boats without anyone knowing it. The last thing they wanted was to spook someone into dumping the unit into the lake. If it disappeared, they would never solve the case.

As the day progressed, hope for an instant answer for the murder diminished. The magnetic blip disappeared after only 20-minutes. By the time law-enforcement was on the scene, they could not be certain which boat it came from – and that was "if" it was from a boat, and "if" it was from a sonar unit. For now, they hoped they had the start of a clue that might lead them to finding the missing unit. If it was still in the area, that would be great news to both the sheriff and the FBI.

Sheriff Bradley contacted Agent Lawson and told him about his results and lack of significant progress. "Keep up the effort," Mark Lawson told him. "I have a feeling we are getting closer to something. If we can get another reading on that sonar unit, it will answer a lot of questions.

* * * * *

Stan wandered around the orchard buildings, until one of the workers asked if they could help him. He answered, "Is Barbara Fontaine here today? I'm a friend of hers, and I was hoping to see her."

"She is up in the office above the Apple Barn. Would you like me to take you there?"

"Only if she is not real busy," Stan responded.

"She is always busy," the worker answered. "She could probably use a break. I'll go knock on the door and see if she can take a breather."

He left Stan in the barn and went upstairs to the office. A few minutes later, Barbara came down the stairs and put a huge smile on her face when she saw Stan.

"You said you would call me this week," she insisted.

"I broke the line on our tin-cans. Did I catch you at a bad time?"

"No! Mother can run this place with her hands tied behind her back. Can you stay a while?"

"Sure, whatever you would like."

"I'll tell mother that she's in charge. She will probably let me know that she has always been in charge." Barbara went back to the office and came back down quickly. "It is great to see you. Let me show you around." She took him for a quick tour of the buildings. Then, they had a chance to walk out into the orchard where they could talk in private.

After a tour of the orchard, Barbara turned and asked Stan, "Can you stay for dinner? We tend to eat a little late. We have a guest room and you can stay the night if you like. Mother would love to see you as well. She's been asking me if you called back. Somehow, I think she actually likes you."

"That's good, I think. I would love to stay and have a chance to talk."

Barbara suggested that Stan park his car up at the house and she would be up there in a few minutes. She went back in to tell her mother that she had a guest for supper, and overnight. After a couple minutes, she joined Stan at the house.

"Can I help you take your things in?" she asked.

"You know me, I travel light, thanks."

She looked down at his white shoes. "Hope we didn't get your new shoes dirty in the orchard."

"No, I stepped in some clay in Bayfield this week. Now I have one red boot and one tan. Had to purchase some cheap shoes that matched."

Barbara was surprised and glad to hear that Stan had been back to Bayfield to finish his book. "Did you get it finished?"

Stan chuckled, "No! Give me six months to a year, and it might be finished. Jean gave me lots of information and I checked out a few places I had missed the first trip, including the lighthouse tour. The excursion boat was not as nice as yours."

As they entered the large two story house, he took off his shoes and noticed a couple other shoes on the mat. One set was obviously Barbara's. They were a lot smaller. The others set was Vivian's. When he was taking his off, he noticed the size on the label on the tongue of Barbara's running shoes – size six. When Barbara turned and headed into the living room, he took off his other shoe and glanced at Vivian's shoe. It was a size eight. He stopped and wondered if Vivian would ever wear a pair of running shoes. Probably not. Either way, he promised Deputy Miller he would check – and he did. He just hoped that the print would not fit either of them.

Barbara showed Stan to the guest bedroom that was on the other end of the house from the main bedrooms.

"It is not the Chateau, but I hope you find it OK. Sorry, there is no view of the lake either. I will let you unpack, while I check on dinner. Mother will join us shortly."

Barbara left Stan to check on food for dinner, which now included a guest. She quickly made a few adjustments that made it a much fancier meal than the two of them had planned.

Stan stayed in the guest bedroom, and called Deputy Miller. He told him the size of Barbara's and Vivian's shoes. The deputy told him that they were off the list as well. You had to subtract two sizes to go from women's to men's shoe sizes, and the print they had was a Nike men's size eight. Stan was relieved. Now he could relax the rest of the evening.

Stan joined Barbara in the kitchen and asked if there was anything that he could do to help with dinner.

Barbara joked, "I suppose you are going to tell me that not only are you a writer, but a gourmet cook."

"I am an expert at dialing the pizza place, and micro-waving eggs," he told her. Actually, he had managed on his own for the past six years and could cook what he needed.

She decided to let him help by setting the table. Besides, she wanted to impress her guest.

Dinner was enjoyable. They talked about Stan's trip to Bayfield, and Barbara's adjustment to leaving Chicago for the rural setting. It was an good evening for all of them. It seemed that they were starting to relax after all the hassles – maybe, it was the company.

By 10:30, everyone was tired from the long day. For Stan, it had been a long drive. For Barbara and Vivian, it was long days with customers. Vivian was the first to excuse herself to head to bed. She thanked Stan for coming.

After cleaning up the table and dishes, Barbara and Stan called it a night. Barbara gave him a big hug.

"See you in the morning. I'll have breakfast ready about 7:00 if that's OK with you," she told him.

In the morning, Stan joined Barbara for breakfast. Vivian was already getting ready for the morning crowd and was making sure everyone reported for work.

Barbara made a great ham and cheese omelet for the two of them. For her, it was nice to have some quiet time for the two of them to talk.

After they finished eating and Stan helped her clean up the dishes, they went into the family room to sit and talk. A short while later, Barbara mentioned to Stan that she found a number of things Anthony had stored when she was packing to move.

"Stan, when I was cleaning out the apartment, I found a hard drive that was in a drawer. I do not know what is on it. Do you know how to check it? I think it is a back-up drive or something that Anthony had."

"Sure, can I see it?"

She led him to the storage area and showed him a box that had the hard-drive in it. It was a 2 ½ inch drive.

"Looks like a laptop drive," he told her. Do you have an external drive for a laptop?"

"No! Just this thing. Can it be read?"

"Yes, I can run into town this morning and get an adaptor cable that will allow us to connect it to your USB slot on the computer."

"Well, whatever you said," she replied. "I'll pay for whatever it costs. It would be nice to know what is on it."

"Don't worry about it. Let's see if we can get into it."

Stan figured it would take an hour to get to town, buy the adaptor and be back. Barbara said that sounded good to her. She could check on the orchard and meet him back at the house.

About 90-minutes later, Stan pulled back into the driveway of the house, and was met by Barbara as she was heading back from the Apple Barn.

"Sorry, had to stop at three places before I found what I wanted," he told her.

They went into the house and over to the computer in the study. Stan connected the adaptors to the drive and to the computer. Then, he started up the computer. He was hoping that Anthony had not put a password on the drive.

When it opened immediately, along with the normal hard-drive, they were amazed.

Chapter 34

The Backup

Stan had purchased the cable adaptor for the hard drive that Barbara had found in their old house, when she cleaned out the drawers. When they connected it up to Barbara's computer, it did not have a password. As a result, they were able to open the programs and files on the drive.

Barbara looked at the files and said, "This does not look like anything I have seen before. I do not recognize any of the file names on the drive."

Stan looked a little closer. Most of the files looked like they were work files. Titles that suggested projects about surveillance equipment. Maybe this was the key to the manufacturer of the sonar device.

He right-clicked the file name and opened the properties on one file to check the date and project information. To his surprise and to Barbara's, it listed an author and it was not Anthony.

Was Anthony using another person's software? Was this the person it was licensed to? Who was that person? Even Barbara had not heard of him. Stan checked a couple more files, and even a file that used a different program. They all listed the same person's name as the author. The couple of files they looked at were progress reports about work on different sonar devices.

Barbara kept asking Stan what it meant. Stan had an idea. It looked like the clue Agent Lawson needed to break the case. Somehow, Anthony must have backed up the hard drive of this individual, and it had information on it about making sonar devices.

This was the individual Mark Lawson and his friend Carl Harris had been trying to find.

* * * * *

Mark Lawson had just gotten back from a late breakfast when he received a call from Stan Moline.

"Agent Lawson, this is Stan Moline. Can I talk to you for a minute?"

"I'm all ears," Mark shouted as he put him on the speaker-phone, so he could do some paper work at the same time.

"I'm at Barbara Fontaine's Orchard in Illinois. She was cleaning out some drawers at her old house and found a bare hard drive. She had no idea what was on it, and asked me if I could open it for her.

"I got some adaptors in town and when we looked at the files, I figured I should call you. I don't think the drive is Anthony's. I think it came from the builder of the sonar."

At that point, Mark spilled his coffee as he reached to turn off the speaker-phone and talk directly to Stan. "Damn!" he shouted. "Not you, I just spilled my coffee. Where exactly are you? I'll get an agent there in one hour."

Stan explained to him the files and the author name on them. It gave Mark something to work on while his agents raced to look at the drive.

* * * * *

Barbara did not know what to do. She had been worried about how Anthony had acquired the sonar. Now it looked like he may have copied someone's computer to get the information. She was almost in tears.

Stan tried to comfort her. Let's see what it is all about, before you get too upset. All we have is a hard drive so far.

Barbara called over to the office and within minutes, Vivian was back at the house. They explained what they had found to her, while waiting for the FBI. Vivian took it in stride.

Just one more reason, she thought, why she had not liked this guy. All these secrets. Not the way you want a marriage to work. She only wished she could have dumped him overboard.

The three of them spent the rest of the morning talking. They were really trying to keep Barbara's mind off everything that had been going on.

* * * * *

It was just after noon when two of Mark Lawson's agent arrived at the house. They showed everyone their identification badges even though everyone knew they were coming. The agents brought a number of electronic adaptors with them and were surprised to see that Stan had already connected it to the computer and had the drive open. It made their work a lot easier.

Vivian made some sandwiches while the FBI examined the drive.

"You say you found the drive in a drawer in your old house?" they asked.

"Yes! I had not seen it before and the files are not the same as any of my files on my computer."

"Do you know this individual, Raymond Sandberg?"

"No! The name is not familiar at all," she told them.

One of the agents stepped outside and used his cell phone to call his office. After 15-minutes, he returned. "I think I have a lead on the name on the file. He worked for a government project. It might explain some things. If you don't mind, we will need to take the drive and examine all the files. I'm not sure you will get it back. If it does contain the information I think it has, we will need to keep it. I'll let you know what I can."

With that, the two agents took the drive and left.

Now Barbara was really upset. "So what just happened? Was Anthony involved with stealing government property? How can they just up and leave without telling us anything?"

Stan put his arm around her. "Listen, if they thought you were involved, they would not have left. We do not know anything yet. I'll call Agent Lawson later. Hopefully, he can give us a hint of what is going on."

Stan had not planned on staying another night. However, as things were taking place, it looked like it might be a possibility. Barbara was so upset that she did not want to head back to the office and just wanted to sit and talk to Stan.

Vivian told her to just stay put and relax. She could keep the apples from falling too far from the trees.

* * * * *

Carl Harris was working with Homeland Security. They had found the manufacturer's marks on a couple pieces of the sonar's equipment and traced them back to determine the purchaser. To their surprise, they came up with a government lab outside Cleveland, Ohio.

It was a lab that designed and made sonar devices for the Navy, specifically for anti-submarine detection. When they checked with the lab, the device did not match anything they were currently using, even though it was definitely ordered by someone at the lab, over three years ago.

It seemed every clue they had followed so far, kept pushing this investigation higher on their watch list.

*   *   *   *   *

Agent Mark Lawson's team did a fast search for Raymond Sandberg. Cross checking that name against the names of some of the projects, pointed them directly to an individual who worked for a Navy lab in Cleveland, Ohio.

When Mark got a call from Carl Harris letting him know the progress so far by Homeland Security, Mark let Carl know that he might have a name.

Mark contacted the lab and asked to speak to the security manager. When he did, he was told that Raymond Sandberg had died almost three years ago.

Mark sank back in the chair. "Can you tell me what happened to him?" he asked.

"Yes! He had a heart attack at work one day. The rescue squad tried to revive him, but they said it was too late. I even went to his funeral. Why?"

"Can't tell you over the phone. I'll have someone at your place tomorrow to do an investigation. I would appreciate it if you would give them all the assistance they need."

"Sure, just make sure they have the proper clearance from the government," he reminded Mark.

* * * * *

Later in the afternoon, Agent Lawson got a call from Stan Moline.

"Agent Lawson, this is Stan Moline. Can you give me a little heads up on what it was that we discovered on the hard drive?"

"Not much," he answered. "All I can tell you is that it was related to a guy that died three years ago. We are checking on it now. You say she has no idea where it came from?"

"No! Until I opened it, she assumed it was a backup of one of her drives."

"It might have been a backup of the computer on the boat that went missing," he told Stan. "We really don't know yet. Any way, that is my hope. It might give us a lead to see how it got there.

"I have your friend Carl working on it as well. He had a link that led to the same lab. Sorry, I can't tell you any more without security clearance. At least we have some good clues now. Thanks!"

Stan hung up the phone and turned to Barbara, "I think they have figured out who wrote the files. He died three years ago. They said they were still working on it."

"That was before we were married," she told Stan. "I wish this whole thing would go away."

They sat and talked for over an hour. Stan reassured Barbara that no matter what had happened that allowed Anthony to get the computer, she was not a suspect.

After a while, Stan told her that he still needed to head back. "I'll call you tomorrow and check up on you," he told her.

"Please make sure you do," she replied. "I miss talking."

Stan left the orchard, and headed back to Minneapolis. Once again, thoughts of working on his book had fallen to the back burner. The whole way back, all he could think of was what Barbara was going through; as she thought about the things her husband had been into without her knowing.

When he was half way back, he called his sister. He realized it was late. When she answered, he asked if they could have a pizza night tomorrow. He wanted to just sit and talk to her. There had been too much going on for the past couple months and he hoped that talking to her would straighten out his mind.

Chapter 35

Surveillance

Two days later, Carl Harris called Agent Lawson early in the morning, about 6:30 am.

"Got another blip," he said. "I requested a jet from Duluth Air Base to do a fly-over. I think we have a picture of the boat. If we are lucky, it may have something shiny behind it. Can you alert the local sheriff to monitor all boat traffic near Sand Island? I'll call you as soon as I see the image."

"I'm on it," he answered and hung up the phone.

Agent Lawson called Sheriff Bradley who contacted the Coast Guard. Within an hour, they were observing a single boat off Sand Island.

They used two boats to watch the boat from long distance. So far, it had just been trolling back and forth off the western tip of the island.

About 9:30 am, Carl contacted Agent Lawson. "Mark, I got confirmation on a shiny object behind the boat. Looks like it's your call."

"Thanks! I'll let you know what we find."

Mark contacted Sheriff Bradley and they setup the observation they needed. Sheriff Bradley would monitor the shoreline from Red Cliff south, while Deputy Miller would monitor Sand Point and west. Whichever way the boat went, they would have it covered. Meanwhile, while the Coast Guard was monitoring it, they would keep it from traveling to Canada or east to other cities. As soon as they had a direction it was traveling, they would set up at the local harbors, well hidden, and wait for them to come to shore. Whoever it was, they were in for a surprise. Everyone hoped it was the sonar device they were looking for and not someone playing with electronics to attract fish.

Around 12:00 pm, the boat started moving towards the west, away from the islands. Sheriff Bradley directed Deputy Miller to setup at Cornucopia Harbor. Meanwhile, he would pull up from Red Cliff and head that way. He was about 15-minutes behind Deputy Miller. If the boat passed the harbor, the next harbor was Port Wing, unless they pulled in at a cabin between the two harbors. The Coast Guard was following from a distance of about three miles out in the lake.

Thirty-minutes later, it was obvious; they were headed into the harbor at Cornucopia. As the boat rounded the break-water and came into the channel, Deputy Miller was inside the harbor office watching it come in. Sheriff Bradley was watching from a spot outside the marina – just out of view. He did not want to come rolling in and spook anyone. He just wanted to let them tie up and exit the boat.

As the boat entered the harbor area, Deputy Miller noticed that there was one person onboard. He asked John Morley, the marina manager who he was.

"That's Charles Ziemanski. He lives just up the hill a little ways. He's been a regular customer for years. In fact, I was talking to him last week. He wanted to know how late we could keep his boat in the marina before we had to haul it out. I told him that a 25-footer would be easy to take out once we got all the big crafts out of the way. Probably could wait for another three weeks or more, if the weather held up."

"Have you noticed anything different about his pattern or behavior?"

"No!" John answered. "He had the boat out a number of times early in the year and then just the past week he has been out again each day. I don't remember if he got out more than a couple times in the summer."

"Thanks! I may have a few more questions after while. You don't remember seeing him hauling anything to and from the boat do you?"

"Everyone hauls coolers and boxes to the boats every time they use them. No, I don't recall anything different."

Charles Ziemanski had exited his boat and was tying it up. Deputy Miller used the opportunity to move over and talk to him.

"Charles, hi, I'm Deputy Miller. I wonder if I can have a word with you. Could you please walk over to the office so we can talk?"

Charles was caught by surprise. He looked like the fox caught in the chicken coop. After stammering a few words, he said "OK." They walked over to the manager's office. Sheriff Bradley drove in and parked outside the door, and briskly walked in, and introduced himself.

"Mr. Ziemanski, I'm Sheriff Bradley. I need to ask you a couple questions about what you were doing on the lake today."

Charles quickly came up with an answer. "I was told the white-fish were schooling over by the islands. I was just searching for schools that I could fish."

"You had your fishing gear with you?" the sheriff asked.

"No, I was planning on coming back later, if I found any."

"And how were you locating them?" Sheriff Bradley asked. So

far, he had just been leading him into giving him the information needed to check out the boat.

"I was using my depth finder."

"And what kind of depth finder do you have Charles?"

He looked around as if he was finally starting to realize what was going on. "It's a new one I bought this summer off a guy in Washburn. He sold his boat and was moving on."

"Do you mind if we look at it?" Sheriff Bradley asked.

"No! Go ahead. Just don't drop it."

Sheriff Bradley asked the marina manager, John Morley, to join him and explained that they were looking for a missing depth finder. Deputy Miller stayed with Mr. Ziemanski.

When they got to the boat, Sheriff Bradley looked at the dashboard. It had an older Hummingbird depth finder on it. "That doesn't look very new," he told John Morley. "Let's see if there is a second unit." He opened up a large cooler in the boat and saw a large metal cylinder inside along with a long set of cables. It was identical in size to the one he had seen on Barbara Fontaine's boat. Even the cable looked the same with several cables twisted together.

"John, if I'm right, there is a unit that operates this thing. I'm going to see if I can find a computer, or some other device to operate it." John watched from outside the boat as the Sheriff checked out the compartments on the boat until he found the laptop under the seat in the cuddy.

"Thanks John. I needed your witness that these items were on board, and that we had permission to look at them." He picked up the computer and headed back to the office.

When he opened the door to the office, Charles just stared at the laptop.

"Mr. Ziemanski, you want to tell me the whole story about this unit? I need to read you your rights first." He read Charles Ziemanski his rights. Unfortunately, Mr. Ziemanski decided it was time for him to shut his mouth while he thought up a good excuse.

"OK, Mr. Ziemanski," Sheriff Bradley said. "Deputy Miller, lets give him time to think about cooperating. Can you drive him down to Washburn and check him into the Hilton? I'll wait here for the crime-lab. I'm guessing Agent Lawson of the FBI will be here shortly as well." He said it loud enough for Charles to hear. He wanted him to realize the jig was up and he might as well talk.

Deputy Miller escorted Mr. Ziemanski to his cruiser, and drove him down to Washburn where he was booked on suspicion of the possession of stolen goods. That would give them time to start gathering the facts they needed.

Chapter 36

Tight Lips

Sheriff Bradley had been in communications with Agent Mark Lawson. As soon as they had confirmation that the sonar unit was onboard, Mark was heading for the airport to take a FBI plane to Ashland. He did not like the thought of trying to land a smaller plane on the grass strip at Bayfield.

Sheriff Bradley had Deputy Miller pick Mark up after stopping at Washburn. By the time both had arrived back in Cornucopia at 5:00 pm, the state crime-lab people had arrived from Ashland. Except for moving the laptop, everything had been left in place.

The crime-lab checked out the laptop for fingerprints before assisting the Sheriff and Agent Lawson in opening it up and checking out the software. When they turned it on, they found it did not have a password. Mark suggested that they check the properties function on a couple files to see if there was an ID. The first file they checked came up with the author name of Raymond Sandberg. This was probably the drive Anthony had duplicated to make sure he did not lose anything if the computer was dropped.

Even though the sun was already setting in the west, the crime-lab spent several hours going over the boat looking for fingerprints and

234

any other identification left behind. Agent Lawson talked to the marina manager John Morley.

"John, did you ever see Charles Ziemanski with any other people? We need to get a list of any other people that he might have dealt with."

John could only remember a couple of times last spring when another person was with Charles. However, he was too busy to remember who it was. Agent Lawson thanked him and asked if he could put the boat on stilts and cover it, until they decided if they wanted it held for evidence.

Then, Sheriff Bradley and Agent Lawson headed back to Washburn for a conversation with their reluctant boater.

On the way, Agent Lawson called Carl Harris and informed him that he had the missing computer and sonar unit in custody. He then asked the sheriff to send a photo of the suspect to Captain George Morrissey of the Royal Canadian Mounties. He was hoping the other two suspects could identify the individual. According to the sheriff, the new suspect did not seem to match the descriptions given by them earlier. There might be another person out there.

* * * * *

That same morning, Stan Moline was feeling caught between a rock and woodpile. Since leaving Barbara's place, they had talked daily by phone. For Stan, this was not the type of relationship he was used to. He had dated a few people, but now he was feeling strongly about a person who lived a long ways away, and lived a different life style than he was used to.

He had hoped that his sister would give him advice when he had pizza with her the night after returning from Illinois; however, she just sat back and told Stan that he had to let his own feelings decide what to do. He also felt uncomfortable about chasing her right after her husband had died.

That was one item his sister, Jane, gave him advice on. She told him, "It sounds like the marriage was built on love at first sight, and not a long term relationship. Go slow and let things progress, if you really want it to."

Stan found himself biking around the lakes in Minneapolis more than writing. It was a way to clear his mind and thinking about what he wanted to do. On the way back from his ride, he saw a floral shop. He parked his bike outside, went in and ordered a large bouquet of flowers to be delivered to Barbara with a note, "Still thinking about you, Stan."

* * * * *

Late in the evening, Sheriff Bradley and FBI Agent Mark Lawson hoped that a couple of hours of sitting in a cell might loosen up Charles Ziemanski's tongue. So far, they really did not have many links to Mr. Ziemanski and needed him to accidentally supply some information they could use.

After a few hours of discussion, Charles was still as silent as he had been in Cornucopia. Whether it was his attitude towards the police, or just his way of life, he figured what he did was no-one else's business. When Sheriff Bradley and FBI Agent Mark Lawson brought him into an interrogation room, he just stared at the table.

Agent Lawson tried to loosen him up a bit, "Charles, you understand that you are in a lot of trouble. If I were you, I would cooperate and see if you can get a lighter sentence."

Charles Ziemanski just sat there and said nothing.

Sheriff Bradley gave it a try, "Mr. Ziemanski, the unit on your boat was stolen. Looks like it might be government property. If you do not help us, they could claim national security and lock you up on espionage charges for most of what you have left in your life. Is that what you want?"

"I didn't steal nothing from the government," Charles answered.

"Well, it was made in a government lab, and we found it in your boat. Want to explain that?"

"I think I need a lawyer," he answered.

That was not what Sheriff Bradley and Agent Lawson wanted to hear. Now, they were back to legwork again to figure out his connections.

* * * * *

The next day, the report came back from Canada to Agent Lawson. Neither of the people of interest recognized Charles Ziemanski's photo. Buzz was still a rather unhappy camper. However, when shown the picture, he said he had never seen him before. The other individual was more cooperative. He said the individual they had met with was much thinner and not as rugged looking. Another piece of bad news for Mark, Charles Ziemanski did not fit the footprint size either.

Sheriff Bradley would have to start running down all his known associates and try to put some links back in the puzzle. It sounded like Deputy Miller was going to be busy again.

* * * * *

Barbara Fontaine was working in the orchard, trying to determine the next rotation for picking. Vivian was in the office when the florist tried to deliver the flowers to Barbara. She took one look at the flowers and decided that she would bring them up to the house, and set them up for Barbara. When she came in for dinner, they would be on the table for her.

It had been a long day for Barbara. She had to schedule some shipments to wholesalers, do payroll, and manage the pickings. By the time she came in for dinner, she was exhausted. Vivian met her at the door. "There's some flowers for you. I put them on the table."

Barbara looked over at the table. On the center was a large bouquet of flowers with a note. It was from Stan. She just stood there and stared.

"You know, of all the guys you knew, I think he's the only one that really seems to care about you," Vivian mentioned. "You might want to keep him around."

Barbara just looked at the flowers. It was true. Most of the guys she dated were interested in catching a good looking girl or hoping that she would inherit a lot of money. She was into the excitement at the time, and probably did a poor job of picking whomever she was with. Her late husband was a good example. He lived the exciting life, and truth be told, she was just now realizing that she never really knew him for what he was.

"I don't think he is that interested," she told her Mother.

"Well, from these old pair of eyes, I think both of you are singing the same tune. Maybe you should step back a little and test the waters. A little encouragement from your side might make it interesting."

Barbara did not say a word. Through most of supper, she just stared at the beautiful flowers on the table.

After dinner, as they were cleaning up, Barbara asked her Mother, "Do you really think I should encourage him? My life is still upside down with the move and re-learning the business. I do not know if I am ready to even consider having my head spun sideways. What if it doesn't work? I'll be a basket case all winter."

"You know, opportunities come and go. If you do not test the water, you will never know if you missed something or not. I'm not telling you to drop everything and camp on his doorstep, but, you might

238

want to tread lightly and see if there is something there. From what I have seen, he does not seem to be after your money, or looking for a cheap cook. In fact, I kind of like him. He did not have to help us out in Bayfield. He dropped everything to help someone that needed help.

"You take your time and decide. Just keep your eyes open rather than shut."

That night, after heading off to bed, Barbara stayed awake for an hour, thinking. Normally, after a tiring day at the orchard, she was asleep as soon as her head hit the pillow. Tonight, it was a different feeling.

* * * * *

Mark Lawson's team was working overtime trying to wrap up this investigation. Nothing seemed to be right. There were no links between Charles Ziemanski and the man who designed the sonar. No links between Charles and Anthony or his family. No links between Charles and the Canadians.

It was starting to look like one of those puzzles where you throw the bones in the air and see where they land. He had assigned a man to work full time at the lab trying to get all the history they could find on the dead engineer, Raymond Sandberg, and he meant everything.

They pulled all the files they could, and checked with co-workers, old friends, and relatives. So far, it was a blank. Raymond was a dependable engineer with a flair for inventing things. He also loved to tinker at home. If any neighbor had anything that was broken, he was the person to take it to.

* * * * *

Deputy Miller was wasting lots of taxpayer money on gas while checking out leads. He was covering all the bases. He checked with Jean to see if she knew Charles Ziemanski's family or anything about him – no luck. He checked with the barbershop, the general store, the bars, and even his neighbors. As far as he could tell, the man lived by himself, ever since his wife died fifteen years ago. He was 55-years old. He would occasionally work with some local fisherman, do some logging in the winter, and assist a few of the carpenters. It looked like he was collecting a pension from the Army and supplementing it, doing odd jobs that were not reported as income.

From what neighbors told him, he had plenty of money when he first moved to the area about 20-years ago. Now, except for a 7-year old boat he bought from a cabin owner who was moving, and an old jeep Cherokee he used to get around, he pretty much just stayed to himself.

The manager of the local general store knew him by name. He told Deputy Miller that he seemed to be a very good, but shy guy.

The bar/restaurant across the street said he was a regular. Came in for lunch often and occasionally for a beer.

Everyone seemed to say the same thing; he was quiet, and seemed like a shy guy. Nothing stood out in the discussions Deputy Miller had.

When Deputy Miller met with the sheriff and compared notes on the case, Sheriff Bradley asked Deputy Miller when Ziemanski bought the boat. That one had slipped from Deputy Miller's radar when he was talking to the neighbor.

Deputy Miller figured the quickest way to an answer was to call John Morley at the marina in Cornucopia. He seemed to remember all the small details.

"He bought that back in July," John told him. Tom Jensen moved and it sat here for a year, before Ziemanski bought the boat. I think he paid about $30,000 for it. Still cannot figure that Charles Ziemanski is involved in anything. He's had an old boat here for years."

Deputy Miller reported the facts and started to wonder where he got the money to pay for it. They did a check of his financials. He did have plenty in the bank. He did not need to live like a hermit. It must have been his choice. However, they did not see any withdrawals. The $30,000 did not come out of his checking or savings.

Sheriff Bradley met with Charles Ziemanski's court appointed lawyer. He explained that they were holding him under the Patriot Act for possession of stolen government property and possible espionage. It was a reach, but if he could get the lawyer to work with him in solving the case, it was worth an effort. At least the stolen property was accurate.

The lawyer really did not like fighting with government espionage lawyers, and wanted Ziemanski to lay it on the table for him. Even with his lawyer, Charles did not want to discuss the case. Almost three days passed since he was arrested at the marina, before he agreed to meet with the lawyer.

The next day, Charles Ziemanski and his lawyer met with Sheriff Bradley and Deputy Miller. With a conditional agreement to keep it in State Court rather than Federal Court if he cooperated, Ziemanski said he was willing to tell his side of the story.

Chapter 37

The Game

Charles Ziemanski said he was at the bar in Cornucopia one day in May, when two guys came in off the lake. It was a cold wet day and they were looking for a warm meal. They sat at a table close enough to him that he could hear the conversation.

"They were excited about something they had found on the bottom of the lake. I couldn't hear everything, but it sounded like they had found some old wreck and were going to dive it the next day. There's lots of old junk on the bottom, so I didn't think anything of it. Well, I went to the restroom, and the one guy comes in. After a minute, he asks if I can help play a trick on his friend. He tells me that the guy thinks there is all kinds of gold on the bottom, and he wants to make it look like they found it. He said he was planning on putting something on the bottom, just so he could find it.

The catch was – he wanted me to dress up like a Park Service Ranger, and threaten to throw the group in jail for illegally treasure hunting.

"Well, I don't like messing with people, so I tell him of a friend he can talk to, if he wanted. I didn't hear from him again, so I don't know what they said.

"Two weeks later, this friend of mine comes up to the house. He said the guy paid him for looking like a Park Ranger and he gave me this fancy depth finder. Said it didn't work. However, if I wanted it, I could have it. He said it was used to see the bottom.

"There was a laptop with it. I figured I could probably sell the laptop for $200, so I said OK.

"I took it to a friend in Herbster the next day, to see if he could sell it. He looked at the depth finder, and told me I was missing some parts. Something about a connector was missing. That was probably why it didn't work. Also, I had been told by my other friend it took three batteries to use it. Hell! I only have one in my boat. Never seen a depth finder that took three batteries.

"Anyway, we tried to get it to work. The laptop worked. Every time we tried to use the depth finder, it didn't boot up. I was all set to scrap it when my friend suggested that it might take more power. He said some of the new bass boats were running on 24-volt batteries. We tried it. When he told me that I had something that was probably not worth the cost of the batteries, I told him to sell it.

"Well, he played with it and sure enough, when he put three batteries in series, the damn thing started working. He called and I picked it up. I told him I might as well try it before we sold it.

"I played with it for almost a month before I figured out how to get the laptop to display the bottom. Great picture, but it kept saying out of memory. My friend suggested it only worked for short bursts. That's what I tried. Five minutes at a time. Then, I erased the data and started it again. It worked.

"The next thing I know, Deputy Dog is at my boat arresting me for National Security. Hell, there was nothing that important on the bottom that I saw."

Deputy Miller asked, "You have the names of your friend in Herbster we can confirm this with? How about your other friend that was going to play the trick on the guy?"

Charles Ziemanski gave them the name of his friend in Herbster. He said he really didn't know the full name of his other friend. All the years, he just called him Shorty. However, he did have his phone number.

Sheriff Bradley and Deputy Miller just sat there and looked at each other. No wonder this case was that hard to solve; everything so far, was done by the accidental happening of amateurs. Real crooks would have been easier to find.

Deputy Miller drove out to Herbster to confirm Ziemanski's statement. It was a 45-minute drive there and 45-minute drive back. Between driving and talking to Ziemanski's friend, it took up the rest of the deputy's day. So far, everything Ziemanski had said about bringing it to his friend, checked out.

* * * * *

The FBI had checked out the hard drive. Except for some new images, the software was an exact duplicate of the drive found in Barbara Fontaine's house. The two were obviously a match. Now the question was; how did Anthony Fontaine get his hands on it? Did Shorty kill Fontaine, and then give the laptop to Ziemanski? Why? Where did the $30,000 come from? Was it payment for the missing salvage? What did they find?

Now, Agent Lawson was down to a couple pieces of the puzzle. Unfortunately, they were the missing links. He really needed to solve how Fontaine ended up with the sonar. He needed to find out what Shorty did with Fontaine. Then, he needed to find out what happened to the loot. On the other hand, was there any loot? Maybe it was all a hoax.

* * * * *

Barbara called Stan, and asked him if he was busy.

"No, just looking at a blank page on my laptop – right under the title line. What can I do for you?"

"I was wondering if you could help us do an article about the orchard during the busy season, to use next summer, sort of an advertisement. You could stay at the house and work from there, if you like. I do not know how long it would take, but I figure about a three page spread is what we need. Do you work by the hour, or by the job?"

"Well, the one I did this summer, for that town on Lake Minnetonka, was by the job. It did not take very long once I got some pictures and a few quotes. When did you want it done?" he asked her.

"It is the busy season now. If you are going to take pictures, this is the best time to do it. The parking lot is full and the trees still have some red apples on them that we will be picking. How about next week? Say Thursday?"

"I'll be there. Say hi to your mother."

As Barbara hung up the phone, her mother turned to her and said, "You won't be sorry. You can find out if there is some magic or not. If you did not do it, you might have wondered for a long time."

* * * * *

Deputy Miller did a trace on the phone number he was given. It was a cell phone, so it took a little longer to get a name and address. The address was a P.O. Box out of Red Cliff. However, with a name, he figured it would not take long to find Shorty.

He drove up to Red Cliff and talked to a couple locals. It didn't take long to get the location of Francis Ramona i.e. Shorty. He lived six miles out of town, toward Sand Point; second driveway on the right, after the sharp curve to the left. Unfortunately, no one had seen him in over a month. The word was, he had gone to see some relatives.

When Deputy Miller checked out the house, Francis Ramona was gone, just as the people in town had suggested. Looking at the lawn, it had not been cut in at least a month, and there were no fresh tire tracks in the driveway.

Deputy Miller called the sheriff and reported his findings.

Sheriff Bradley said he would get a search warrant for the location by tomorrow. Meanwhile, he would ask for a trace on the cell phone as well.

Deputy Miller did some checking with the neighbors, and back at the casino sports bar. The story seemed to be the same; hadn't seen him for at least a month. At the bar, one patron told the deputy that Shorty had purchased a new pickup, just before he left – a black Ford F150.

Deputy Miller put a check on his computer to see if he could find a Ford F150 registered to Francis Ramona. It came back as a match. Now, he had a license number as well.

He sent the information back to the sheriff. He knew what the sheriff's next words were going to be - have the FBI do a financial trace on Francis Ramona. See how he paid for this new truck. He did not bother to wait for the words. So, he called Mark Lawson and gave him the information and the license number of the truck.

The next morning a judge signed the search warrant and the request for the location of a cell phone belonging to Francis Ramona. The request was given to the cell provider for tracing.

At the house, they found that Francis Ramona – Shorty, had left rather quickly. He had packed some of his clothes – mainly his underwear and socks, along with some of his shirts and pants. The closet was still half-full. All of his coats were still hanging in the back entry. The thing that told him he left in a hurry, the refrigerator was still full, and there were things growing that did not need to grow in a refrigerator. As they opened the door, the odor hit them immediately. Sour milk!

They took some items for evidence including a pair of shoes.

Chapter 38

Tracing

The cell phone provider was slower than molasses in the Apostle Islands in January. It took three days before they came back with information. They showed a few calls the last week in June in the area, then, it appeared he headed south.

There were only two calls made – from Missouri, then none until recently. The last call was from southern Texas. It looked like he was heading for the Mexico border. The last call was two weeks ago.

Agent Mark Lawson checked with the Border Patrol. They had an automatic camera reading of a license matching the description one week ago on their computer. It had crossed into Mexico – near Brownsville, Texas. *At least we know where to look,* he thought.

He sent a request to the Mexican authorities to look for a new, black Ford F150 pickup, with Wisconsin license plates. He also sent along the photo from Francis Ramona's driver's license. He marked it; wanted for questioning for murder, known to be in northeastern Mexico as of last week.

Now, until they heard from the Mexican authorities, all they could do was wait. They had a few phone calls to follow up on from Francis Ramona's cell phone, and they sent a picture of him to Canada.

Maybe this was their match. Mark's biggest concern was that they would say "Yes, that's him," just to get them off their backs.

When Mark checked Francis Ramona's bank records, he found they had been emptied. Not that there was much to take out. He had apparently withdrawn about $500, close to the time he left town. What they did not see, was any money movement to coincide with the purchase of a truck.

*   *   *   *   *

Mark Lawson got a message back from the Canadian Mounties quickly. Both people of interest, Jacques and Buzz, had identified Francis Ramona – Shorty, as the person that they met in the Park Service uniform. Mark was hoping that was good news. He was worried that they had seen too many pictures and were not accurate. However, if both identified him, perhaps they finally had their man.

One more piece of good luck came their way; the shoes that were picked up at Shorty's house appeared to be the same size as the prints found in the sunken boat. Now, all they needed was the missing suspect. He was somewhere in Mexico. The question was where, and whether or not the Mexican Police could pick him up.

While they were waiting for word from Mexico, they still had a couple of mysteries on their part to solve. What did they find in the water? Where did they sell it to raise cash? There was the issue of a boat and a new truck.

Mark asked the Sheriff to track down the Ford dealership and see how the truck was financed. Francis Ramona did not appear to have a good line of credit.

*   *   *   *   *

Deputy Miller was staying a very busy person. He had only a couple local dealerships in the area, so he started with the one in Ashland.

He got a hit right off the bat. The sales manager remembered selling Shorty the black, Ford F150. He said it was a demo with all the options on it. In fact, his finance manager had been driving it, and it only had 500 miles on it.

The sales manager told him, "I was shocked. He looked at it in the morning and came back later in the day with a cash down payment, and we financed the rest."

"How much down, and how did you finance it?" the deputy asked.

"He gave us $8,000 cash, and we did a risk loan for the rest. He didn't even complain about the interest rate."

"Well, I would not be looking for that loan to be paid in full," Deputy Miller told him. "Last we heard, the truck was down in Mexico."

Deputy Miller called Sheriff Bradley and told him the news. The question was; where did he get the $8,000.00?

* * * * *

Deputy Miller was still talking to Shorty's neighbors. Someone must have a clue as to where he got the money for a truck, and what he had been doing.

There was some speculation. One farmer thought he had leased out his fields. Another thought he had cashed in a life insurance. Deputy Miller still could not find the source.

He was checking out a couple of Shorty's back buildings, looking for clues, when he noticed several crows in the old oak tree, on the edge of the field. They were making enough racket that even a blind person would know they were there. As he watched, he noticed there were eight crows. They would fly down to the ground, and then fly back up. He decided to go check it out.

When he crossed the open field, he saw the crows were picking on something in the brush, behind a tree. As he got closer, he realized what it was. Someone had buried garbage or something close to the surface, and the animals had uncovered it. As he looked, he realized it was a body that was uncovered in a shallow grave.

Deputy Miller called Sheriff Bradley. "Sheriff, I think I've got a body on the Francis Ramona place. Animals uncovered it and the crows drew me to it."

"Deputy, I'm going to fire you yet. Every time I try and shut the book on this case, you write another chapter. Heck, I might as well permanently assign you to the case. I'll send the team out to meet you. Let me know what you find."

It took about an hour for the investigation team to show up at the farm. They took pictures and dug up the body. On first glance, it looked like the male body had been hit over the head, and buried in the shallow grave.

Deputy Miller took a look at the body. It was hard to tell, but it looked like the photo he had seen of Francis Ramona - Shorty. The other thing he observed, it had tennis shoes on, one was dirty white, the other was reddish white. They were Nike shoes.

He called Sheriff Bradley. "I think you better fire me before I give you the news," he told him. "I think the body might be Shorty."

Sheriff Bradley just shook his head in amazement. What else could happen to this case? Now, he had two bodies and no suspects. Time to bring Agent Lawson up to speed.

Chapter 39

Mexico

The next morning, Sheriff Bradley got a call from Agent Lawson.

"Sheriff, hate to ruin your lunch, but I got one more tidbit for you. I got a call from Mexico this morning. Apparently, they saw your pickup truck on one of the back roads about 50-miles south of the border. The driver tried to run from the officer and flipped it over on a corner. He's dead.

"I asked them to send up a picture of the driver. Should have it by late afternoon. It should help confirm that the body you have up there is Francis Ramona – Shorty."

"Any more rabbits in your hat?" the sheriff asked him.

"Guess you will have to start all over with this guy's photo. We'll run it through our computer as soon as we get it," Mark replied.

"Thanks! I'll buy Deputy Miller another tank of gas."

* * * * *

It was the next morning before Agent Mark Larson sent the information to Sheriff Bradley. They had a photo, however, the scan through the FBI computer did not come up with a match. Whoever it was, he did not show up in the Federal database.

Deputy Miller thought the guy looked familiar. He could not put a name to the face, but he had seen him before, and probably had a run in with him. Since Shorty was from northwest of Red Cliff, and he had Shorty's truck, he figured that was a good place to start his search. He drove up there and started with the bar.

Several people said he looked familiar. However, they did not have a name for him either. That meant he was probably from the area, just not Red Cliff. Deputy Miller decided he would take the picture to the places he visited on his route the next couple of days. Someone would have to recognize him. One thing on his side, he did not have to worry about this guy getting away. The sheriff had also asked his other deputies to show the picture to people.

* * * * *

Late in the day, one of the other sheriff deputies got a lead. One person he showed the picture to, thought it was a guy that lived near Siskiwit Lake. He lived back in the woods about a quarter mile from the lake.

Sheriff Bradley drove over to Siskiwit Lake and helped his deputy follow-up on the lead.

After talking to a few people that lived in the area, they finally put a name to the face. He was James Dufault.

His neighbors said that they had complained about him in the past. Apparently, he was prone to helping himself to an occasional chicken dinner – fresh chicken. Also, when gas prices went up, several people thought he might have been helping himself at their expense – at night. No one appeared to be on his friends list.

Sheriff Bradley called Agent Lawson and informed him that they had a positive identification on the photo. Agent Lawson said he would pull all the financial records of James Dufault and see if they could find any links.

By the end of the next day, the FBI had a full list of records belonging to James Dufault. He had not filed a tax return in five years. Did not look like he had any large income either. Bank accounts were cancelled years ago. Probably kept whatever cash he had in a coffee jar.

It looked like he might have lived off the land for the past few years with an occasional job helping some farmer or chopping wood. Where Shorty knew him from was a real guess. Somehow, he had Shorty's truck.

* * * * *

Stan drove down to Barbara's early that morning from Minneapolis. It was a wonderful day, and Stan wished that he had driven down the night before. The sun was shining, and there was not a cloud in the sky. Perfect day for picture taking. He pulled into the orchard just before noon.

There was a line of cars turning off the main road into the orchard parking lot road. Most of the spaces were already taken and people were forced to park in a grassy area along the road, near the trees. Stan motioned to the parking assistants that he was heading up to the house.

When he reached the house, he parked in the driveway. Then, he walked over to the office to see if he could find Barbara or Vivian.

The place was packed with customers. It looked like a great time to work on an advertising spread.

It did not take long for Stan to find Barbara in the office. Her face lit up with a smile as he walked in. Vivian was there also, and greeted Stan with a hug. Then, Vivian told Barbara, "I can take care of things. You two get lost for a while."

The two walked downstairs where Barbara offered Stan a snack from the food concession. The smell of apples was enough to make anyone hungry, and after trying an apple-crisp bar, and a piece of apple pie, Stan washed it down with some apple juice. He was amazed at how many people were purchasing foods, along with buying a bag of apples. "Wow, you must do a great business during apple season," he told her.

"Well, the season is short, so we have to make whatever we can in about three months. If you have a good product and present it well, the customers come back each year."

Stan suggested that they make use of the perfect day for photography and get some pictures in the afternoon. Barbara agreed. After she helped Stan bring his things into the house, Stan picked up his camera and they walked out into the orchard, to get some pictures of the workers picking apples.

Stan shot some great pictures. The bright red apples on the trees, with the green leaves and blue sky, made a perfect promotion shot. After shooting a few pictures of the apples and the workers picking them, he took a few pictures of Barbara holding an apple in the orchard, and of her picking an apple off the tree.

Stan almost stopped taking pictures after a few shots. The sun, coming from slightly behind Barbara on a few shots, made her blond hair glow. It reminded Stan of the picture he shot on the iron bridge in Bayfield, of this beautiful jogger that was just coming onto the bridge. She was definitely a distraction.

After a few more pictures, Barbara suggested that they could head further up into the orchard. There was a high spot that they could get a larger view. They walked down the rows of apple trees. It was almost as thick as a forest, only decorated green and red.

It was a quiet, peaceful walk through one type of apple tree, and then through another. The noises of the crowds disappeared as the heavily loaded trees muffled out the sounds. It was almost as if they were alone in the orchard.

As they walked, Barbara showed Stan the different trees and the order they were picking them. They had some apples that were ready early in the season. Others, would still be picked in late October, after the frosts.

When they reached the top of the hill, there was a wagon ready to be loaded with bushels of apples. They sat on the wagon and looked over the orchard. Stan stood on the wagon and took a few pictures from their perch, and then sat back down next to Barbara. He reached out and held her hand. "I missed seeing you the past week," he said. "Even though we talked on the phone, I'd rather talk to you in person."

She glanced over at him and said, "Can you find an excuse to make this job last a few days? I really missed you too."

Stan put his arm around her and held her tight. "If you can convince your mother its OK, I'll find the time."

Barbara replied, "I think she has already let the air out of your tires. She would make you walk back if you tried to leave today."

For the first time, Stan leaned over and gave her a kiss. "Is it OK to do this to your boss?" he asked.

"If it's not, you're fired," she replied and gave him a much longer kiss.

Somehow, the time seemed to fly by. Before they realized it, it was almost time for dinner. Stan took a few pictures using the evening sunlight, as they walked back down the row of trees.

This time, they held hands all the way back.

When they got back to the house, Vivian was making dinner. "Everything OK?" she asked.

"Absolutely," Barbara answered.

Vivian took one look into Barbara's eyes and knew exactly what she meant. She did not have to say another word. She could see by the way the two of them walked close together that Barbara had already been swept off her feet.

After supper, Vivian and Barbara discussed with Stan how they wanted to create a marketing insert for a local magazine. Stan asked which areas they wanted to emphasize. He told them that he would wander a little tomorrow and get some selected photos. After that, they could sit down together to look at them on the larger computer monitor, and see if they liked what they saw.

As the evening progressed, Vivian noticed that Barbara was not in the house. Stan and Barbara were outside on the wrap-around porch of the old farmhouse, which had been refurbished on the inside. They just sat out there talking and holding each other's hands.

Later, Vivian got tired and went up to bed. She left a light on inside for Barbara.

They were still out on the porch.

Chapter 40

Warming up

Morning rollout was normally around 5:30 am, for Vivian and Barbara. The orchard opened at 9:00 am, and they had a lot of preparation to oversee. This morning, Barbara came down for breakfast at almost 6:30 am.

"Late night?" her mother asked.

"Sorry! I guess I wasn't watching the time. I'll get moving shortly."

"Take your time. I see you were enjoying the time with Stan last night. Did he enjoy it as well?"

Barbara looked at her. "No comment. I told him you would let the air out of his tires if he tried to leave."

Vivian laughed! "Nonsense! I would just park a tractor behind his car. Might even put a chain around his bumper. I can manage things today if you want."

"Thanks, but he wanted to just wander around today. Maybe later if he …"

"I know," she said. "I'll be over in the office. See you later."

Stan popped his head out of his room around 7:00 am. Barbara was waiting for him. She had fresh rolls on the table along with orange juice. Stan could smell the rolls baking in the oven from his room.

"Good morning," she greeted him.

"Good morning," he answered as he looked around for Vivian. When he did not see her in the room, he walked over and gave Barbara a warm kiss.

"That the way you greet all the women you meet in the morning?" she asked.

"If they have a beautiful smile like yours," he answered.

They sat and talked as they ate breakfast. Then, Barbara excused herself to go help Vivian with opening.

Vivian noticed that Barbara was not quite her old self all morning. She seemed distracted and was constantly looking around. She just chuckled, *"She's lost."*

About 11:30, Barbara found Stan and suggested that they could have lunch in the orchard. She had a bag with her that contained sandwiches, juice and apples.

Stan laughed. "You mean with all the apples on the trees, you needed to bring some along?"

"I washed these," she answered. Actually, she hand picked them earlier, making sure she had perfect apples, which were at the exact stage of ripeness.

They walked out to the orchard and found a picking wagon that was not being used that day. It made a great spot to sit and eat.

"I'm getting spoiled with all the beauty here," he told her. "I know you wanted to work in oceanography, but this is something special as well."

"I know. The first week back, I started to see the things I missed while being away. I do like it here. Mom made it sound like she really

259

needed me back. In reality, she's running it. She would be lost if she gave up control. Someday, she will quit. However, I doubt that day will come for a long while. There is always enough new projects to keep me busy. That way she does not have to worry about things like any new marketing and technology needed in the future.

"In the off season, it will get a little quiet around here. I guess I will have to take up cooking."

They sat and talked for almost two hours before Barbara forced herself to head back to the office.

Vivian just peered over her glasses as she walked back in.

* * * * *

Around 7:00 pm, just before dinner, Vivian walked up to Barbara and suggested that the two talk as they headed back to the house for dinner.

"I have not seen you taken off your feet like this since you were in high school," she told her. "Am I reading this right or am I missing something?"

"I don't know. Part of me says yes, and yet I guess I am afraid to let go, only to have one more problem. I think you are right; he is probably the nicest guy I have gone out with. I just don't know how I can fit in his plans."

"Well, that's what I wanted to talk to you about. You know how sometimes the beautiful girl has problems getting a date because all the gentlemen figure she is looking for something higher than them. He may be having the same problem with you. You are financially well off, and your husband just died. He is far too sensitive not to respect that and worry that he is not your type. If you really want him around, you might have to gently let him know."

"That sounds easy, but it is hard enough for me to decide," she said.

"Take your time. Just let him realize you are still there," Vivian advised her.

Soon they reached the house. Stan was sitting on the porch watching as they approached.

"I've been sitting here trying to pick up girls for the last hour," he said. "So far, the two of you are the only ones to stop. I guess the best come last."

They headed in for dinner.

After dinner, Stan showed them some of the pictures he had taken, on Barbara's computer. There were many possibilities. Vivian pointed out six of her favorites. Then, she told Barbara that she had some work she needed to do on the computer up in her room. "I'll let you and Stan decide what would make the best presentation."

She excused herself and went to her room.

Stan and Barbara spent the rest of the evening out on the porch watching the stars, and talking about what things were like when they were growing up.

* * * * *

Agent Lawson had driven up to Washburn to meet with Sheriff Bradley late the evening before. He wanted to see if they could put together something that explained what happened to Anthony Fontaine. So far, it looked like most of it would have to be guesswork.

The next morning the two of them met with Deputy Miller, and used a chalkboard to try to map out all the clues and people involved. So far, it looked like the butler did it with the candlestick.

"The clues and evidence are all over the map," Mark Lawson stated. "We have a dead body – Anthony Fontaine from Illinois, who was found, anchored in a gunnysack off Sand Island. We have two Canadians – who admitted they purchased the gunnysack in Cornucopia, and were with Anthony Fontaine. Coroner says Fontaine was dumped in the water days after our Canadians returned to Canada. We have the mysterious imitator of the Park Service Ranger, which turns out to be Shorty, whose footprint was in the scuttled boat in the lake.

"Then, we have the sonar unit that Charles Ziemanski claimed he got from Shorty. Charles claims that Fontaine asked him to impersonate the Park Service Ranger, and he gave him Shorty's phone number. Oh, Charles just incidentally purchased a boat for $30,000 this summer.

"There is another dead body – Shorty. Somehow, James Dufault steals Shorty's new truck, which he had mysteriously come up with $8,000 in cash to buy. Then, James turns up dead in Mexico.

"Oh yeah! We have this designer in Cleveland that made the sonar – only to have a heart attack over three years ago and dies.

"Did we leave out anyone?" Agent Lawson asked.

"You left out the wife that shows up with the duplicate sonar unit, and later finds the backup hard drive in her husband's drawer. And, for the heck of it, Stan Moline shows up to drive their boat. Yeah, that comes close to covering it," Sheriff Bradley replied. "Heck, we might as will throw in the whole town in this one."

"Well, Dr Watson and Mr. Hyde, you forgot a couple more clues," Deputy Miller added. "The Canadian had some gold crosses. That meant they did find something. Were the gold coins there too? Why did they rent the boat with a phony name and pay cash for the inn, while using a credit card we could follow to purchase gas?"

"I think we need our fiction writer, Stan, to put all this in a book and tell us the answer," Mark Lawson said with a smile. "So far, my hunch is still in following the money. If we can find the source of the money, we will have the answer."

Sheriff Bradley asked, "Let's suppose they did find some coins. Where would they sell them?"

"I would guess the internet, pawn shop, gold shop, or a collector," Mark replied. "I'll run a search on the internet, and check the shops within 150-miles. Any local collectors might be harder to find. Can you see if anyone knows of any in the area?"

They sat and stared at the board for an hour. The answer was probably there, but there were too few clues to link them together.

Mark Lawson drove back to his office in Minneapolis that evening.

Chapter 41

The Purchase

About half way back to Minneapolis, Mark received a call on his cell phone. The agent in Cleveland might have found a clue.

"Mark, I did some more hunting on our designer. There was absolutely nothing in his history to say he would take a candy bar out of a vending machine without paying for it. That was the clue.

"So I checked with his employer's records department. The parts that were in the sonar unit, he bought them through the company. They were not government property. In fact, they were not covered by any secrecy agreement, as they were not used on any of the projects before that time."

"Oh my, more good news," Mark replied. "I'm not sure I can take one more today."

"Well, you might want to."

"When I had talked to his friends, they had mentioned that they would go out on his boat, in the harbor, once and a while and relax after working long hours on a tough project. I forgot about it until the other night. I called the harbor and found he did have a boat. It was foreclosed on after his death. The bank took it back.

"It took the bank some time to find the auction record, but here's the catch. The $200,000 boat was auctioned off for $125,000."

"OK, so are you going to tell me, or do I have to drive over there and hang you by the heels until you cry uncle?" Mark told him.

"Hold on to your hat, the winning bid was Anthony Fontaine. It was almost a year after the designer – Raymond Sandberg's death."

"Let me get this straight, the man gets a great deal on a 45-foot boat, and gets a million dollar sonar for free?"

"That's my guess," the agent told him. They probably had no idea what it was at the bank. Sold it 'as-is.' That's pretty standard on repossessions. The guy had no relatives to claim the boat and no one else knew he was working on the sonar."

"Congratulations! You get the gold star for the day. Good work," Agent Lawson told him.

The rest of the way to Minneapolis, Mark's mind was spinning. This whole case is dumb luck, with the exception of the dead people.

He decided to call Barbara Fontaine and see if she knew anything about the purchase of the boat.

It was about 8:30 pm when he called. Barbara had just finished dinner with Stan and Vivian.

"Barbara, this is Agent Mark Lawson of the FBI. Sorry to bother you this late in the evening, however, I have a question for you that may solve a problem I was working on. Did your husband ever mention to you where he bought your boat?"

"Well, yes. He said he was watching the broker ads on the internet and found an auction with some bank repossessions. Why?"

"Well this might put your mind to ease. We think the sonar unit was on the boat when he purchased it. In fact, my guess is that both units were on board, as well as the laptop.

"The laptop may have been stashed away on the boat. The broker sold the boat as is. The bank never knew what they were, and the original owner had passed away. As far as I can see, you do not have to worry about selling stolen merchandise. It was never stolen. Hope that makes your day a little brighter," agent Lawson told her.

"Thank you! It really does. Thanks for calling."

* * * * *

Barbara turned to Stan and her mother, and told them about the conversation she had with Agent Lawson. You could see the instant relief in Barbara's eyes.

"You know that map compartment, down below, Anthony used to have his computer in there. I wonder if that was where it was, if he found the laptop? I remember him saying that he had to replace the lock."

They talked about Anthony and the mysteries that had surfaced, for the next couple hours. It was obvious to Stan that Barbara was quickly moving from the grieving stage; to one of unbelief that she had not seen any of the signs earlier.

She had really enjoyed the time together. However, Barbara told Stan, "I have to cover the office tomorrow. Vivian has a standing lunch with her friends Marcella and Edna every other week. As much as I wish mother could just skip a week, I understand that these are her long time friends, and they have been real close over the years. By the way, they said to say hi to you, from them."

Stan remembered them from the funeral. They made a lasting impression.

"I should probably head back tomorrow morning. I need to spend a couple days putting together the presentation for you. I can call you when it is finished and we can look it over."

They spent a slow hour saying they should get some sleep, only to steal an extra kiss goodnight and talk a little longer.

The next morning, after breakfast, Stan headed back to Minneapolis.

For Barbara, the day seemed a lot longer than normal.

* * * * *

When Mark Lawson got to his office the next morning, he put his agents to work checking out all listings for gold coins from May 3rd until September 1st. If anyone sold them, it would have been in that time frame. They may have sold them one at a time or tried to sell the whole lot.

The FBI also contacted a long list of pawnshops and shops that buy gold covering Illinois, Wisconsin, Minnesota, and Michigan. Somewhere, they had to get lucky. If there was a sale, they wanted to find it. If not, someone must have had a conversation about it.

After a few days, they had still come up blank, without a lead.

Chapter 42

Gold Fever

Sheriff Bradley had his deputies out talking to everyone in sight, looking for anyone that might be a rare coin collector. If they were lucky, they might find someone that was willing to purchase or resell the coins.

Deputy Miller was having breakfast with Jean one morning and mentioned to her that they were trying to find a coin collector.

She paused and mentioned to him, "My hair dresser mentioned the other day that a friend of hers was trying to purchase a gold coin. She said some guy showed it to him, and try as he could, he could not get him to sell the coin. He knew they were fairly rare. I guess he offered him $40 for the coin, and he turned it down. I think she said it was some $20 coin. I've seen them advertised on TV. Sounded like a fair offer to me."

Deputy Miller sat up in his chair.

"Jean, this is important. Do you know who saw the coin or who had it?"

"No! But, I can find out in an hour when they open the salon," she said.

If Deputy Miller could physically move the hands of the clock to get to opening time, he would have.

At 9:00 am, Jean called the hair salon, and the operator told her the name of the individual who saw the coin.

"I know him," Jean said. "He lives on a farm just over the hill from the ski area."

"You want to drop a hint of the name?" Deputy Miller insisted.

"Only if you take me along," she replied. "I've been hearing about this case all summer. I want to hear who has the merchandise."

After a little bargaining, Deputy Miller convinced Jean that she could not go on official police business. However, he would call her before he left the farm, if he got an answer.

"Deal!" she told him.

Deputy Miller got in his cruiser, headed down the small blacktop road south of town, and quickly turned into a gravel road. Around the second hill, he turned into a small farm and walked up to the door. It was his lucky day; the owner was home.

After a short discussion, Deputy Miller was told that he was shown an old $20 gold piece at the bar. The guy had been drinking, and he tried to convince the owner that he would like to buy it. However, the guy would not budge.

Deputy Miller asked him, "Did he have one, or more than one coin?

"Sorry, I do not know."

When the deputy asked who the man was, he told him the man's name was Chuck. He did not know the man's last name.

Deputy Miller asked him if he would look at a picture on the computer in the cruiser.

He followed him out and the deputy pulled up a few pictures on his laptop.

"Yeah! That's the guy with the coin," he answered.

The photo he had just identified was Charles Ziemanski.

Deputy Miller thanked him for his help, and had him sign a statement about the conversation. Then, he called the sheriff and arranged a meeting – just south of Cornucopia, where Charles Ziemanski lived.

He almost forgot the most important call – he needed to call Jean and thank her.

* * * * *

Charles was caught by surprise when he saw Sheriff Bradley and Deputy Miller pull into his driveway. He had no idea that they knew about the coin he had flashed at the bar.

Sheriff Bradley met him at his front door.

"Mr. Ziemanski, I'm hear to arrest you. You have the right to remain silent …"

After reading him his rights, he took him into his cruiser where he and Deputy Miller talked to him. They did not have a search warrant yet and did not want to search the house illegally.

Deputy Miller told him that they had an eyewitness's statement that he had in his possession a gold coin that was taken from Anthony Fontaine before his death. If he wanted to see his farm again, now was the time to tell the truth.

Charles had been worried that he probably had too much to drink a few nights ago and showed a coin to someone. Now, he realized it was going to be impossible to hide it.

"Ok, I have a gold coin. However, I did not kill anyone to get it. It was like I said, the guy asked about someone to play a trick on someone and I gave him Shorty's name and number."

"Then, how did you get the coins?" the sheriff asked. He still did not know if Charles had one coin or many coins.

"Well, like I told you before, I met Shorty at the Casino's sports bar in Red Cliff one night. He told me he had this sonar unit that I could have. He didn't know how to work it and thought I might want to try and fix it.

"Then he said he was going to head to Arizona, and wanted to know if I knew anyone who wanted to buy some old coins. He said he had some old gold coins and wanted to sell them.

"I went over to his place with him. Sure enough, he had this old box full of coins. They were all $20 gold pieces. I asked him what price he wanted for them. He said he saw this commercial on TV, saying they had some of these coins that were found in a bank in mint condition. They wanted $50 each.

"We counted them. He had 500. I told him I would buy them from him. It would take a couple days. He said no problem.

"Then, I told him I wanted the box they were in as well for that price. He took the offer. I figured they were probably worth double that amount.

"I cashed in one of my life insurance policies. My wife's dead, I didn't need them. I got a cashier's check for almost $15,000. Signed it over to Shorty, along with just over $10,000 I had on hand. Took a few days longer than I promised, but Shorty got his money.

"I don't know anything about the dead guy. Shorty never said anything about him. I guess he never will, now. Too bad. Who killed him?"

"We were going to ask you," the sheriff said. "We figured you might have had a hand in it."

"No way! That's the truth. That's all I did and all I know. The coins are in the box, in the steel box on the bottom of the wood pile in the shed," he told them.

Sheriff Bradley left Charles in the car with Deputy Miller and returned a few minutes later.

He carried an old wooden box with metal latches that were just starting to rust after being exposed to the warm moist air the past few months. Inside were the $20 gold pieces.

"Charles, I need to take you to jail. We'll sort this through and see if there is more to the story than you told us so far," the sheriff told him.

"Deputy, will you close up Charles's door, until we can get a warrant to check for additional evidence?"

Sheriff Bradley took Charles to the jail in Washburn. After they searched his farm thoroughly and found nothing else, he called FBI Agent Mark Lawson, and gave him the information Mark wanted to hear.

Mark had felt that if they found the money source, they could start to put together the whole story. The only thing missing was the proof – why Shorty was killed. Seeing that he liked to frequent the bars, they felt he probably bragged about the trickery one too many times.

Did Shorty have a partner or did James Dufault kill Shorty and perhaps Anthony Fontaine because he had heard them bragging, followed them home, then stole Shorty's truck and maybe his money? Where was Anthony Fontaine those few unaccounted days?

Mark figured that he would probably never know for sure. It looked like they had brought the case to a weak close.

Charles would probably get a "slap on the wrist" from a local judge for obstruction of evidence, for not telling the police that he had the coins. They doubted that he would get any time in jail, other than the time he had served while being questioned.

Chapter 43

Relocation

Mark Lawson was almost ready to file his report, when one of his agents stopped in his office.

"Mark, did you ever find the missing money on that Fontaine case?" he asked.

"No! Don't know if the guy in Mexico had it on him and it disappeared like everything else down there, or if Ziemanski told us the real truth this time. Why?"

"Just wondering. I was checking out your dead man in Mexico – James Dufault. It took a while, but I found that his fingerprints did not match his name."

Mark's eyebrow lifted. "And?"

"Well, I checked the files and we have this guy's fingerprints listed in our relocation files – dating back 20-years earlier. Turns out, he was involved in some gang activities in Chicago. In agreement for turning in evidence, we relocated him to northern Wisconsin. Looks like he lived a very low profile for the past 20-years, up in the woods. Maybe he finally got bored. His relocation payments ran out a few years ago.

"When I checked his phone records, I didn't see anything that stood out. He had used Shorty's cell phone on the way to Mexico. Unfortunately, those calls were just local area code calls with no importance.

"However, I just got his cell phone records from 'his' phone. He had the phone number listed from a different area code in a different state, so no one would know where he lived. It was also unlisted. It really threw me off for a little while.

"Anyway, once I found it, it looks like he made a few calls to someone in Chicago the past few months. I have a phone number, but no name so far." He dropped the file on Mark's desk.

Mark shook his head.

"This case will never end. Well, you found the lead, let me know what you find, "handing him back the file." I'll tell the sheriff to keep the key handy on his filing cabinet. Who knows where this we lead to, or it might just be an old girlfriend he was calling."

* * * * *

Stan got back to town and spent the evening with his sister Jane. He told her all about the couple days he spent with Barbara. He was afraid that if he didn't, Jane would tie him to a tree infested with ants and spread jelly on him until he finally did.

"So, did you sleep in separate bedrooms, or who shared who's?" she asked him, watching his expressions.

"That's kind of personal don't you think," he replied. "Besides, her mother lives there also."

"So, is this a going thing or not?" she asked.

"It's getting warmer. I think her mother even likes me. We will have to wait and see what happens. Right now, I am working on a magazine spread for her. When it is done, I might have to go back down there and show them the finished work.

"I think their busy season starts to slow down in another two weeks. Hopefully, I can spend some time with her when she does not feel she needs to be watching the business constantly."

"From what you said earlier, it sounded like her mother was more than happy to fill in and give the two of you time together. Better not screw this one up," Jane told him.

"I'm still concerned about getting involved with someone that is financially well off. I probably look like another gold digger to all their friends," Stan told his sister.

The rest of the evening was spent talking about the wedding plans Jane was making. Once she had the low-down on her brother, she wanted to tell him about all the wedding plans she was working on.

* * * * *

It took a few weeks for the FBI to sort through all the records and find the contacts. Seemed that everyone was using unlisted phone numbers that were blocked. To an FBI agent that was used to dealing with someone in the protection program, that usually meant that James Dufault was dealing in his old games.

Mark got the report a few days later. It showed a few phone calls made to a cell phone on Chicago's south side. The person listed for the phone had a long record for almost anything you could think of, mainly thefts, extortion, robbery, and assault. Nothing on his record sheet had put him away for a long time. Each time, a sharp lawyer had gotten him off with a minimal sentence. The name listed was Arthur Jones, however, he had a number of other names listed that he had used in the past.

Was there a link to this case? That was going to be hard to establish.

He started by pulling the phone records for Arthur Jones along with his financial information. He needed to find something solid that linked him to the case.

* * * * *

The mad rush of apple customers was slowing down rapidly by the time Stan drove back down to see Barbara. He had talked to her on the phone nearly every day since he had last seen her. Now, with the rush almost over, Barbara had suggested that he come back down and show her what he had put together for the magazine. It was an excuse on both their parts to see each other in person.

As Stan drove into the orchard, he noticed the difference quickly. The lines of cars were gone, the trees were stripped of their apples and even the leaves were gone. The signs of fall were rapidly feeling as though winter was just around the corner.

Stan got there about 4:00 in the afternoon. Barbara was at the house waiting to greet him as he arrived. With the lack of customers, she did not have to watch the apple barn until late every day.

"What took you so long?" she asked as he got out of the car. "I've been waiting all afternoon for you to drive in."

Stan was not sure, if she was joking or if she really expected him earlier in the day. "Sorry, no cars to follow to find the place. Took me a while to find the driveway." She got a laugh out of that answer. To Stan's relief, that meant she was probably joking about her comment.

Barbara gave Stan a big hug, and he responded with an even bigger kiss. "Missed you," she told him.

"If that's the case, I can get back in the car – drive out and drive back in, to see if I get the same reception twice," he told her.

Barbara gave him a big smile and then helped him carry his things into the house.

"Mother has her lunch thing again tomorrow with her friends. I told her the two of us can hold down the fort while she is gone. She said to call her when I got supper ready. Mother is figuring out the scale-down work schedule for a few people who will stay working for the next month."

Stan helped Barbara set the table and finish getting the food ready for supper. It was nice having her relaxed and enjoying the moment.

When they were all set for dinner, they called Vivian at her office to tell her to be back for dinner by 6:00 pm.

Vivian got back at 5:50 pm, and gave Stan a hug when she saw him. "It's nice to have you back."

They enjoyed sitting and talking at dinner.

After dinner, Stan was going to take out the presentation he had put together.

Vivian stopped him. "Let's look at it in the morning. I will let the two of you enjoy the evening. We don't need to work 12-hours a day until next fall." After watching a show on television, Vivian excused herself to go finish a book she was reading.

"I told her she didn't need to disappear," Barbara told Stan. "We'll be alone all afternoon tomorrow, when she gives her friends the low-down on everything that is going on."

Stan put his arm around her shoulders as they sat tight together on the davenport, and watched another show. He was enjoying the soft leather furniture. Somehow, it seemed a lot warmer than his furniture – maybe it was the company.

Barbara did not seem to mind either. In fact, the tighter they sat, the better it felt. Neither one could remember the finish of the next show. About 1:30 am, they decided it was probably time for some sleep.

The next morning, after a late breakfast, Stan showed Barbara and Vivian the presentation he had put together. He had put a lot of effort into cropping the right pictures that made the place look exciting.

"It's perfect," Barbara said. "Don't change a thing."

"I like it also," Vivian replied. "We can send it in to the magazine just like it is – just before spring. That way we will be ready to have it run in late summer."

About 10:45 am, Vivian left to have lunch with her friends Marcella and Edna.

"I guess we are on our own," Barbara told Stan.

"I thought you needed to cover the orchard," Stan said.

"It's covered. I'm not needed all day."

"After last night, we might need to use your walk-in cooler before your mother gets back," Stan suggested. "I almost followed you to your room last night."

"I wouldn't have kicked you out," she whispered.

* * * * *

The FBI had several people working on the records of Arthur Jones. By trying to link the phone calls from James Dufault to other calls out, they tried to see if there was any other links to the case. They also searched for any direct bank transfers. So far, the money was hard to trace. If there was any, it was probably a cash deal.

Looking at the phone records, there were a couple records that seemed to have a pattern. They found one phone number that showed up around any communications with Arthur Jones and James Dufault. The number was for a house in Elgin, Illinois. When they did a search on the number, it came up for Rosemary Baron.

The FBI did a follow-up search on Rosemary Baron and came back with some information that they passed on to Agent Mark Lawson.

Rosemary Baron was a 62-year old woman who lived at the same address for the past 5-years. Her name was familiar. As they dug a little deeper, they found the name of her husband – Raul. He had passed away 7-years ago at 64-years old. Raul was very well known to the Chicago police. He had been a major player in organized crime for years before his death.

The question before them was; how were the records related? They did the same search they had done on Arthur Jones on Rosemary Baron trying to see if they could find any links using her phone or bank records.

Chapter 44

Links

Vivian had her luncheon that day with her friends. Vivian's friends – Marcella and Edna, grilled Vivian for any gossip on Barbara and her new friend. They wanted to know what Stan was like, was he dependable, and was Barbara interested in him. As long as Vivian knew them, they were always playing matchmaker or at least keeping track of all the kids that were part of the close families in their old neighborhood.

Vivian filled them in on all the news along with the fact that Stan was staying at their house this week. That got an "oh" from her friends.

Edna told Vivian, "You better start looking for a dress for the wedding. You don't want to be caught unaware like last time."

Vivian just laughed. "I think I will have time to look this time."

"Better keep control of the orchard, until you really know about this one," Marcella told her. "You think he can smell the money?"

Vivian tried to convince both of them that so far Stan looked like an honest gentleman. "I don't think he is interested in cashing in Barbara's money," she told them.

They spent the next hour catching up on all the other gossip.

* * * * *

By the time the FBI was done digging, they had a lot of information, however, no facts. It was one thing to establish probable phone links between people. It was another to try to prove something happened. The agents realized that the best they could do was try and establish that some communications were conducted between Rosemary Baron, Arthur Jones, and James Dufault. If it was about Anthony Fontaine, they were not sure why. They definitely did not have any evidence to support a case.

Finding the link was proving to be very difficult. When they looked into their financial records, they did trace two checks from Rosemary Baron to Arthur Jones for $5,000. One was dated mid-April. The other was May 30th. The time frame was right. Was it a coincidence or was it the smoking gun that might point to something? Could these provide the links they needed? They kept looking. So far, they were really grasping at straws.

* * * * *

When Vivian returned from her luncheon, she was wondering if Edna was right. Barbara and Stan had definitely made some unconscious decisions. Both were lost in each other's gazes.

At dinner, Vivian commented that her friends were tracking every move the two of them made.

Barbara joked, "I better give them blinders for Christmas."

That evening, the three of them played a few card games before heading off to bed.

When Barbara and Stan finally went to bed, Stan heard a light tap on his door. It opened slowly, and Barbara asked, "Did you request turn down service?"

She looked even better in a short nightshirt than in her swimsuit.

In the morning, Vivian noticed Barbara head back to her room. "Someone enjoyed themselves last night," she commented.

"More than you know," she answered.

"I asked Stan if he wanted company. He said he only slept with women he was married or engaged to.

"I asked if that meant he wanted me to sleep in my own room. He suggested there was another option."

Vivian shook her head. "I thought I said slowly."

"You told me to pay attention to him and let him know I was interested. I guess he decided he really was interested," Barbara told her mother. "In the past few weeks, I realized that Stan was the first guy that really cared about my feelings and that I could just talk to. Besides, I thought you approved of him?"

"I do. Congratulations! Just promise me that you will get to know him fully, so you can discover any hidden secrets he might have. Spend some time with him, before you get married."

"I am. I do not want to make the same mistake twice. We are planning on waiting until after the first of the year to even start making wedding plans. Stan wants to let his sister keep her spotlight."

* * * * *

The links between the phone numbers were getting longer and longer. The FBI just kept digging.

There was still no evidence – just patterns and maybe's. Agent Mark Lawson was starting to wonder if they had dismissed some suspects too early.

They found another set of links with a set of similar checks from Vivian's friend – Marcella, to Rosemary Baron. When they followed the possible links from Marcella's phone, it showed them a correlation that led them to Edna, and finally to Vivian.

Mark started to wonder – *did the mother-in-law get rid of the guy that stole her daughter?* It was a weak possibility earlier. Now, there was a set of phone links and perhaps a money exchange that led his theories back in that direction.

Mark could not find a money link between Vivian or Barbara and Marcella. However, cash could have easily changed hands. At this point, he was not going to rule Barbara out, either. He learned a long time ago that sometimes the least suspected individual was the culprit.

He told his agents to dig in as far as they needed to see if they could make a case. The question now; who was the weakest link to start questioning. Someone had to give up a lead that would solve this thing.

Since the money transfers between Marcella and Rosemary Baron could be documented, he decided to start with Marcella. One of the two of them had to talk. If there was something going on, he would push money laundering charges in their face until they explained everything. At their ages, they would not want to spend a lot of time in jail if they were given the option to bargain their way out of it. Alternately, these ladies might just be stubborn enough not to tell on their friends.

Mark hated to think of the fact that there was the possibility that Marcella might have just purchased something from Rosemary with the money. So far, the evidence was still just a hunch.

* * * * *

Marcella was going about her normal morning routine, and was startled to see an FBI agent knocking at her door.

After Marcella let him in, they sat down in the living room. Mark Lawson introduced himself, and suggested that they needed to talk.

"I am investigating the murder of Anthony Fontaine, and the trail has led me to your door. You did know Anthony?"

Marcella was not sure what to say. "Do I need a lawyer?" she asked.

"Your choice," he answered. "If you cooperate now, we might be able to work a deal. If one of the others on my list talks first, you might want a lawyer."

He was hoping that she would take the bluff. He could see that she was thinking about it. That was a good sign. Mark was hoping that he was finally on the right trail.

"I have a money trail that leads directly to your door," he told her, figuring that it might help with her decisions.

Finally, Marcella spoke up.

"I didn't have anything to do with his death. We just paid someone to tail him and nail his hide, if he was cheating or doing something dishonest."

Mark sat back in his seat. That was not what he expected. He was hoping for a confession. Now, he had another fork in the road. So far, this case had a full set.

"By we, do you mean you and Vivian or Barbara?" he asked.

"Oh, neither. Edna and I figured someone needed to catch that weasel before he hurt Barbara."

Mark hated to do it, but he decided to ask Marcella to discuss this at the FBI office. He could get some general information on the ride over there, while asking another agent to pick up Edna. He knew there was something here, and he had a feeling that he would need this story on tape to prove anything. If he was going to get to the bottom of this, he would have to look for the slightest slip of the tongue to build his case.

At the office, Marcella gave him the whole story.

"You see Vivian, Edna, and I grew up together in Chicago. Our families have been looking after each other all this time.

"When Barbara met Anthony, he caught her hook, line and sinker. He knew a good thing when he saw one. This one came gift wrapped – good looking and rich.

"The first time Edna and I met him, we saw right through him. Too many years of seeing fast-talking men taking women for a ride. Even Vivian did not care for him – though she had to keep her mouth shut around Barbara.

"Anthony got Barbara to get married in Las Vegas, so none of us could say anything to Barbara. It tore Vivian's heart, not to be part of her only daughter's wedding. He did not even like Vivian visiting her after they got married.

"When we heard about him leaving Barbara to go on a sailing trip up north – in April, Edna and I figured he was up to no good. No one heads that way to go sailing with a new wife left at home. We were guessing – perhaps another girl on the side?

"We asked a friend of mine if she could contact someone that could trail him. You see, Rosemary Baron married a person a long time ago, that became sort of an enforcer for the mob in Chicago. Even though he passed away years ago, I figured she still had some contacts that could follow Anthony and record what he was doing.

"It took some talking. Reluctantly, Rose agreed even though she hated those people, she would talk to some guy with connections. As a favor to the wife of an old friend, he said they would do it. It would cost $10,000. We gave the check to Rose, to give to him.

"That guy had someone in Wisconsin follow Anthony, after he confirmed that Anthony was heading that way. We got reports every couple days. We did not know what Anthony had planned. We just did not trust him.

"I don't know any names. They did not tell us. Rose and I sort of understood why.

"Anyway, the guy told us that Anthony was staying with some Canadian in a cabin, heading out in a sailboat each day. Edna and I were shocked. Anthony was actually up there sailing. The guy even rented a couple old boats to keep an eye on Anthony from a long way off. He would trade off boats each day so no one would be the wiser. He had an expensive camera with a long lens like the ones they use for wildlife photography. I was getting worried that we had wasted $10,000.

"Then, one day I get this call. Anthony had made contact with some other man in a bar, and discussed pulling a bait and switch on the Canadian. He thought Anthony and the Canadian had found something in the lake, and he was going to send the Canadian packing.

"Whatever they told the Canadians, they packed up and left in a hurry. He shot some pictures of them with a long zoom lens, from over two miles away. Then, I don't know why, but Anthony scuttled the sailboat, and came in with the other guy. They stayed over at the other person's house for a week. Apparently, they had a number of items they found on the bottom of Lake Superior. Edna and I were right. He was up to something.

"Edna and I were wondering what to do at that point. It was getting expensive following him and we still did not know what game Anthony was playing. They told us it might cost us another $10,000 by the time it was over. It was getting expensive. If it was someone other than Barbara, we would have probably call it off and called the police."

"Why didn't you?" Agent Lawson asked her.

"We would have had to tell Barbara we called the police on her husband. We weren't sure she would understand. Besides, we didn't have any evidence that he broke the law other than scuttling a boat.

"Well, the next report we got from the guy, said that Anthony and the other person he was staying with, had a fight one night after drinking. He said he could hear them arguing about splitting the money from out in the woods, where he was watching them. Apparently, Anthony had not told the guy about how much the stuff was worth. He heard them say they had 1,000 gold coins and some other stuff.

"The next morning, he saw Anthony being dragged out of the house and hauled to a boat. He took the boat out into the lake. When the guy came back, Anthony did not.

"That's the last report we got. They didn't charge us anything additional."

"Why didn't you tell Vivian what you knew?" Mark asked.

"When the scum was killed, what was the purpose? Barbara had enough grief, she didn't need to know more," she answered. "She thought he was a great guy."

"What if he hadn't been killed?" Mark asked.

"Then we would have had to decide what to do."

"She left that option open," Mark thought.

So far, everything Marcella said matched the events as Mark and Sheriff Bradley had guessed they occurred. It was detailed enough to make Mark believe someone was tailing Anthony Fontaine, and that he was a pro at it. It was either a well-planned story or another unbelievable twist to this case.

He had Marcella sit in the office, while he talked to Edna. Could she tell the same story? Perhaps she would slip up. Marcella was far too polished in her story. Mark had figured that she would have been extremely nervous and make mistakes. So far, Marcella's story was concise and unweaving.

Edna was far more nervous than Marcella. However, after an hour he came back with a matching story. Edna told it slightly different. It was from her perspective. The basic facts were the same.

It looked like the only thing left to figure out was the missing coins. Shorty only sold 500 gold pieces to Charles Ziemanski. That left the other 500 coins. Mark was getting an idea where they might be.

To Mark's complete surprise, Vivian and Barbara had not been implicated by either Edna or Marcella. Neither story put them in the investigation. Amazingly, they did not even appear to know what their friends had done.

Before the day was over, the FBI had picked up and questioned Rosemary Baron and Arthur Jones. The four stories matched.

Agent Lawson obtained a warrant to search Arthur Jones's Chicago house. Attempts to put him away for mob activities in the past had not been very successful.

Inside his house, Mark found a shipping box with 500 gold coins. This was the reason Marcella and Edna were not charged any extra fees. Arthur Jones had figured out a better way to collect his payment.

Arthur was held in the complicity in the murder of Shorty. Without direct evidence, the FBI could not prove that he had any active part in the actual murder. They did have evidence of what appeared to be a theft and receiving stolen merchandise.

Arthur would probably get a good lawyer and end up with a few weeks at the workhouse.

The others were released. There was no evidence that they committed a crime.

Mark still wondered why Anthony scuttled the sailboat. Mark realized that if Anthony brought it back without the Canadian, the marina would have probably asked questions and Anthony would have been stuck with paying the rental.

They never did find Anthony's leased car.

The next day, Mark received an email from Captain Morrissey of the Royal Canadian Mounted Police. Captain Morrissey finally found the answer to what Buzz was hiding.

After a lengthy investigation into his curious behavior, they discovered that in his dredging job, Buzz had found several unused, thick old phone cables on the bottom of one of the bays in Lake Superior. When they were between jobs, Buzz had been salvaging the old cables and selling the copper for scrap. He had made considerable money without reporting his efforts or profit.

Chapter 45

Invitations

Stan had been at the orchard for four days. It seemed longer. Too many things had happened in such a short time, and it caught both Barbara and Stan by surprise, not to mention Vivian.

Stan suggested to Barbara that she should come to Minneapolis to meet his sister, and see what his life was like. He was still concerned about how their life styles would merge. It was important to Stan that Barbara and Jane became friends. So far, all Jane knew about Barbara was what Stan had told her.

He told Barbara that both she and Vivian would likely be invited to Jane's wedding. This was important to Stan, and he would especially like to have them there to meet his parents and the rest of his relatives.

They made plans for Barbara to fly up to Minneapolis in a week, and stay with Stan for the weekend. Vivian could handle things at the orchard for a spell while she was gone.

It was almost as if Barbara and Stan had been swept up in a cloud and their feet were off the ground. Things were changing so fast. Barbara kept thinking about what her mother said – go slowly. Well, they had not set a date yet, so she still had time to make sure she knew what she was doing. However, so far, she was not about to make any changes. Stan had caught her love, and she was not going to do anything that might alter things.

* * * * *

Right after lunch, Barbara got a phone call. It was Agent Lawson. He was closing the investigation and wanted to talk to Vivian. Barbara handed the phone to her.

After a minute or two, Vivian excused herself and took the phone to another room to talk to Mark.

Mark Lawson spent the next 15-minutes telling Vivian about her friends participation in the event. Vivian could not believe what she heard. When Mark was done with the story, Vivian was in shock - but not surprised.

She knew her friends very well, and knew what they would do to protect family and friends. They had never gone to this extreme, as far as she knew, but they were definitely capable of it. Vivian was amazed that they would spend 10,000 dollars of their money, without telling her what they were doing.

Mark felt it might be better for Vivian to tell Barbara what her friends had done.

"Thank you for letting me know," she told Mark. "I will talk to Barbara, and discuss this with Marcella and Edna. As far as you told me, I think their intentions were on the right side."

After she hung up the phone, she told Barbara and Stan the long story that Mark Lawson had told her about her close friends Marcella and Edna. Barbara just sat there in shock. "They meant well," Vivian told them.

"I'm glad Marcella and Edna didn't tell us what they were up to until now," Barbara told her. "I would have been furious. I don't think I was ready to hear anything negative about Anthony until lately. I guess

I was the only one that did not know what he was like," she said with a tear in her eye.

She turned to Stan, "Promise me one thing – no secrets. I don't think I can go through this again."

"I'll promise you two things; first – no secrets, second – everyone will be invited to our wedding. If they want to stand up and say 'no' during the wedding, it will be their last chance."

Vivian smiled. "You mean I'm invited this time?"

"Sure, did Barbara tell you we were planning the wedding on a cruise boat that goes around the tip of South America?"

"I'll sic Marcella and Edna on you if you do."

Stan knew one thing; he was not going to cross Vivian or her two friends in the future. He wanted them on his side.

The conversations had started to lighten up considerably since Mark Lawson's phone call had shattered their thoughts earlier.

After a while, Stan and Barbara took a long walk to the end of the orchard and back. They wanted to discuss things and make sure they were doing the right thing.

Barbara was still concerned, "Are all the events of the past year, which keep coming back, going to be an anchor on our relationship?"

Stan assured her, "Before we get married, the past will be old history, and you will know me better than anyone you have ever met. That's why I wanted you to come for the weekend and meet my sister. You need to feel that you are part of my family, too.

"Hmm! That reminds me, I guess that means that I need to call my parents and bring them up to date.

"Any idea on how I am going to tell Jane? She is going to pump me for all the facts the second I talk to her."

"I think she will figure it out the second she starts talking to you," Barbara answered. "She will probably hear it in your voice long before you say anything. I don't think you could hide it for even a couple days. You probably would not be very good at bluffing in poker, either."

* * * * *

The next morning Stan left for Minneapolis. He had a lot of things to do before Barbara came up for her first visit. That started with cleaning up his apartment.

On the way back, he decided that he would reserve a room at the Chateau for Jane and her husband, as a wedding gift. He called up to Bayfield and ordered it as a gift certificate, just in case Jane had other plans.

Then he had another thought. He wondered if Jean knew he was engaged.

* * * * *

That day, Vivian had an "interesting" conversation with her friends at her luncheon.

David Fabio is the author of two youth adventure novels –
The Hidden Passage and The Second Summer.
He has also written a historical fiction novel centered on life on the
Mississippi River – Tales of a River's Bend.
Now, his two mystery novels – Search and Seizure and Secret of
the Apostle Islands challenge the reader's imagination.

He is an educator, photographer, and an outdoor enthusiast. His
love for nature and learning about the outdoors, show up in many
of his writings.

Breinigsville, PA USA
25 February 2011
256329BV00001B/4/P